**Also available from RaeAnne Thayne
and HQN**

The Cliff House
The Sea Glass Cottage
Christmas at Holiday House
The Path to Sunshine Cove

Haven Point

Snow Angel Cove
Redemption Bay
Evergreen Springs
Riverbend Road
Snowfall on Haven Point
Serenity Harbor
Sugar Pine Trail
The Cottages on Silver Beach
Season of Wonder
Coming Home for Christmas
Summer at Lake Haven

Hope's Crossing

Blackberry Summer
Woodrose Mountain
Sweet Laurel Falls
Currant Creek Valley
Willowleaf Lane
Christmas in Snowflake Canyon
Wild Iris Ridge

For a complete list of books by RaeAnne Thayne,
please visit www.raeannethayne.com.

Look for RaeAnne Thayne's next novel,
coming October 2021 from HQN.

RaeAnne Thayne

The PATH *to* SUNSHINE COVE

HQN

ISBN-13: 978-1-335-66543-0
ISBN-13: 978-1-335-91636-5 (ITPE)

The Path to Sunshine Cove

HQN
22 Adelaide St. West, 40th Floor
Toronto, Ontario M5H 4E3, Canada
www.Harlequin.com

Printed in U.S.A.

While a writer's life sometimes feels like a solitary one,
wrestling the characters in my head onto the page,
the reality is far different. This book would not have been possible without
an entire team. As always, a huge thank-you first to my amazing editor,
Gail Chasan. We have worked on sixty-one books together now
and I hope for sixty-one more!

Everyone at Harlequin works incredibly hard to get my book
into the hands of readers and I am deeply grateful to every single person
who worked on this book, from the art department to the sales team
to everyone in editorial.

Thank you also to my literary agent, Karen Solem,
for her wisdom and guidance through the years.

For this particular book, I owe a huge debt of gratitude to my friends
and fellow beachside plotters, Marina Adair, Skye Jordan and Jill Shalvis,
who helped me shape a nebulous idea into one with bones
and especially heart. I dearly miss all the laughter, creativity
and peanut brittle and can't wait until we can meet again.

I could not have written this book without my family, especially my
wonderful hero of a husband, Jared, who has been my biggest cheerleader
and supporter for thirty-five years. I love you dearly.

The Path to Sunshine Cove

1

Jess

IF NOT FOR ALL THE EMOTIONAL BAGGAGE CLUTTER-
ing up her Airstream, this wouldn't be a bad place to park
for a few days.

As Jess Clayton drove through the quiet streets of Cape Sanctuary on a beautiful May afternoon, she couldn't help being
charmed anew by the Northern California beach town vibes.

She had been here before, of course. Several times. Her sister
lived just down that street there, in a large two-story cottage
with gables, a bay window and a lush flower garden. Rachel
loved it here. Every time Jess came to town, she was reminded
why. What was not to love? Cape Sanctuary was a town de-
fined by whimsical houses, overflowing gardens, wind chimes
and Japanese fishing balls.

And, of course, the gorgeous coastline, marked by redwoods,
rock formations, cliffs.

She drove past Juniper Way, her sister's street, but didn't turn down. Not yet. She would see Rachel, Cody and the kids soon, after she was settled.

They were the whole reason she was here, after all. She didn't see her nieces and nephew enough, only on the rare holidays and birthdays that she could arrange a visit. When a prospective client reached out from the same town as Rachel and her family, Jess saw it as a golden opportunity to spend more time with the kids.

And her sister, of course.

She sighed as she made her way to her destination, Sunshine Cove, still a mile away, according to her navigation system.

Rachel was the reason for all that baggage she was towing along. Jess loved her younger sister dearly but their relationship was like a messy tangle of electric wires, some of them live and still sparking.

She would be in Cape Sanctuary for two weeks on this job. Maybe she would finally have the chance to sort things out with Rachel and achieve some kind of peace.

The road rose, climbing through a stand of redwoods and coastal pine, with houses tucked in here and there before the view to the ocean opened up again.

In five hundred feet, your destination is on the right: 2135 Seaview Road.

She couldn't argue with Siri on this one. That was a spectacular view. The Pacific glistened in the afternoon sunlight, with only a few feathery clouds above the horizon line.

She turned at the orca-shaped mailbox Eleanor Whitaker had told her to seek. Through more coastal pine, she could see the house. She recognized it from the pictures her client had sent. One level, made of stone and cedar, the house looked as if it had grown out of the landscape fully formed.

She knew the house was more than five thousand square feet, built at the turn of the century by a wealthy ranching and logging family in the area. It featured seven bedrooms and eight bathrooms, all of which she would come to know well over the next two weeks.

From the picture Eleanor had sent, Jess knew Whitaker House was beautiful. Elegant. Comfortable. Warm.

The kind of place where Jess had once dreamed of living, free of shouting, chaos, pain.

She could see, tucked into the trees overlooking the ocean, a smaller house on the property that was almost a miniature of the big house, with the same cedar and stone exterior as well as windows that gleamed in the afternoon sun.

A big dark blue pickup truck was parked there but she couldn't see anyone around.

Jess pulled her own rig over to the side of the driveway in case anyone needed to come in and out, then scouted around for a place she could unhitch.

From their phone call earlier that morning as she was driving, she knew Eleanor wouldn't be here, that she had taken her teenage granddaughter into a nearby town to an orthodontist appointment and then to catch a movie they had both been wanting to see.

Make yourself at home and set up anywhere that works, Eleanor had said.

As she cased the property, she instantly found the spot a hundred yards from the house that would give her a perfect view of the water, almost as if it had been created exactly for her twenty-four-foot 1993 Airstream, affectionately nicknamed Vera by Jess's business partner.

This job was meant to be. She had already bonded with Eleanor Whitaker over their weeks of email and phone correspondence. This view sealed the deal.

When she was done working each day, she could go to sleep to the restful sound of the ocean. She climbed back in her pickup and backed the trailer with the ease of long practice. Some people struggled with trailering but Jess didn't. The seven years she had spent as a driver in the military still served her well.

When the Airstream was in a good spot, she hopped out and was reaching in the back of the pickup for the chocks when an angry male voice drifted across the manicured lawn to her.

"Hey. This is private property. You can't park that here!"

She instinctively wrapped her hand around the chock. Angry male voices always brought out the warrior princess in her. She could blame both her childhood and those years in the army when she had to go toe to toe with people twice her weight and a foot taller.

The chock was heavy and could do real damage in the right hands.

Hers.

"I have permission to be here," she said, her voice cool but polite.

He frowned. "Permission? That's impossible."

"I assure you, it's not."

"This is my mother's property. She would have told me if she had given somebody permission to camp here."

Ah. This must be Nathaniel Whitaker, Eleanor's son. Her client had mentioned that he lived in another house on the property and would probably be in and out as Jess went about her work.

Hadn't Eleanor told him Jess was coming?

She relaxed her grip on the chock but didn't release it. "You must be Nathaniel. Eleanor has told me about you."

Her words didn't have an impact on his expression. If anything, his glower intensified, his frown now edged with confusion that she knew his name.

Despite his sour expression, she couldn't help noticing he was an extraordinarily good-looking man. Eleanor hadn't mentioned that her son had dark hair, stormy blue eyes, a square jawline. Or that his green T-shirt with a logo over the right breast pocket that read Whitaker Construction clung to his muscles.

Jess found it extremely inconvenient that Nathaniel Whitaker happened to hit every single one of her personal yum buttons.

"Who are you?" he demanded. "And how do you know my mother?"

Ah. This was tricky. Eleanor was her client. She must have had her own reasons for not telling her son Jess was showing up. Jess felt compelled to honor those reasons. Until she could talk to the woman, Jess didn't feel right about giving more information to Nate than his own mother had.

"My name is Jess Clayton. Your mother knows I planned to arrive today. I have her permission to set up anywhere. I thought this would work well."

Beautifully, actually. The more time she looked around, the better she liked it. A twisting path down to the ocean started just a few yards away, leading down to what looked like a protected cove.

"Set up for what? Why are you here?"

"You really should ask your mother," she said. It would be so much better if he could hear the explanation from Eleanor.

"I just tried to call her when I saw you pulling in. She's not answering."

"Probably in the middle of the movie. She told me she and Sophie were going to a matinee after the orthodontist."

If she thought this further knowledge about his family would set Nate's mind at ease, she was sadly mistaken. His gaze narrowed further. "How the hell do you know my daughter had an orthodontist appointment?"

"Your mom happened to mention it."

"Funny, the things my mother told you. I talk to her several times a day, every day, and she hasn't said a word to me about a strange woman setting up a trailer in the side yard. Tell me again what you're doing here?"

She *wanted* to be finishing her trailer setup so she could unhitch and go into town for groceries. She would rather not be engaged in a confrontation with a strange man, no matter how hot, who didn't need to know every detail of his mother's life.

Why hadn't Eleanor told him already? It's not as if the woman could keep their efforts a secret for long.

Still, it was not up to *Jess* to spill the dirt.

"I'm afraid that's between me and your mother. You really need to get the answer to that question from her."

"Sorry, ma'am, but that's not good enough. Right now, you're trespassing. If you don't move this out of here, I'm calling the police. The chief happens to be a good friend of mine."

"Yes, I know." Done with this discussion, Jess reached down to wedge the chock behind the passenger-side wheel. "You play poker with him every other Friday night. Your mother told me."

"What else did she tell you?" He had moved beyond suspicion to outright hostility. She probably shouldn't have said anything about the poker. She certainly wouldn't want someone she didn't know poking into her business. If he hadn't been so blasted good-looking, she might have been able to handle this whole thing better.

She forced a smile, trying to take a different tack. "I assure you, Eleanor knows I'm coming, as I said. She told me to settle in and make myself comfortable until she gets home. You can try calling her again."

Or you can accept that maybe I'm telling the truth and give me a break here. I've been driving for hours. I'm tired and hungry and I would really like to make a sandwich, which I can't do with you standing there like a bouncer at a nightclub in a bad part of town.

"I've tried multiple times. She's not answering. You're probably right, her phone is probably on silent."

"Look, when Eleanor and Sophie come back from the movie, she can tell you what's going on. Until then, I would really like to finish setting up here."

"No matter what I say?"

She didn't want to challenge him but she was starving.

"This is your mother's house and she invited me here," she said simply. "It will be easy enough to prove that once Eleanor returns. If I'm lying for some unknown reason and just happened to make an extraordinarily lucky guess about your mom and a daughter named Sophie who had an orthodontist appointment today, you and the entire Cape Sanctuary police force can boot me out."

He didn't look at all appeased, his features still suspicious. She couldn't really blame him. He was only trying to protect those he loved. She would probably do the same in his shoes.

"Would you like a sandwich?" she said, trying another tack. "I make a mean PB and J."

For the first time, she saw a glimmer of surprise on his expression, as if he couldn't quite believe she had the audacity to ask. "No, I wouldn't like a sandwich."

"Suit yourself. I've had a long day already and I'm ready for some food. And I need to see how Vera survived the drive."

As she might have expected, his frown deepened. "Who is Vera?"

She patted the skin on the Airstream. "It was, um, a pleasure to meet you, Nathaniel."

"Nate," he muttered. "Nobody but my mother calls me Nathaniel."

"Nate, then."

She nodded and without waiting for him to argue, she slipped into the trailer and closed the door firmly behind her.

The curtains were still closed from the drive and she didn't want to open them yet to the afternoon sunlight. Not when Nate Whitaker might still be lurking outside.

Instead, she sank onto the sofa that doubled as her office, dining room and guest space, astonished and dismayed to find her hands were shaking.

What was *that* about? She had a familiar itchiness between

her shoulder blades and could feel a little crash as her adrenaline subsided.

Nate Whitaker wasn't a threat to her. Yes, he might be angry right now but he wouldn't hurt her. She already felt like his mother was an old and dear friend. Eleanor surely couldn't have a son who was prone to random violence.

Instinct told her he wouldn't physically hurt her, yet Jess still had the strangest feeling that Nate posed some kind of danger to her.

Ah well. She likely wouldn't have much to do with the man. She was here to help Eleanor, not to fraternize with the woman's gorgeous offspring.

She only had to make sure she didn't lose sight of her twin objectives here in Cape Sanctuary—spending time with her sister's family and helping her client—and she would be fine.

2

Nate

NATE GLOWERED AT THE CLOSED DOOR OF THE trailer. Who the hell was this woman and what was her business with his mother?

More important, why hadn't Eleanor told him she was expecting company?

He didn't doubt Jess Clayton when she said Eleanor was expecting her. How could he? As she had pointed out, she knew details about Eleanor's schedule she could only have received from his mother herself.

That didn't mean the woman wasn't some kind of scam artist. His mother was a vulnerable widow still dealing with the loss of her husband from cancer six months earlier. Someone with nefarious motives might consider her ripe for the plucking.

He would only find out by getting in touch with his mother.

Nate had intended to return to his job site, the new town library and city hall, but maybe he would change plans and work from home for the afternoon so he could keep an eye on his mother's guest.

A half hour later, he was set up in his office, which happened to have a clear view of the Airstream, when Eleanor finally called him back.

"I'm sorry, darling. I turned off my phone when the movie started. That's what they tell you to do, isn't it? Turn off your devices so you don't disturb others in the theater?"

His mother's innocent tone didn't fool Nate for an instant. "Right."

"Is something wrong? It appears I've missed four phone calls from you. We told you we would be at the matinee this afternoon after the orthodontist, didn't we?"

He had known, he had just forgotten. Until Jess Clayton reminded him. "You told me."

"Then I assume something terrible must have happened if you needed to reach me so urgently."

"Not terrible. Only somewhat concerning. You have a visitor. A strange woman set up a trailer on the property, on the flat piece of land next to the beach path."

"She made good time. Oh, that should offer a lovely view of the ocean for Jess. I was thinking that might be the very place. I couldn't have picked a better spot for her myself. I'm so glad."

Nate tried not to grind his teeth. That wasn't the point, was it?

"Obviously you were expecting her."

"Yes. And I'm embarrassed I'm such a poor hostess that I couldn't be there when she arrived. Jess originally hadn't planned to reach Cape Sanctuary until this evening. After she told me she changed her plans and was leaving earlier, I had to explain about the orthodontist and the movie I had already promised Sophie. Thank you for helping Jess settle in, son."

He waited for his mother to offer some other explanation but she didn't elaborate. Eleanor had been acting strangely of late.

Really, since his father died six months earlier after a long and painful battle with colon cancer.

"Will she be visiting for long?"

"As long as it takes," Eleanor said cryptically.

"Which tells me exactly nothing about who she is and what she's doing here."

She laughed, though it sounded forced and perhaps even a bit guilty. "I should have told you she was coming. I'm sorry. I suppose I wasn't sure how you would feel about it. And to be honest, I couldn't figure out how to tell you."

"Try."

Eleanor sighed. "Do you remember when I told you my child-hood friend Lucinda in Seattle hired a lovely woman to help her clean out her house before she put it on the market and moved into that retirement village in Florida?"

"Yes," he said slowly, looking out the window at the silvery Airstream glinting in the sunlight as he tried to process the con-nections. "But you're not moving into assisted living, Mom. You're not moving anywhere."

Her sigh was deep and heartfelt. "Not right now, but who knows what might happen in the future? Your father was here one moment and gone the next."

"Dad had colon cancer. He had a terminal diagnosis for two years before he died."

"I'm aware of that. But none of us were ready for him to go. My point is, I don't want you to have the burden of cleaning out years of accumulated crap. Whitaker House is a cluttered mess and I'm tired of it."

"Tired of the house or tired of the mess?"

"The mess. Not only do I have all your father's things that I haven't been able to part with yet but I still have boxes left over from your grandparents' day when *they* lived in the house. Things your father didn't want to get rid of out of some mis-guided sense of loyalty to them."

He knew there was truth to that. Five generations of Whitakers had lived in the house. Six, counting the years when he and Sophie had lived there before he finished gutting and renovating a small abandoned house on the property into a comfortable three-bedroom cottage about six years earlier.

"I need help clearing it all out," Eleanor continued. "I'll never do it on my own so I've asked Jess to stay for a few weeks to hold my feet to the fire, as it were."

"Sophie and I could have helped you. You didn't need to turn to a stranger."

"Yeah, Gram. We could help."

He heard his daughter in the background and was glad she was on his side. About this, anyway. He and Sophie didn't agree on too many other things these days.

"That is a lovely offer. I do appreciate it, but I also know how busy you both are. Nate, you're running a construction company with more projects than I can keep track of and Sophie is plenty busy with school."

"We can still find time to help you," he started to say but his mother cut him off.

"This is what Jess does for a living. Lucinda told me hiring Transitions was the best decision she had ever made. She said Jess made the process of cleaning out years of clutter as painless as possible."

Eleanor paused, then added quietly, "I think I've been through enough pain, don't you?"

Her words stripped away all his objections. He had worried for her physical and emotional health since his father died. She was only now beginning to smile again over the past month or so, to find some enjoyment out of life.

If she was excited about cleaning out Whitaker House, how could he argue?

"Who knows?" Eleanor went on with a small laugh. "It might

turn out that I'm not able to part with a single dishcloth and Jess might find she wasted her time coming all this way up here."

Jess Clayton. He grimaced, remembering his surliness when she arrived. "I wish you had given me some warning that you were expecting company. I wasn't very welcoming to her when she pulled in and started parking her trailer."

"I know. I should have told you. I'm sorry I put it off. I suppose I've been afraid to tell you. I know how much you miss your father, too. I wasn't sure how you would feel about me clearing out all his old things when he's only been gone six months."

He did miss his father, though their relationship had always been somewhat complicated.

"I don't care about a few old shirts and sweaters, Mom."

"I know I'm being silly," Eleanor said. "Change is always so hard."

"But inevitable."

"Whether we like it, or not." His mother paused. "I hope you weren't too hard on my guest. She's giving me two weeks of her very packed schedule so we can go through the house. She'll be staying on the property for that time. You're bound to run into her again. I would hate for things to be uncomfortable between you."

"I'll talk to her and try to clear the air," he said.

"Come for dinner," his mother suggested. "I planned to make that lemon shrimp pasta you like."

He sighed. "I'll have to see. I'm behind on a couple of projects and might be late but I'll try. Don't wait for me."

"Of course."

They said their goodbyes. As he disconnected the call, he saw their guest backing her pickup truck out of the spot and driving down the street.

She left her trailer behind, so he could only assume she would return at some point.

He needed to apologize.

The realization wasn't a pleasant one. He had been rude and unwelcoming, treating her as if she were trespassing. Had he really threatened to call the police on her? He could be such an overprotective ass sometimes.

He needed to apologize as soon as possible. Eleanor had pointed out that Jess Clayton would be staying at Whitaker House for two weeks, living only a few hundred yards away from him. For his mother's sake, he had to make things right.

That didn't mean he had to like it.

3

Rachel

"FOR THE LOVE OF CHRISTOPHER ROBIN, CAN YOU please give me five more minutes? That's all I need. Five minutes."

"But I'm *starving*!" Her five-year-old daughter, Ava, whined, just as if she hadn't finished a mozzarella stick and several apple slices a half hour earlier. "If I don't eat something, I'm going to *die*. Can I have one of your cookies?"

"Eat." Her brother, Silas, echoed the sentiment if not the words.

Rachel Clayton McBride closed her eyes and released a heavy breath to keep from snapping back. She dredged up a calm smile. "Give me five more minutes and I will be done taking pictures, I promise. Then I can make you some macaroni and cheese."

"I don't want macaroni and cheese. I want a cookie."

Of course she did. If Rachel had said she would give her a cookie, Ava would have said she was in the mood for macaroni and cheese. She was in training for the debate Olympics, apparently.

"I don't need a cookie, Mama," her other daughter, Grace, said from the kitchen table in a prim voice that seemed out of place in a seven-year-old girl.

She knew her oldest well enough to be quite certain Grace would quickly change her tune if Rachel actually did start doling out cookies to Grace's younger siblings. That wasn't going to happen with these particular cookies. She had worked too hard on them to see them gobbled up by little mouths that wouldn't appreciate the nuances of flavor.

"Grace, could you please grab a granola bar for Ava and Silas?"

"I don't want a granola bar," Ava whined. "I want one of those. It's purple and pretty."

Ava pointed to the tray of perfectly decorated almond sugar cookies Rachel had been working on all afternoon.

"I told you when we were making them. These are for my book group tonight. I made some for only us and you can have one after dinner."

"But they're so pretty. Why can't I have one *now*?" Ava whined.

"Because you can't." It was the worst sort of maternal response but she was just about out of patience for the day.

Undeterred, Silas reached on tiptoe for one but still couldn't reach. If she hadn't been focused on the photographs for her blog and social media properties, she might have seen the telltale signs of a tantrum. The jutted-out lip, the rising color, the obstinate jawline.

He grunted and tried to reach.

"See? Silas wants one, too," Ava informed her. "Daddy would give us one."

"I'm sure he would. But Daddy's not here right now, is he?"

All right. She was heading straight into full-on bitch mode.

It wasn't Ava's fault that her father seemed to be spending more and more time working these days.

She wanted to think it was simply an uptick in the construction business that had him leaving before sunrise and coming home after dark most days. As the owner of a successful roofing company, her husband had plenty of obligations outside the home—which meant most of the work *inside* the home fell on Rachel's shoulders.

She hoped work was the reason Cody was gone so much, anyway, and that he wasn't trying to avoid the hard realities of home life, especially their son's early diagnosis of autism two months earlier.

When Cody *was* home, he seemed distracted, as if he couldn't wait to be somewhere else. Anywhere else.

She shoved down the low, constant thrum of anxiety to focus on her children. "A granola bar or nothing," she told Ava. "Those are your choices until dinner. Silas, you can't do that. No. Play with your car on the floor."

As she might have expected, her son ignored her. She might as well have been talking to one of those flower-shaped cookies. He continued driving his car along the edge of the island.

At least he hadn't had a meltdown over not getting a cookie. Rachel decided to focus on the positive as she took a few more shots of two cookies on a piece of antique china she had picked up at a thrift store.

This would make a beautiful post about spring baking when she shared the recipe on her blog, she thought.

Her phone rang with Cody's distinctive ringtone, a jazz song they had danced to on an amazing trip to Sonoma for their anniversary some years back.

She was quite certain she had conceived Silas on that trip.

Even though doctors had told her it wasn't the case, Rachel still wondered whether Silas's autism was a result of all the wine she had consumed, in between magical afternoons spent making love.

"Hi," she said breathlessly. Oh, how she missed sex. It had been weeks, for one reason or another.

"Hey, babe. I'm going to be late again. I'm sorry. I'm down two guys and the job is taking longer than we thought. It's supposed to rain overnight and we can't leave the Tanners with a hole in their roof."

"Again? You promised you would be home on time tonight! I have my book group, remember?"

Rachel had been holding on desperately to the idea of a little adult conversation. Okay, most of the time her group rarely actually managed to make time to discuss the book. It was more about drinking wine and having a discussion that didn't involve her wiping someone's nose or telling someone else to stop jumping on the furniture.

"Oh, damn. I completely forgot about book group. Maybe my mom could sit with the kids until I get home."

He could remember the batting average of every single hitter on the Giants lineup but didn't bother to remember the one night a month when she could pretend to have a life outside her kids.

"Your mom will be at the book group. I can't ask her to miss it to tend my kids. So will your sister and Jan."

Those were about the only people she dared entrust with all three of her children, especially considering Silas's behavior issues.

"What time is it over? I should be able to wrap things up here and leave the rest of the job to the guys so I can be home by eight. You would only be a little late."

"Don't bother. It's fine. Finish the job."

"No. I'll see what I can do. I don't want you to miss book group."

"You said it yourself. You can't leave the Tanners with a hole in their roof with rain in the forecast. Do what you need to do. I'll be fine."

"I'll do what I can," he repeated. "I've got to go. Love you."

It sounded so practiced, so casually offhand that she suddenly wanted to cry.

"Bye," she said, tapping her wireless earbud to end the call.

She stared into space, aching inside for everything that had gotten in the way of the vast love they used to share.

She was distracted from her grim thoughts by a clatter and matching squeals from the girls. When she whirled around, she found Silas and Ava standing over her tray of beautiful sugar cookies, now a jumble of broken glass, crumbs and frosting all over the floor. An entire day of work. She had been working on them all day and had finally perfected the lavender-infused icing.

"Look what you've done!" she exclaimed. The stress of the day chasing kids seemed to pour over her like water gushing over the cliffs to the ocean.

"I'm sorry, Mommy," Ava said, tears dripping. "We didn't mean to ruin your cookies. I was trying to look at one when you were on the phone. Only look. And Silas grabbed it and the whole tray fell down."

"They were so pretty." Grace wandered over to look at the disaster with a mournful look. "Now they're trash. Should I clean them up and throw them away?"

Grace was being helpful, she knew, but Rachel still couldn't like the way her daughter was always so eager to throw away anything that wasn't perfect, whether it was a coloring page where she went outside the line or a toy with a broken piece.

Silas sat down and picked up a cookie piece from the floor. Before Rachel could stop him, he popped it into his mouth.

"Silas, stop. Don't eat that. There's glass."

He looked at her, barely acknowledging she was there, and picked up another broken cookie to eat.

She wasn't even sure he would notice if he ate glass. His reactions to things were sometimes so far out of the realm of what most people would consider normal. He could hold his hand under hot water without making a sound but have a complete meltdown if she left a tag on his shirt that bothered him.

"No," she said again and swooped around the kitchen island to pick him up and physically move him out of harm's way.

As she might have expected, Silas didn't like that. He wriggled to get down, grunting his displeasure at her. "You'll hurt yourself on glass," she said.

He started banging his head back against her, something new and fun he had recently discovered.

"Stop," she ordered. How did he manage to wriggle his body and buck his head like that at the same time? Sometimes keeping him from danger was like wrestling an angry baby alligator.

She had finally managed to restrain him and calm him a little when the doorbell rang, starting him up again.

"I'll get it." Ever helpful, Grace sailed to the front door before Rachel could remind her that they didn't always have to answer the door every time it rang.

Great. Just what she needed. Someone to witness what a disaster she was making of her life.

Silas continued to fight so that he could be free to eat sugar-coated broken glass while Ava sat on the floor sobbing quietly, though Rachel couldn't tell whether she was crying because of what she and her younger brother had done or because of the cookies she could no longer eat.

She almost forgot the doorbell had rung until she heard a whoop of excitement out of Grace. A moment later, the last person she expected to see that day walked into the kitchen.

Jess, her older sister. Jess, who lived a rambling life and was usually on the other side of the country.

Jess, who hadn't given her one single whiff of warning that she might be coming to Cape Sanctuary.

Her sister surveyed the chaos of broken cookies and upset children with the impassive expression she always seemed to wear whenever she was around Rachel and her family.

"Looks like I've come at a bad time."

"Aunt Jess!" Ava exclaimed. Her tears miraculously dried as she launched herself at her aunt, who hugged her with a little laugh.

Rachel couldn't seem to stop staring.

Jess was as stunning as ever, her sun-streaked hair shorter than Rachel remembered. She wore hardly any makeup but was still beautiful. Lean, fit, with a flat belly that had obviously never had anything to do with giving birth to three children.

Her sister lived almost the length of the state away and rarely even came for a *scheduled* visit, let alone an unexpected one.

"Jess. What are you doing here? Why didn't you call and let me know you were coming?"

"Surprise." Her older sister smiled, though it seemed forced. "I picked up a job in this area so that I can spend time with you and the kids."

"A job?"

She knew Jess helped people, usually senior citizens, clear out their houses before moving. Rachel considered it a strange occupation but her sister seemed to thrive on it.

"Yes. I'll be here for a few weeks cleaning out a place over near Sunshine Cove."

Rachel knew a handful of people who lived in that area of Seaview Road but didn't have time to figure out who might have enlisted her sister's help. She was too busy trying to figure out what her sister was *really* doing there.

And also trying to face the fact that her relationship with Jess was yet one more area of Rachel's life where she was failing. Their bond had been broken for a long time and at this point she didn't know how to repair it.

"That's great," she said now. "So great."

Did her voice sound as hollow to her sister as it did to Rachel?

Could Jess tell her presence was a shock on par with a UFO landing in the backyard?

"I haven't spent nearly enough time with the kids. A few phone calls and visits here and there during the holidays. I'm looking forward to spending more time with them."

"Wow. They'll love that." Rachel tried to infuse her voice with warmth and delight but it took every iota of her limited acting skills.

How could she pretend to be overflowing with joy when her insides felt as hollow as her words?

She was tired, frustrated, afraid for her marriage, worried about her son's future and upset about her book club cookies. She didn't know if she had time to deal with all the guilt and pain inextricably tangled with her sister.

"I wish you had told me you were coming. I could have planned dinner for you or something. I was just about to make some macaroni and cheese for the girls. I can cook extra, if you would like."

"Not necessary," Jess said with that same blasted smile that Rachel couldn't read. "Thank you, but I just went grocery shopping and have plenty of food back at my trailer. I can help you clean up that mess, though. Looks like we had a cookie accident."

"Eat," Silas demanded, his voice more urgent.

"You can't eat those," Rachel said again. "They have glass on them. Yucky. Owie."

"Eat!" Silas said, more loudly and forcefully. He had temporarily stopped wriggling in light of their surprise visitor but continued his efforts now to be free.

"You deal with him. I'll clean this up. Point me to your broom and dustpan," Jess said.

Rachel didn't want to accept her help, which she knew was stupid. Her sister was only being kind. There was just so much painful history between them, so many unresolved issues that hung in the air like their father's cigar smoke.

The truth was, she *did* need help. Silas was gearing up for a full-on meltdown if she didn't head it off first.

"In the closet off the mudroom."

With her chin, Rachel pointed vaguely in the direction she meant.

"I can show you," Grace said, ever helpful.

Jess followed her. Rachel gave in and found the tin containing all the less-than-perfect cookies she had saved for the kids and Cody. She pulled one out for Silas, and two more for Grace and Ava, then pulled another for her sister.

While Jess cleaned up the mess, Rachel held her son at the table while he enjoyed his cookie as Grace and Ava regaled her sister with a play-by-play of what had transpired a few minutes earlier.

"These look like delicious cookies," was Jess's only comment. "Were they for some kind of special event?"

"I was supposed to have book club tonight. But I guess it's fine that they're ruined. Cody has to work late so I can't go anyway."

She tried for that same cheerful tone that she was far from feeling. As she might have suspected, Jess wasn't fooled. Her sister gave her a careful look that Rachel met with an impassive smile of her own. She refused to let her sister see the cracks in the foundation of her marriage.

"He's got so much work right now, it's crazy. We're having a construction boom in this area, plus you wouldn't believe all the people who had storm damage from nasty weather this winter and decided to get entirely new roofs once they received an insurance check."

"That's great. It's good that he's staying busy."

"Super busy."

"These cookies are fantastic," Jess said. "What did you do differently from usual sugar cookies?"

"To start with, I use the finest quality ingredients and I like almond extract instead of vanilla. But a lot of people do that. The real secret is in the icing. I add powdered culinary lavender to give it an extra pop. Some people add that to the dough but I like the flavor it brings to the icing instead."

"I never would have thought of adding lavender to cookies. I didn't know you could even do that. But it's really delicious."

Jess looked at the cookies then back at Rachel. "You know, I could probably stay with the kids until Cody gets home so that you don't have to miss your book group."

The offer shocked her almost as much as the fact that Jess was sitting here at her kitchen table eating one of her imperfect lavender sugar cookies. She was instantly tempted. Friends, conversation, alcohol. Mostly a few hours away from the unrelenting work involved in trying to stay sane amid the chaos of three children under the age of seven, including one with special needs.

Before she could agree, Silas wriggled off her lap and zeroed straight for his car, flapping his hands as he had started to do.

She couldn't leave Jess with Silas. Not now, when his behavior was so out of control. She shrugged. "It's fine. I haven't read the book anyway."

"I really don't mind. As I said, I've been looking forward to spending more time with them while I'm here in Cape Sanctuary."

"No. But thank you," she said firmly, then changed the subject to avoid further argument. "You said you're staying near Sunshine Cove. Are you helping Eleanor Whitaker?"

Jess made a face. "I try not to talk about my work, for the client's privacy. But since that's where my trailer is parked right now, which is easy enough to find, you will eventually figure it out. Yes. I'm helping Eleanor clean out Whitaker House."

"Oh, I love that place. It's so gorgeous and dripping with history."

"Yes."

"I had no idea Eleanor was cleaning it out. Is she putting it on the market? I have many contacts online who would jump at the chance to buy that house, right on the water with those views and that gorgeous Craftsman architecture."

"I don't know her plans. I only know she's asked me to help her clear out years of accumulated stuff."

"Is she having an estate sale? Oh wow, the treasures I bet you could find in there."

"We still have to figure all that out. I don't know her plans. And I couldn't share them, even if I knew. My clients trust me not to talk about their business."

"I totally get it. No problem. I'll just ask her myself. Eleanor is one of my good friends. In fact, she's supposed to be going to book club tonight."

"Except you're not going to book club because you don't think I can handle staying with your kids."

"I never said that," Rachel protested, though of course that was absolutely what she thought.

"It's fine. Don't worry about it. I'll have plenty of other chances to hang out with them."

"Yay!" Grace exclaimed, already gazing with hero worship at her aunt. "Did you see my coloring page? I only messed up one place. See, on the dog's head? I wanted both ears to be brown but I forgot and did one ear black. You can't erase crayons."

"That is an unfortunate truth," Jess said. "But I like a dog who has different-colored ears. It gives him a little more personality."

Grace glowed under the praise, making Rachel painfully aware that she didn't give her child enough of it.

"Are you sure you won't stay for dinner?" she asked. "It's no trouble."

"That's very kind of you, especially when I showed up out of the blue, but I should probably head back. Unless Eleanor decides to take off for book group, we're supposed to be meeting when she returns to town so we can figure out a few things before we start working tomorrow."

Rachel was ashamed of the relief she felt that she wouldn't have to continue making awkward conversation with a sister who had become a virtual stranger over the years.

"I wouldn't want you to keep her waiting, then. Eleanor is pretty special."

"Do you have to go?" Ava whined, tugging on Jess's hand. "I haven't even showed you my new stuffed dog."

"I'll be around for a few weeks. I'm sure I'll get the chance to see it soon."

"When will you come back?" Ava asked.

"I don't know for sure. But soon."

"Tomorrow?" Grace pressed.

"Maybe not tomorrow since I'll be working that day."

"What about the day after tomorrow?" Ava asked.

"Girls, give your aunt a break," Rachel said before Jess could reply. "She's here to work, not play with you guys."

"But I'll find time to play with you while I'm here, I promise," Jess said. "I would love to spend time with the kids in the evening, when I'm done helping Eleanor. Maybe you and Cody could get out for a night away or something."

"That would be great," Rachel said. The only trick would be persuading her husband to leave work for five minutes, a task at which she did not expect she could succeed. That also left the issue of Silas, who didn't do well with other people.

Still, it was nice of Jess to offer.

Rachel walked her sister to the door, where they exchanged an awkward sort of hug that made her heart hurt.

Once upon a time, Jess had been her best friend. They had been inseparable, united by their shared experiences. Living with a harsh father in the military who moved his family every two or three years had drawn them closer together than typical sisters. Making outside friends had been a challenge in that environment.

That was only one of the reasons they had come to depend entirely on each other.

Everything had changed the year Rachel turned thirteen, that horrible summer when the world fell apart.

She didn't want to think about that time. She preferred to block it out of her mind—the fear, the pain, the shared trauma.

Instead, she preferred to focus on what she had, the life she had rebuilt brick by brick out of the rubble that had been left behind.

"I'm glad you're here," she said now to Jess. Her sister gave her a surprised look and for the first time she thought she saw something beneath the careful facade of politeness.

"Same," Jess said, her voice gruff.

"Eat!" Silas demanded, wriggling again to be free.

"I'll call you soon and we can get away, the two of us, to catch up."

"Sounds good," Jess said, then walked with her purposeful stride out the door and down the walkway to the pickup truck she had parked at the curb, leaving Rachel to wrestle her child and her demons at the same time.

4

Jess

JESS DROVE BACK TO HER TRAILER AND WHITAKER House with a strange ache in her chest, an echo of an old injury.

So much for joyful reunions. The interaction with her sister had been awkward, stilted, like bumping into an old friend with whom you now have nothing in common.

What had she expected? That Rachel would drop everything and throw a party for her?

Admittedly, her timing hadn't been the greatest. Rachel had been in the middle of what looked like a chaotic situation, with Ava howling, Silas throwing a fit, and glass and cookies all over the floor.

Still, she might have hoped her sister could at least *pretend* she was happy to see Jess. Rachel likely would have been more welcoming to a bat flying into the house. Bats at least ate mosquitos.

That ache in her chest seemed to throb in rhythm to her

truck's tires spinning on the asphalt as she made her way up the hill.

What had she expected? Her relationship with her sister was as broken as that plate she had cleaned up. Was it irreparable? She didn't know. The chasm between them seemed so wide, as impossible to breach as the Grand Canyon.

The sight of her trailer gleaming in the early-evening sunlight lifted her heart. It wasn't big, only twenty-four feet long, but the classic curved lines and aluminum skin always made her happy, especially because she knew how far Vera had come.

She had barely turned off her pickup and opened the door when a figure walked down toward her from the terrace of Whitaker House.

Her nerves bumped. Was it Nate again, ready for another confrontation? No. She relaxed when she recognized an older woman, tall and graceful with steel-gray hair cut in a classic pageboy.

She was followed closely by a small dog with curly hair and spaniel features.

This must be her new employer. The woman, anyway. Not the dog. The dog must be Charlie, Eleanor's Cavapoo.

"Oh, Jess. You're here at last!" Eleanor exclaimed. The other woman reached out and folded her into a huge embrace.

Jess stiffened, momentarily uncomfortable with the hug before the sheer genuineness of the gesture disarmed her.

Here was the welcome no one else but her nieces had given her in Cape Sanctuary, warm and enthusiastic and kind.

The constriction around her heart after the visit with her sister seemed to ease slightly. "Yes. Here I am."

"I can't tell you how happy I am to have you here at long last. I feel like the luckiest of women that you were able to find time for me in your schedule. I've heard you can be booked out a year in advance."

Jess and her partner, Yvette, both had bookings that far out and had started turning down clients. "Business is booming right now."

"That's what happens when all those in my generation get sick and tired of living with all the clutter we always thought was so important."

"I guess so."

She smiled, charmed when Eleanor plopped onto one of the two bistro chairs. The small, cute dog collapsed at her feet as if too tired to take another step.

"How was your drive? You came up today from Los Angeles, right?"

"Yes. Mission Hills, actually. Traffic was fine. I got an early start before it could get too bad." She had actually left at 4 a.m. so she could avoid the heaviest traffic in LA County but had hit more around the Sacramento area.

Towing the Airstream through rush hour crowds could sometimes be a pain.

"I understand you had a run-in with my son. I'm so sorry about that."

"Apparently he didn't know I was coming."

Eleanor winced. "I should have told him. I meant to, it's just that… Well, he loved his father very much, though their relationship was complicated. I suppose I was afraid he would think I was trying to box away all of our memories of Jack."

That did nothing to change her impression of Nate Whitaker as a tough, albeit gorgeous, man. He had to be oblivious not to see his mother was clearly conflicted at taking this necessary but painful step.

"I'm sure everything will be fine. I've explained to him what's going on. He shouldn't give you a hard time now."

"Good. I'm glad to hear that."

"That's why I'm here, actually. Other than to meet you in person, which I'm so happy to do. I'm making lemon shrimp pasta and I'm here to ask if you might be interested in joining us for dinner. I thought it might be a good chance for you to meet my son under better circumstances, as well as his daughter, Sophie."

For a moment, she was tempted. She liked Eleanor already from their weeks of correspondence and wanted their working relationship to be a smooth, comfortable one. The social lubrication of food and likely wine would ease the conversation and might help her feel less awkward around Nate Whitaker when she saw him next.

"What about your book group?" she asked. "I stopped to see my sister, Rachel, and she told me you are supposed to be meeting tonight."

"We are, but to be honest, I haven't read the book. One of our, er, snootier members picked it and I couldn't finish the stupid thing. I found it pedantic, moralistic and boring as beige wallpaper. Much like the person who picked it, if I can be catty for a moment."

Jess had to smile. "I don't know anybody in town except you and Rachel, so you can be as catty as you want."

Eleanor's laugh was low and infectious. "Rather than discuss a book I couldn't finish that I can only recommend for drying flowers from your garden, I would rather have the chance to get to know you better. Your life sounds so fascinating, traveling the country and helping, ahem, seasoned citizens like me clear out their clutter."

She was only here for two weeks, Jess reminded herself. While Eleanor seemed like exactly the kind of woman Jess wanted to be when she grew up, she probably shouldn't socialize with her more than absolutely necessary.

What was the point in establishing a connection when Jess would only be a temporary presence here at Whitaker House?

"Thank you for that kind invitation but I've had a long day of driving, leaving before dawn, and I'm pretty beat. We will have another long day tomorrow so I should probably turn in early."

Eleanor looked disappointed but hid it quickly. "I totally understand, though I'm still not going to book club. You can be darn sure of that."

She waved her hand. "You'll have plenty of other chances to meet Sophie and hopefully get a better impression of Nate."

She didn't need a better impression of Nate. Really. She should probably stay far away from any man who could annoy her and make her insides shiver at the same time.

"I'm sure I will."

"I'll try to persuade you to have dinner with us another night soon."

"Do you eat with Nate and Sophie every night?"

"Oh no. Usually only once or twice a week with all three of us and maybe another time or two with Sophie and I alone when Nate is working late. It's been lovely to have them so close, especially during those long months when Jack was so sick. I honestly don't know what I would have done without them."

Her chin wobbled but Jess was impressed when she seemed to shove aside the emotion to offer up a firm smile instead. "We'll make time for dinner another night when you haven't had such a long day of driving."

"Thank you."

To Jess's shock, Eleanor gave her another warm hug. "I really am so grateful you were able to find time in your schedule to help me. If you need anything in the night—snacks, towels, anything at all—don't hesitate to come up to the house. I'll text you the security code. I've become a light sleeper since my husband died and I'll hear you, no doubt."

"Thank you. I appreciate that."

Eleanor's warmth and friendliness went a long way toward ameliorating the uncertain welcome she had received in Cape Sanctuary thus far from Nate Whitaker and from Rachel. Maybe taking this job hadn't been a mistake, after all.

"So tomorrow, bright and early, I'll come to the house and we can get started."

Eleanor gave her a rather guileless look. "Are you sure you wouldn't rather take the morning off to rest after your long drive?"

The suggestion veiled in the form of a question wasn't completely unexpected. Though Eleanor had hired her to help her clear out the house, she was clearly ambivalent about the process. Her reaction wasn't unique among Jess's clients. Change was hard, especially when it involved sorting through a lifetime of memories.

Many older people preferred not to deal with it but to leave the process of sifting through their lives to their heirs after they passed.

She gave Eleanor a reassuring smile. "Once I have a good night's sleep, I will be fresh and energized for the day ahead. You should make sure you have plenty of rest, too. You're going to love your house when we're done."

"Right, then. First thing in the morning. Should we say eight?"

"That works for me."

"I'll see you then. Good night. Sweet dreams."

Eleanor headed back to the house. Jess watched her for a moment then walked up into the Airstream. She had left the windows open when she headed over to Rachel's and the curtains fluttered in the breeze. She had turned down two dinner invitations but knew she still needed to eat. She decided on another sandwich, this one toasted French bread topped with burrata and marinated cherry tomatoes. She ate it out on her folding turquoise bistro set under the awning of the Airstream to the low song of the ocean and the sound of birds in Eleanor's lovely flower garden.

It was messy and delicious, creamy, drippy perfection.

While she ate, she worried again about Rachel. Her sister

had seemed worn-out, as if she were barely holding together the frayed edges of her life. Was it because of Silas's recent autism diagnosis? Rachel had seemed so matter-of-fact about it a few months earlier when she had messaged Jess to tell her. Jess had immediately called, not wanting to have this important conversation over text.

Rachel had seemed not nonchalant exactly. More like reconciled. *It's a very early diagnosis but his case is fairly clear-cut. We're going to be meeting with a team of specialists at UC Davis in a few months to come up with a therapy and treatment plan. It feels good to have a few answers about some of the things we've seen and to know that we are on a path to find out more,* Rachel had told Jess.

Despite Rachel's positive attitude in that first phone call, Jess had to assume it couldn't be easy on their family. Rachel and Cody must have been struggling to come to terms with the diagnosis and its implications for Silas's future.

Shortly after Jess had found out about Silas, Eleanor had reached out to her asking about a possible opening in her schedule. The chance to come to Cape Sanctuary and spend more time with them had seemed serendipitous during this challenging time in her sister's life so she had rearranged her schedule to make it happen.

Now that she was here, Jess realized how falsely optimistic she had been. Rachel didn't want to open her life to her. She wouldn't welcome Jess's concern or any effort she made to support her.

Her sister had made that clear more than a decade ago. She was perfectly happy to build her life here in Cape Sanctuary without Jess.

Jess lifted her face to the ocean breeze, wishing it could carry away the old pain in her heart.

5

Nate

WHEN HIS MOTHER RETURNED FROM VISITING JESS Clayton at her trailer, Nate told himself that odd feeling in his chest was relief. He certainly wasn't disappointed.

"Your guest didn't want to come to dinner?"

"She had a long day of driving," Eleanor explained. "She wanted to get some rest so she'll be full of vim and vigor tomorrow."

"Is that seriously what she said?" Sophie looked up from her phone long enough to give the world a general look of disgust at the idea of someone using such an old-fashioned term.

His mother laughed. "Okay, those are my words. Jess said she wanted to rest up for tomorrow. We have a lot of work ahead of us."

Sophie frowned at that. "I don't get why you have to do this now. I mean, it's not like you're using all those other rooms."

"I might if they weren't so crowded with old things."

"What would you use them for?" Nate was genuinely curious. He had a strange feeling about this whole thing, especially since his mother was being so closemouthed about hiring Jess to help her clean out Whitaker House.

Why hadn't she told him? Eleanor wasn't usually so secretive about things. He wasn't naive enough to believe he knew every detail about his mother's life but this seemed like such an odd thing to conceal from him.

Eleanor gave them both a breezy smile. "Oh, I don't know. Maybe I'll start a yoga studio. Or open a bed-and-breakfast for starving artists or something."

That actually didn't sound as far-fetched as it might. The house would be perfect for something like that, set on a small cliff overlooking the Pacific, with a terraced pathway that led down to a small cove.

The beach was open to the public but because the only access was across property that had been in the Whitaker family for generations, only townspeople in Cape Sanctuary knew about it and used it.

To Nate, Sunshine Cove had always felt like his own private refuge. He had loved waking up before school and taking the long, winding path down to the beach to surf the cold waters.

Sometimes friends from town would meet him but he was often on his own, though more than once he had been joined by a pod of dolphins playing in the surf.

In retrospect, it hadn't been safe at all for a teenage punk to be down there by himself but he wouldn't trade those moments and memories for anything.

He hadn't surfed in a long time. His work schedule had been demanding lately as the construction market in the area boomed. He should do something about that.

"How was the movie?" he asked them.

"Fine," Sophie said shortly.

He fought down his annoyance at her succinct response. Over

the past two or three weeks, one-syllable responses had become the norm for her, at least in her interactions with Nate.

He wasn't sure what the hell had happened to his sweet, talkative, fun daughter. After she hit thirteen, she had somehow become surly and short with him.

Was he at fault or was it hormones? Or was it something else entirely?

He had no idea. He only knew he was getting seriously tired of it.

"Only fine? You've been looking forward to that one for weeks."

"The book was better," she said.

"Books are usually better than movies," Eleanor said. "I remember how disappointed I was when I watched *Doctor Zhivago* after reading the book."

"I also don't like that all the people who never bothered to read the books are stanning all over the movie. So lame."

While Nate didn't consider himself the hippest of parents, he at least knew *stans* were superfans.

"Regardless of the movie's quality or lack thereof, we had a lovely girls' day in the city," his mother said. "The orthodontist appointment went well and then we did a little shopping at a couple of our favorite shops. I bought a new purse and some yarn, of course, and Sophie found some cute new earrings. Show your dad," she said.

Without bothering to look at him, Sophie flicked one dangly earring that looked like it ended in an arrow.

"Fun."

She shrugged, not shifting her gaze from her phone, and Nate again fought down his irritation and, yes, hurt.

He felt like the sweet, kind girl with whom he had spent thirteen years building a loving relationship had rolled out with the tide one day, leaving this angry, sullen stranger in her wake.

During dinner, Eleanor and Sophie talked more about their

trip to town and the last few weeks of school for Sophie while they ate. When they finished, Sophie cleared her plate and loaded it into the dishwasher then claimed homework.

"I forgot all about an essay I have to write for English class. It's due tomorrow," she claimed.

He might have told her maybe she should have made sure she was caught up on schoolwork before taking the afternoon off with her grandmother to go to a movie but he didn't want to cause more tension so he let it slide.

"Gram, can I use your computer?"

"Sure. It's already on, since I was using it before dinner."

"Thanks. This won't take long." Sophie raced into the other room.

"So," he said to his mother after she left, "tell me about Jess Clayton."

Eleanor busied herself with transferring the leftover vegetables into a glass container. "What do you want to know?"

Who is she? What put those shadows in her eyes? Is she involved with anyone?

He couldn't ask any of those questions so he focused on the dozen other things he wanted to know.

"How did you hear about her? And how do you know you can trust her not to rob you blind?"

Eleanor's mouth tightened with annoyance. "You might not believe this but sometimes I know what I'm doing. I did my research. She comes highly recommended and not just by Lucinda. I called other clients, who all had nothing but good things to say about her and her partner."

That was something, at least. "That's good to know. It's not a question of me not believing that you know what you're doing. I just worry about you. It's kind of in my job description. I don't want to see you get scammed by an opportunist out to take advantage of your kind nature and willingness to believe the best in people."

Eleanor's expression softened. "Jess isn't like that. She doesn't take any kind of commission on anything I might sell down the line. Her fee is standard and more than reasonable for the services she provides. Oh, and she's Rachel McBride's sister."

He stared. "Seriously? The Rachel McBride we know?"

"Yes. Cody's wife. Mom to those darling kids. The Rachel McBride who lives in town and has all those social media followers."

That was certainly unexpected information. Rachel was tall, willowy, with a warm, friendly smile and long dark hair. She tended to wear flowered dresses and lived in a house with a literal picket fence.

He had only had one brief encounter with Jess but she had struck him as sharp-edged, independent, tough. Jess had short, choppy honey-colored hair, lean, sculpted features and a vague air of restlessness.

On reflection, he thought he could picture a resemblance in the eye color, that green that reminded him of the ocean on a stormy afternoon.

Rachel had moved to town around high school age, he thought he remembered. She had lived with Kurt and Jan Miller. He only knew that because the Millers' older daughter had dated one of his friends.

"I didn't know Rachel had a sister."

"I wouldn't have known about the connection myself, though I think Rachel had mentioned Transitions in passing to me. But my friend who recommended Jess mentioned Cape Sanctuary to her and Jess told her about her sister here."

Rachel was married to one of the subs who often did work for Nate at his construction company. He had always found Cody a good guy, honest and hardworking. He had even socialized with the McBrides on occasion.

That made him feel slightly better about the whole thing. If nothing else, he would probably be able to track her down if she absconded with any of his family's valuables.

"You've already gone through your father's bookshelves and taken the books you wanted. Do you want to go through his office one more time to see if there's anything else you would like to keep, before we start purging things tomorrow?"

No. He wanted his father back, he didn't want to try holding on to the memory of Jack Whitaker through inanimate objects.

"I'll take a look," he said.

He hadn't spent much time in his father's study in the six months since his death. The scent of dusty old books and leather furniture hit him like a two-by-four to the gut.

He stood helpless for a moment, lost in his grief for the man who had wanted so much for Nate to follow in his academic footsteps.

He was picking out a book on tying flies and another collection of short stories by an author they had both admired when Sophie came in.

"It smells like Grandpa in here," she said.

"Yeah."

She inhaled, closing her eyes as if to absorb it into her skin. When she opened her eyes, he thought he saw glimpses of his sweet daughter before she looked away.

"I'm done with my assignment. My friend Maria texted while I was working and asked if I could go to a slumber party at her house."

"When?"

"Friday. Her mom will be there so you don't have to worry about that."

Which gave him only about a million other things to worry about when it came to his child.

"Who's going to be at this slumber party?"

"Just some kids from school."

"Which kids?"

"I don't know all of them. She goes to the Catholic school and some of her friends from there will be going."

He raised an eyebrow. "Boys?"

"I don't know. She hasn't told me everyone who's coming. Do you need every single name on the list?"

By her defiance, he suspected there was far more to the story than she was letting on. "Yes. Or at least the number of Maria's mom so I can ask her."

"That is so stupid. You don't trust me. I feel like I'm living with the NSA or something. Why do you have to know every detail of my life? I'll be fourteen years old in only five months."

"Right. So that's four years and five months longer during which I'm still responsible for keeping you safe and out of juvenile detention."

"I might as *well* be in jail. Even prisoners get time off once in a while for good behavior."

Maybe you could show some good behavior once in a while. Then we can talk.

He opted not to inflame the situation more by saying that. "I'm sorry you feel that way. I'm only concerned for my daughter's physical and emotional safety."

The look she gave him would have soured the milk of a whole pasture full of cows.

"I'm going home. My head hurts."

"Fine. Put your phone on the charger when you get home. I'll be there in a minute."

She glared at him and stomped out. He followed and saw that she at least lifted her cranky mood long enough to hug her grandmother.

"Night, Gram. I had a really fun day today."

"So did I, darling."

After Sophie left with their black Lab, Cinder, in tow, Nate turned to his mother.

"You think I'm too hard on her, don't you?"

She shrugged. "I think you've never been a thirteen-year-old girl."

"Thank the Lord."

She laughed. "She's a good girl, Nate. But if you push her too hard to be who you want her to be, she's going to instinctively run in the other direction."

"What happened to my sweet little girl who a few weeks ago thought I was the coolest person in the world?"

"She's growing up. Finding herself. Figuring out who she is. If you'll recall, you and your father certainly butted heads plenty when you were around Sophie's age."

"And after that. For quite a few years. You don't have to say it. I was a little shit, wasn't I?"

Eleanor smiled. "I wouldn't go that far. You wanted your own way and didn't want to listen to us or follow any of our house rules. But we made it through and by the time you left for the army, you and your father had a good relationship. He was so proud of you."

"I'm sorry I put you through that."

"We all survived. And you'll survive Sophie's teenage years, too."

"I hope so." He hugged his mother, too, feeling the thinness that hadn't been there before his father was diagnosed with cancer. Caring for him in his last days and then grieving him the past six months seemed to have aged her beyond her years. She had turned seventy a few months earlier and had never felt so fragile to him.

"Don't overdo tomorrow," he advised her. "I know you've been feeling under the weather lately."

Her mouth thinned briefly before tilting into a reassuring smile. "I'll be fine. Don't worry about me."

"I told you, that's part of my job description. Let me know if you need my help with anything, once you start sorting through what you're keeping and getting rid of. I can help with the big items."

"Thank you, my dear. Don't worry about things here. I'm sure between Jess and I, we will have everything under control."

"No doubt," he said. After he said good-night to his mother, he walked the short distance to his and Sophie's house. The lights were off in the little Airstream and he tried not to picture Jess Clayton stretched out inside, hair tousled, sleepy.

His conversation with his mother hadn't shed much light on Eleanor's reasons for taking on this project right now. Whatever her motives, he would support her. If she trusted Jess, he didn't have any reason not to.

Eleanor had been withdrawn and sad for months since his father died. Perhaps clearing and organizing her house would invigorate her and help her shake off the grief.

If that happened, he would owe Jess Clayton far more than merely an apology.

6

Jess

THE NEXT MORNING, JESS DRANK HER COFFEE while she watched the sunrise send ribbons of pink and amber across the water.

California was most known for its sunsets, of course, the sun's nightly slide into the Pacific, but she was particularly fond of the sunrises. They might not hold the same drama as the sunsets, but she loved the way the morning light played on the water.

She tidied up her trailer, which took all of about three minutes, then grabbed her supplies and headed up to Whitaker House.

Eleanor answered the door only a few seconds after she rang the bell. Her features wore the peculiar mix of excitement and trepidation Jess was accustomed to seeing in her clients.

"Good morning. Can I get you some breakfast?"

"I've already eaten, thanks. I'm all ready to go."

"Are you sure? I made blueberry muffins this morning."

That did sound—and smell—delicious. Still, Jess shook her head. "No thank you. Maybe we could save them for a mid-day snack."

"Right."

"Should we take a look around the house so we can see where we want to start?"

"Yes. That would probably be best. What do you want to see first?"

"We can start here and then work our way through the house."

This was always the most tense part of every job, when the client teetered on the edge of uncertainty and the wrong move by Jess could send them tumbling down the wrong side.

It was a delicate dance. Sometimes when she came into a job, it was inevitable that her clients would be moving, like when health problems required a different living situation.

Sometimes it was voluntary, when clients wanted to down-size in their golden years.

Eleanor's case was a little tricky. She seemed to want to only clean out her house so that her son wouldn't have to do the job after she died.

After her initial hesitancy, Eleanor entered into the tour with enthusiasm, showing Jess behind closed doors of the house.

"There are seven bedrooms in total, right?" she asked, after they had seen three.

"Yes, counting the master. I told you things were a real mess. I'm embarrassed that I let the clutter take over and get to this point."

"I have been at this for five years, Eleanor," she said gently. "Please believe me when I tell you Whitaker House is nothing compared to most of the jobs I've done."

Eleanor seemed heartened by that information. "Jack didn't like to throw things away. He wasn't a hoarder by any means. I don't want you to think that. But while his family had this lovely house, his parents were cash poor when he was growing up. Jack liked to reuse and recycle where he could. After he died, well, I honestly didn't know where to start so it was easier not to do anything."

"I totally understand. That's not at all an unusual reaction upon the loss of a loved one."

"It's been six months, though. I thought things might become somewhat easier as the months pass. Instead, the loss seems fresher every day."

The pain in her voice made Jess's throat tighten. She remembered going through that after her parents died. For the first few years, the pain seemed to get worse instead of better. The regret and guilt haunted her sleep and turned her angry and hard.

Finally, right around the time she had enlisted, the ache inside her began to fade. She couldn't point to any single event that had turned things around. But one day she had woken up feeling as if a cloud had lifted, as if the sun seemed to be shining a little more brightly and the world seemed a little more beautiful.

She still had moments of raw grief sometimes.

Did Rachel?

They didn't talk about their parents. It was like a huge, painful topic neither of them wanted to broach.

"I'm sorry," she murmured, laying a comforting hand on the other woman's arm.

"Thank you." Eleanor patted her hand, then seemed to push away the sadness.

"Are you comfortable helping me go through your husband's things?" she asked when Eleanor led the way to an office space facing the water, the desk crowded with loose papers and the bookshelves overflowing.

"I don't know."

"I can do it on my own if you want."

Eleanor didn't seem to like that suggestion either so Jess offered one more. "If you would like, we can save this room until later and start working through some of the empty bedrooms first."

"Let's do that," Eleanor said with alacrity. "That way I can have Nate go through one more time to make sure he takes any of his father's effects he might still want. He was here last night but only went through quickly. I would like to give him another chance."

They would have to get around to this man cave eventually but Jess could wait. "All right. Why don't you show me the other bedrooms and we can pick one to start."

"Perfect," Eleanor said.

Whitaker House was truly lovely. Built into the hillside, it featured large, airy rooms and stunning woodwork. Most rooms opened up to views of either the ocean or the surrounding forest of redwoods and coastal pine.

Eleanor had described the house as cluttered and dark but Jess didn't see that. She saw a structure that had provided a home for multiple generations, where each had left a mark.

She would have loved to wander through every room admiring both the view and the contents but knew their time was limited.

"How long has this house been in your husband's family?"

"Since it was built. Jack's great-grandfather came from banking money back East and wanted to make his mark in California. He was a haphazard rancher at best, from what I understand. By the time Jack and I married, much of the surrounding land had been sold off over the years, leaving just these two acres, the main house and a few run-down guesthouses."

"I didn't notice any run-down guesthouses."

"We tore one down years ago because it couldn't be saved and Nathaniel fixed up the other one after he came back home with Sophie. Basically he completely rebuilt it, saving only the bones. We had plenty of room for them here, of course, and he lived here when she was little. When she started school, he felt like it was important that the two of them have their own place. It's a darling house. No more than a thousand square feet but he's done a great job with it."

Where was Sophie's mother? She wanted to ask but didn't want to be nosy. She was here to help clean out Whitaker House, not pry into the business of the inhabitants, no matter how intriguing she might find them.

"It's nice that you know all this history about your husband's family."

"Oh, we can trace back generations. My late mother-in-law was obsessed with Whitaker genealogy. On my own side, I can't keep track past the great-grandparents."

Jess couldn't trace her family even that far. She knew her father had been orphaned young and her mother had run away from home to marry him when she was seventeen. Neither had ever talked about their parents much.

Maybe Rachel knew more than she did. Her sister had always been interested in that sort of thing.

Eleanor opened a door at the end of the hall. "This was Nathaniel's bedroom. Let's leave this one for now, too, so he can go through it one more time himself. I think he's taken most of the mementos he might have wanted. His surfboards, favorite books, that sort of thing. What's left are things he probably doesn't mind leaving behind."

Jess stood inside the door, scanning the room to mentally catalog the work ahead of her. It smelled like him, an outdoorsy mix of soap and cedar. Which was completely irrelevant to anything.

"He's a surfer?" she asked. There was a gorgeous framed photograph of a surfer on the wall across from the bed, the figure tiny as it made its way through a huge translucent green curl of water.

"Yes. That's him in high school when he went to Hawaii with some friends. He never competed, only for fun, but he was good enough to be on the professional circuit, if you ask me. Of course, I'm his doting mother. What else am I going to say?"

Eleanor gave a rueful smile that Jess couldn't help returning.

"In some parts of California, the schools have surf teams but Cape Sanctuary is too small for that and the surfing isn't all that great. After high school, Nathaniel was torn between moving to Southern California to pursue professional surfing or joining the military after high school. The military won."

She had suspected he was ex-military. It wasn't any one thing she could pinpoint, more his general bearing.

Yet one more reason, if she needed it, to ignore her unfortunate attraction to the man. She had nothing against the military in general. She had given years of her life to the army, after all. In that time she had known mostly good, honorable men and women who worked hard to uphold the ideals of their particular branch of the military.

But she had also been sexually harassed more than once and had even physically fought off a sergeant who wouldn't take no for an answer and thought his higher rank allowed him to touch whomever he wanted, whenever he wanted. She had defended herself with a well-placed knee and an even better-placed warning that the asshole needed to keep his hands to himself around her and any other female recruits or she would personally make sure he received a dishonorable discharge.

She had spent too much of her life being an unwilling victim to her father's emotional abuse and complete dominance in their family to tolerate male hegemony in any form.

"It's probably for the best if we have, er, Nathaniel help us clean this out."

Eleanor chuckled. "He won't appreciate you calling him Nathaniel. No one does but me, now that his father's gone. It's been 'Nate' to just about everyone since he was in school."

Jess forced a smile. "I'm the same way when people want to

call me Jessica. It's my name but Jessica ought to be wearing frilly dresses and have her hair perfectly curled. That's never been me."

"Isn't it wonderful that our names do not always have to define us? Everyone called me Eleanor Roosevelt when I was a girl. I'll admit, I might have become a bit more outspoken, with that sort of role model, but they were hard shoes to fill. Jack just called me Ellie."

Her smile wobbled and Jess worried she might be on the brink of tears. She pretended to mark something on her checklist to give the other woman time to recover.

"All right," she said. "We have ruled out the two rooms we're *not* clearing out yet. While I am enjoying the tour and the history immensely, maybe you should point me in the direction of one we can start on."

Eleanor's laugh sounded shaky but no longer tearful. "You caught me. This is harder than I thought it would be. My whole life since I was twenty-five years old is wrapped up in this house. My husband's entire life was wrapped up in it. Sifting through a legacy is *hard*. Now I understand why some people leave this until after they're gone."

"If you have changed your mind about doing this now, I completely understand. I have other jobs I can do. I'll charge you my travel fees and for my time today and we can leave it at that."

For an instant, Eleanor looked tempted by the offer but she finally shook her head. "That would be the coward's way out. Eleanor Roosevelt was certainly not a coward and neither am I. No. This won't be easy but I think I just have to push my way through the hard, don't I? That is what life is all about."

Oh, she liked Eleanor. The woman's grace and dignity made it very tough to maintain a cool, impersonal business relationship. Jess wanted her as a friend.

"Come on," Eleanor said. "I'll show you the rest of the rooms, then we can decide where to begin."

In the end, they both chose to start in one of the spare bedrooms on the south, lesser-used wing. That took most of the morning, during which they cleared away several boxes of old holiday decorations that hadn't been used in years as well as various knickknacks from previous generations.

She carried some of the boxes down to her pickup truck, which left several more boxes and an old velvet rocker recliner in the room.

"I don't want you to have to carry everything by yourself. Let me get Nathaniel to help you."

"It's my job, Eleanor."

"But it's all my old junk. I can call him. He might be busy but he can probably come later."

"How about this? Now that this room is mostly cleared out, let's use the space for a clearing house of sorts for this wing of the house. We can put the things going to a charity shop on one side and the things you might want to sell yourself at an estate auction on the other."

"I don't know about an estate auction. Unless you or your partner can run it for me, the whole thing seems like so much bother for a few hundred dollars."

"From what I've seen, you might be looking at substantially more than that."

"I wouldn't mind being able to donate to Sophie's college fund. Her grandfather would love that."

"Good idea. You don't have to decide that right now. We can sort through things and you can make up your mind later. If you decide it's too much bother, we can donate everything to the charity shop."

Eleanor sighed. "You're trying to make this as painless as possible on me, aren't you?"

"That's the idea." Jess smiled.

They broke for lunch shortly after that. Eleanor looked tired and said she needed to rest for a half hour before they started up again.

"Perfect. Would you like me to take Charlie for a walk?" Jess suggested.

"Oh, he would love that. His harness and leash are by the back door of the mudroom. Thank you, my dear. I only need a few minutes, then I should be right as rain."

Jess quickly found the dog's leash and a chest harness that took her a moment to figure out while the dog watched on with clear anticipation.

Finally they were ready and she headed with the little hybrid dog on a trail that wended through the trees along the rocky cliffs overlooking the Pacific.

The air was sweet with the scent of redwoods and pines, with a salty underlayer from the ocean.

She would never get anything done if she lived here, Jess thought. The scenery was just so beautiful, she wanted to sink onto a fallen log and just watch the waves.

"Should we go back?" she asked Charlie after a few moments. He gave her a quizzical look but trotted ahead of her back toward the house.

This was one of the downfalls of her itinerant life. She had always wanted a pet but didn't think it was fair to leave one in a tiny trailer all day while she worked. Clients who had pets were her favorites because she could shower all her pent-up cuddles on them.

When she returned to the house, she found Eleanor back in the kitchen, looking much more energized.

"How was your walk?"

"Beautiful. I can't get enough of your views here."

"Aren't I lucky?" Eleanor said with a smile.

Jess had to agree.

The next room they worked in after lunch turned out to contain a treasure trove, a big walk-in closet that was filled with clothing of every possible style and color. It was like something out of a vintage boutique.

"For years, I've been throwing everything I don't know what to do with in this closet," Eleanor confessed.

"These have some value. Vintage clothing in this kind of condition is always hot and I'm sure we could find a vintage clothing store maybe in one of the bigger communities that might take some on consignment."

Eleanor snorted and stuck on a particularly ugly yellow hat. "I remember my late mother-in-law wearing this to church on Sundays, without fail. She was quite a dragon, trust me. She didn't want me to marry her precious Jack because my blood wasn't nearly blue enough."

She looked at herself in the mirror. "All I see when I look at it is her frowning face at Sunday dinner, criticizing me for not using enough yeast in my rolls. I can't believe anyone would want this ratty old thing."

"You may be surprised. It looks like something you might find on a Paris runway right now. I'm not an expert on fashion so I'll leave that determination to my partner."

Yvette had a fantastic eye for design and fashion and they typically consulted together frequently. Jess would snap a picture of several of the items and send them to her to see if her instincts were right, that they carried resale value.

They spent a few more hours going through the clothing, with Jess taking pictures here and there of things that caught her eye.

She could tell Eleanor was tired, though the older woman refused to rest when Jess suggested it.

"We're almost done with this room. It will be so nice to say we have two rooms done."

"It would, but I need to stretch and I think Charlie needs to go out."

Eleanor shifted her attention to her cuddly little dog, who was staring at both of them from the doorway with an intent look.

"You're probably right."

"I'll take him out."

"Thank you. I believe I could do with a snack. And I just realized Sophie should be coming home on the school bus soon. She usually hangs out here in the afternoons until Nathaniel comes home from work."

How wonderful of Eleanor to be there for her granddaughter, Jess thought as she opened the door for the dog into the fenced area of the gardens.

Charlie finished his business then ran back inside quickly. When they both returned to the kitchen, she found Eleanor setting out a snack of fruits, vegetables and cheeses.

"This looks good."

"I didn't eat much lunch and realized I was hungry. Help yourself."

She grabbed some grapes and a few cubes of what looked like a good Havarti and set them on one of the plates Eleanor pulled from the cupboard.

"We've been so busy this morning that I really haven't had time to ask you about yourself."

Jess tensed. She really didn't like talking about her past. "Not much to tell," she said. "I joined the army out of high school and then a friend and I started Transitions when we both got out."

"I know that much. I'm more interested in what you did before that. Where did you grow up?"

She swallowed a grape then gave some of the glib narrative she had developed over the years. It was the truth, anyway.

"Our father was in the military so we moved around a lot."

"You probably lived in some interesting places, didn't you?"

Years later, they all tended to run together in her memory. "We spent some time in Hawaii, Germany, England. All over the place."

"Would you say you consider any one of those home?" Eleanor pressed.

"Tough question. I don't know. I liked Monterey quite a bit."

"Who doesn't?" Eleanor said with a laugh.

"Cape Sanctuary reminds me of that area. The same dramatic coastline and scenery."

Eleanor nodded. "I've always thought so. The landscape here is a bit like the Monterey and Carmel area but without the crowds. The best of both worlds. Of course, we don't have the same number of quality restaurants and art galleries but we do all right here."

Better than all right. Jess knew her sister loved it here. Rachel had stayed through high school, hadn't she? Even when Jess had tried to convince her to move to Southern California with her.

"Did you grow up in this area?" Jess asked. She was genuinely curious but was aware she also used the question as a diversionary tactic to keep Eleanor from probing too deeply into Jess's own history.

"No. I was raised in Europe and Asia, mostly. Like you, I don't have any one place I could call home. My parents were both in the foreign service."

"That sounds exotic. I imagine you have fascinating stories."

"I was in boarding school, for the most part. It was rather lonely, if you want the truth. I went to Stanford for university and ended up meeting Jack my senior year. He was the assistant professor for an English class I was taking. He was seven years older than I was and we both knew it was a completely inappropriate relationship but we fell in love anyway. It was quite scandalous, as I'm sure you can imagine. It was his first university teaching job and he was so afraid we would be found out. Lots of clandestine meetings at my apartment, hotels off campus, that sort of thing."

Her dreamy expression gave Jess an odd feeling. Envy, she realized.

Why? She didn't want that kind of passion. Ever. Her mother had clearly demonstrated how disastrous it could be to love someone that completely.

"Jack and I eloped the day after my college graduation," Eleanor went on with a laugh. "It was the only way he could keep his job."

"Did he stay at Stanford?"

"Another few years and then his mother died and his father grew ill and we decided to move back here to help him. He transferred and we've been here ever since. He commuted to Redding to teach there. It wasn't quite Stanford, but it was the students he loved anyway."

Was Eleanor aware her whole expression softened whenever she talked about her husband? Jess found it charming.

Before she could answer, she heard the front door open and a young voice call out. "Gram? Are you home?"

"In the kitchen, my dear."

An instant later, a young teenage girl came in, maybe thirteen or fourteen. She had light brown hair and bright blue eyes. Jess knew instantly this must be Nate's daughter, Sophie.

The girl stopped short in the doorway. "Oh. I didn't know you had company."

"This is my friend Jess Clayton. I told you about her. Jess, this is my granddaughter, Sophia."

"Sophie," the girl said. She tilted her head, studying Jess with interest. "You're the one who has that adorable trailer parked by the beach trail."

"Guilty."

"It's so cute. Is it an antique?"

"It's a vintage Airstream from the 1990s but I'm not sure I would call it an antique exactly."

"I've seen them on Instagram. Did you restore it yourself?"

"Most of it. It's been a labor of love for the past few years."

"Can I see inside it sometime?"

She blinked at the unexpected request. Not very many adolescent girls would be interested in a restored Airstream.

"Sophie has an emerging interest in all things design," Eleanor explained.

"That's terrific," Jess said. "Good for you. I should tell you that while I did most of the physical work except what I had subcontractors help with, my friend Yvette made all the design choices. It would have been a disaster if I had tried to decorate it myself."

Sophie offered her a tentative smile. "I still want to see it sometime. If you don't mind."

"Why don't we go now?" Eleanor suggested. "I wouldn't mind seeing it myself."

"Can we?" Sophie asked.

Jess felt guilty, thinking of all the work they still had to do here at Eleanor's house, the rooms they hadn't yet touched.

On the other hand, Eleanor was paying for her time. If she wanted to take a break so her granddaughter could see a restored travel trailer, Jess didn't know that it was her place to argue. Anyway, the Airstream was only twenty-four feet long. The tour only lasted about two minutes.

"Sure. Let's go."

She did love her little house, with its clever uses of space and the generous light pouring in through the windows encircling it. Eleanor and her granddaughter seemed enthralled with the cabinets and the bathroom wet room that gave her adequate space to shower.

"It's so cute. Seriously. The cutest tiny house I've ever seen. You really live here all the time?" Sophie asked.

"Technically I keep an apartment outside LA but I usually only sleep there a few weeks out of the year. The rest of the time, this is home."

"That's so awesome. Maybe I'll buy one when I graduate from high school and travel around the US and Canada."

"After college, you mean?" Eleanor asked pointedly.

Sophie shrugged. "Or before. Who knows?"

"Your dad won't be very happy with that idea," Eleanor said with a laugh.

"By then I'll be eighteen and he won't get any say in what I do," the girl retorted.

The defiance in her voice reminded Jess so painfully of her own stilted relationship with her father at this age. Jess's father had earned her antagonism. Had Sophie's?

She didn't know the man well enough to make a guess about that.

"Are you really Rachel McBride's sister?" Sophie asked as they were heading back to the house. "You don't seem very much alike."

Yes, she had been hearing that for most of her life. Rachel had been sweet and kind, traits Jess could never claim.

"Yes. Since the day she was born. I'm two years older."

"I follow her on Insta. Someday I want to have as many followers as she does."

She blinked at this information. It still took her by surprise to be reminded that Rachel had become a social media influencer, mixing images of her kids and her home with charming pictures of the landscape around Cape Sanctuary. Jess didn't spend a lot of time on social media but she had found that following her sister was the best way to keep up with her nieces and nephew.

"Rachel is quite a celebrity around here," Eleanor added.

"Not just around here," Sophie said. "My friend Jaycee lives in Florida and her mom follows Rachel. She was excited that I live in the same town as her."

"I'm glad she found her niche," Jess said.

"She should feature your Airstream. Seriously, it's so cute."

Jess wasn't sure she liked the idea of all those prying eyes looking into her space.

"Maybe," she said in a noncommittal way.

"Can I help you guys clean stuff out?" Sophie asked when they returned to the kitchen.

"We're mostly done for today. I'm only taking a few pictures of some clothes we found in one of the rooms to send to my partner. She's better than I am at guessing value."

"You can help us, if you'd like. But don't you have homework to do first?" Eleanor asked.

Was the older woman looking pale again or was it only the difference in light after moving from the sunshine to the indoor lighting?

"Not much. Half a math worksheet that I didn't have enough time in class to finish. I'm caught up with everything else."

"You can certainly join us, then."

As they started toward the wing they had been working in, Eleanor stopped, resting her hand on the edge of a table in the hallway. "On second thought, I'm not feeling the best. Would you mind terribly if I stop for the day and take a nap?"

Jess frowned, worried all over again about Eleanor's health. "Am I wearing you out?"

"It's not your fault. I was ill a few weeks ago and I don't quite have my strength back yet, I'm afraid."

"Want me to stay with you, Gram?" Sophie asked.

"No. I'm fine. I'll just take a snooze in my favorite chair with Charlie on my lap and be good as new in a half hour or so."

"Are you sure?"

"Positive. Don't you worry about me. Go take your pictures." She kissed her granddaughter's head and shooed them down the hall.

"Is that unusual, for your grandmother to tire so easily?" she asked Sophie.

The girl shrugged. "Yeah, she gets tired a little more often lately, maybe. Like she said, she was pretty sick a few weeks ago. She didn't get out of bed for about three days. She hasn't been herself since then."

Jess found it odd that Eleanor had been so energetic first thing that morning and then had tired as the day wore on. She seemed frail, somehow.

Not her business, Jess reminded herself. She was supposed to be keeping a safe emotional distance from Eleanor, Sophie and everyone else here in Cape Sanctuary.

Too bad she was having such a hard time remembering that.

7

Nate

WHEN NATE LET HIMSELF INTO WHITAKER HOUSE in the early evening, he expected to find his mother dozing in her easy chair in the TV room, a talk show on and her dog, Charlie, stretched out next to her, wedged into the smallest of spots, while Sophie did her homework or messaged friends nearby.

Instead, the room was empty. So was the kitchen.

He was about to call out when he heard female voices coming from the end of the hallway, in a seldom-used wing of the house.

After a quick stop in the kitchen, he followed the sound. He couldn't hear what they said, he could only pick up the low murmur of voices and a sound he hadn't heard in a while, at least not shared with him. His daughter's laughter.

The sound hit him hard, as did the laugh he assumed must be coming from Jess Clayton. It was low and genuine and infinitely appealing.

What had she said to make Sophie laugh? His daughter didn't even know Jess. Why would she be so open and happy with a strange woman while treating her own father like some kind of pariah?

He was half-tempted to go back the way he had come and leave them to their fun but then he heard his mother's laughter join in and couldn't resist seeing what had amused them all so much.

The door to the room was open and he peeked in to find a startling sight. Jess sat on the bed while his mother was in a rocking chair in the room. Both of them were focused on Sophie, who was dressed in a fancy blue dress he didn't recognize.

"Well? How do I look?" she asked.

"Smashing, darling," his mother answered. "Like you stepped right off the cover of a 1920s copy of *Vogue*."

"It looks like it was made for you," Jess Clayton added with a smile that made him catch his breath. She looked bright and vibrant and beautiful.

Sophie giggled. "I should have one of those long cigarette holders to complete the look."

Eleanor laughed. "You won't find that here amid these things. Your great-great-grandmother might have been a flapper once upon a time but she hated smoking with a passion. I only met her a few times before she died but I knew she thought it was a nasty habit fit for only floozies."

"Ouch," Jess said.

"I know. I had to hide my own cigarettes when I first met her after Jack brought me here to meet his parents."

That was news to Nate. He couldn't resist chiming in. "I never knew you used to smoke."

All three females in the room looked at him with varying expressions. His mother looked startled but pleased, Jess immediately took on a guarded expression and Sophie simply looked away, as if she couldn't bear the sight of him.

"It was a long time ago." His mother shrugged. "I only picked it up in college because all my friends were smoking. I quit shortly after I married your father."

What else didn't he know about his mother?

"Sorry to interrupt the fashion show. Looks like fun."

"Oh, it has been. We've found so many old treasures, haven't we, girls? Things I had forgotten I still had. It's been quite a day."

"I'm glad you were feeling better enough to join us, after all," Jess said.

Eleanor quickly changed the subject, making him wonder if she had been under the weather.

"We made good progress today. Two rooms down, anyway."

"That's great."

"At this rate, it won't take us long at all to work our way through the house."

"May I keep this dress, Gram?" Sophie asked.

"It's yours if you want it. You can keep anything else you find, too."

"Keep in mind that our house isn't as big as this one," Nate pointed out.

"I know that."

How did she manage to convey so much disgust with just a few words? She seemed to have perfected that tone over the past month.

He sighed inwardly and forced a smile. "I happened to be driving past The Mandarin on my way home and decided Chinese takeout sounded good. Anybody interested?"

"Ooh. Me!" Eleanor said.

"Did you get orange chicken?" Sophie asked.

"Yes. I know that's your favorite. And kung pao and teriyaki chicken as well as beef with broccoli. Plus rice and their delicious chow mein."

"That sounds so good," Eleanor said. "How did you know I was in the mood for Chinese?"

"Lucky guess." He gave Jess a smile, hoping she could take this as the olive branch he intended after his rudeness the day before. "I picked up enough to feed everybody here and about a dozen more people. You're welcome to some, if you like Chinese."

She looked surprised at the invitation and he realized guiltily that he still hadn't officially apologized for his boorish behavior.

"You have to join us," Sophie said. "I want to hear more about the hoarder house you cleaned out."

"Yes, my dear. Please join us." Eleanor added her voice to Sophie's entreaty.

"I don't want to intrude on your family dinner."

"You're not intruding at all," Nate assured her. "Anyway, you have to eat. Nothing wrong with a free meal, is there?"

"I suppose not," she finally said.

"I just need to change out of this dress," Sophie said. "I don't want to spill food on it. I might wear it to school tomorrow. We're supposed to dress up from our favorite decade and this would be *perfect*. I can't believe I didn't think to ask you before if you had anything I could wear, Gram."

"Glad you found it before we give everything to Goodwill."

"Or send it to the consignment shop," Jess added.

"It's a lovely evening," Eleanor said. "Why don't we take the food out to the terrace so we can hear the ocean?"

"Good idea. I'll grab some plates and utensils."

"I'll do that while you and Jess carry out all this food. Sophie, join us as soon as you change out of that dress."

"Okay."

"Wow. You did buy a lot," Jess said, looking at several bags, each holding containers of food.

"I can never decide what sounds best. Anyway, it makes good leftovers for a day or two."

"True." She looked at Eleanor. "Can I carry out some glasses and beverages for people?"

"Oh, good idea. There's a pitcher of fruit-infused water in

the refrigerator. That's what I'll have and I know Sophie likes it. What about you, son?"

"I'm not picky."

By the time they carried everything out to the patio, which was a lovely spot in the May evening air, surrounded by vibrant spring flowers overflowing their pots, Sophie had changed her clothes and joined them.

He usually loved eating al fresco with his family. This was a place that generally left him with a great sense of peace, especially after a long day of wrestling with subcontractors and struggling with suppliers.

It was hard to feel peace with Jess Clayton around, especially given the awkwardness of their last meeting.

He wanted to apologize now to clear the air between them but couldn't figure out a way to do that while his mother and daughter were there.

To his vast relief, Sophie managed to put away her new surliness toward him for the evening, too busy being fascinated by their guest. Gone was the moody, intense thirteen-year-old girl he walked on eggshells around these days. Instead, she was bright and animated.

He had forgotten how funny and vivacious his daughter could be. He found himself just watching her and marveling that she was his child, this amazing human who had somehow survived being raised by a clumsy single father and her grandparents, losing her mother before she could even remember and her beloved grandfather six months ago after a long illness.

Nate was damn lucky to be her father and didn't take enough chances to tell her that.

"That was delicious," his mother said, pushing her plate away with satisfaction. "Thank you for being so thoughtful."

"You're welcome."

"It really is a lovely evening," Jess said, looking out at the ocean. "If this were my terrace, I think I would eat out here every night."

"We should, but the weather doesn't always cooperate. We are often chilly, so close to the coast, and we get plenty of rain," Eleanor said. "But you're right. I'm afraid we take the view for granted sometimes. Sometimes entire days go by when I only have to pinch myself once or twice a day that I really live here."

Jess laughed, a low, enticing sound that slid across his skin like a warm breath.

"I love it here," Sophie said. "I know Sunshine Cove isn't really our own private beach and other people can use it if they want to. But hardly anyone ever does so it kind of feels like ours."

"It is one of the best things about Whitaker House," Eleanor agreed.

"The tide is out," Sophie said suddenly. "We should go see if we can find a sea glass stopper. It's been forever since we've even looked."

Nate felt a pang in his chest at her suggestion, which reminded him so much of the days when she used to adore him.

They used to love beachcombing on *their* beach at low tide to see what new treasures the sea had delivered to them.

She was right. It seemed like forever since she had wanted to.

"A sea glass stopper?" Jess asked, looking confused.

"It's one of the most elusive of beachcombing treasures," Eleanor explained. "The stopper from a bottle or a jar. It's easy enough to find agates and your average, everyday sea glass washed smooth by the ocean. But an intact stopper is almost impossible to find. We've been on the hunt for years."

"We never find one, but it's still fun. We might not find what we're looking for, but we always find *something*," Sophie said.

"What a good idea and the perfect end to a delightful day," his mother said. "Let me change into my beach shoes."

"Are you sure you feel up to that?" Jess asked.

Again, his mother looked slightly perturbed at the question, though she quickly concealed it.

"I've been traipsing up and down that path since long before you were born. I'll be fine. You can go ahead without me, if you want."

"We'll clear away the food while you change your shoes," Nate said.

While they carried the dishes and the take-out meal inside, Sophie kept up a long-running conversation with Jess about surfing, about the end of the school year in a few more weeks, about her plans for the summer.

In about five minutes, she freely spilled out to this virtual stranger more info about her world than Nate could drag out in a week.

"Okay. I'm ready," his mother announced as they were loading the last few dishes into the dishwasher.

They set out on the walk that made three hairpin turns down a fairly steep hill to reach the bottom.

California's beaches were all public up to the high tide mark but access to them was sometimes closed when they were surrounded by private property. In the case of Sunshine Cove, the only egress was through the land surrounding Whitaker House.

The Whitaker family had always allowed townspeople to park on the road and walk through to reach it but as there were easier beaches to reach without the longish walk, few visitors ever found their way to the small beach.

Sophie was right. In many ways, it still felt like their own private little cove, shared only with the seals, otters and seabirds who sometimes visited.

"What will you do with a stopper if you find it?" Jess asked as they made their way down.

"I don't know. Maybe a necklace or something, don't you think, Gram?"

"Yes. We could find something fun to do with it."

"Gram makes jewelry with the sea glass and agates we find. I have a bunch of cool earrings and a ring she made. She also has a display case in her house that contains some of the things we've found in our cove."

"I'll have to remember to show that to you," Eleanor told Jess. "I believe that's not something I plan to get rid of anytime soon."

"Cherished treasures should definitely stay in the *save* category."

Sophie held the leashes of both dogs as they trotted down the path first. That was another family rule. Though they could let the dogs off leash as it was basically their own private spot, his parents had always insisted dogs remain leashed until they reached the cove to make sure there weren't any seals or sea turtles on the sand that the animals might bother.

Eleanor was next in line, which left him taking up the rear with Jess walking beside him. She didn't seem particularly comfortable with the arrangement but he decided this was his best chance to apologize.

"I'm glad to have the chance to speak with you privately," he said when his mother and Sophie had moved farther down the pathway ahead of them.

"Are you?"

Her tone wasn't at all encouraging but he pressed forward anyway.

"I'm afraid we got off on the wrong foot yesterday. I owe you an apology."

She raised an eyebrow. "Whatever for? Threatening to call the police on me?"

Had he really done that? He winced. "I'm afraid I didn't exactly roll out the welcome mat for you. I do apologize. I was hoping I would have the chance to apologize last night, but you didn't come to dinner."

"I'm sorry I inconvenienced you."

Her dry tone again made him wince. "I'm doing it again."

"Doing what again?"

"Stepping in it. I'm trying to apologize and not doing a very good job of it. Let me try again. I'm very sorry I was a jerk. The last thing I expected to find when I came home to grab some blueprints and a sandwich was a stranger parking a trailer on the property."

"Did Eleanor explain why she didn't tell you I was coming?"

"Not really. Only that she was afraid of my reaction, that I might think she was trying to close the book on the chapters of her life involving my father."

"Is that what you think?"

"No! Of course not. She loved my father very much. She was a loving, caring wife to the end."

"I've only known your mother through correspondence for a month or so and in person for only a day but I received the same impression. She doesn't want to forget those years, she only wants a fresh start as she prepares to move on with her life alone."

He looked ahead at Eleanor smiling down at something Sophie was saying to her. Where would he have been after Michelle died without his mother's calm, steadying presence?

"I've become a bit protective of her since my father died. She lives alone here. Though Sophie and I are technically on the property, our house is through the trees. Plus, I work long hours and Sophie has school and her friends. We're not always here."

"She has Charlie."

He snorted. "Right. Her killer Cavapoo, who is more likely to lick an intruder's face off than bite him."

Jess smiled slightly, just enough for Nate to feel as if he had accomplished something remarkable. "Even without Charlie, your mother strikes me as someone who can take care of herself."

"In most situations, yes. But she has a soft heart."

"You say that like it's a bad thing."

"Not at all. It's one of the things I admire most about her. But she can be too ready to always believe the best in people. I could easily see her opening up her property to someone down on his or her luck whom she met online or through her volunteer efforts. Someone who might have an ulterior motive for staying on the property of a widow who is financially comfortable."

Jess gave him a sidelong look that made him realize how his words could be interpreted.

"I'm not suggesting you have any ulterior motive. My mother explained all about hiring you to help her clean out the clutter in the house. She told me you come highly recommended."

"And let me guess. You checked out my credentials."

He debated how to answer that before deciding honesty was really his only choice.

"Guilty. And I learned she was right. Your reviews are all positive."

"Good to know."

"So far my apology isn't going very well, is it?"

To his surprise, her smile widened slightly. "Don't worry about it. You're not the first suspicious family member I've had to deal with since my friend and I started Transitions. Children aren't always happy when their parents decide it's time to downsize."

He frowned. Who said anything about downsizing? Eleanor had simply said she was clearing things out. Was she planning to move out?

She wouldn't sell the house without speaking to him first. He knew that much. But she could be making all these arrangements in a roundabout way of telling him she wanted to leave Whitaker House.

No. He and his mother had a good, loving relationship. She wouldn't keep a secret like that from him. Or at least he didn't *think* so.

He decided to change the subject away from his own disquiet. "Helping people declutter seems an odd career choice for a former staff sergeant."

She frowned. "Is that something you found in your research?"

"Indirectly. When I was looking at your company's Facebook page, I ended up on your partner Yvette's profile and saw an old picture of her in uniform with another soldier who was unmistakably you. I wasn't cyberstalking, I promise."

He really was making this worse.

To his relief, she didn't seem upset. "Yvette and I went through basic training and were deployed together."

"How did you decide to go into the, er, transition business."

"We both got out at the same time, around the time her grandmother was about to enter a nursing home. I didn't have anything else pressing to do so I agreed to help Yvette clean out her grandmother's house. We both realized we enjoyed the process. A couple of Yvette's older relatives asked us to help them, as well, and by the end of the summer, we realized we both had found something we love. I'm good at sifting through a house, parsing out what might hold value financially or emotionally and what can go in the bin or to Goodwill. Yvette is fantastic at marketing and design and has made connections in the resale market so our customers get the best prices for their excess items."

"You do this full-time?"

"More than full-time, if you want the truth. We really need to think about taking on someone else to help us. We seem to have an endless waiting list of people who don't know where to start."

"What do you like about it?"

She looked surprised by the question, as if she had never stopped to think about it.

"This may sound silly or even grandiose but I feel like I'm making a difference, one job at a time. People have a hard time with change. If I can facilitate that a little and give them one less thing to stress about, it's worth it."

They had reached the sand by now.

"Can I let the dogs off the leash?" Sophie asked.

He scanned the area to make sure they wouldn't disturb any fragile sea life. Charlie and Cinder were both well-mannered dogs and would back off on command but he didn't like to take any chances. When he couldn't see anything but a couple of seagulls pecking through a string of sea kelp washed up on the shore, he gestured to Sophie.

"Go ahead."

The moment she unclipped them, both dogs raced around the sand like they were kids out at recess.

Eleanor headed straight for the bench he and his father had built a few years earlier, just above the high tide line.

"You're not going to beachcomb with us?" Sophie asked her.

"You go ahead. I am perfectly content here, watching the sunset and the dogs. You have fun."

His mother sat down, gazing out to sea with her head slightly bowed.

She was thinking about his father. He didn't need to see her expression to know. Since his father's death, he had felt closer to Jack Whitaker here by the ocean than anywhere else.

Grief was a horrible thing, sometimes a living, breathing beast constantly prowling through a person's heart.

It was lovely to let the worries of the day go. His day had been a busy one, with multiple meetings on the various projects Whitaker Construction had a hand in right now.

Jess seemed to share his feeling as she walked beside him, looking out to sea more than she was perusing the sand for treasure.

"This is a truly lovely way to end a busy day. If this were my cove, I would be here every night. In fact, I think I would pitch a tent right there between those trees."

He had done that when he was a kid, plenty of nights when he was tired of butting heads with his father.

In retrospect, Nate felt stupid and childish at his own obstinance, especially now that his father was gone. Jack Whitaker had not been overly controlling. He only had high expectations for Nate, as most parents did for their children.

Whether it was grades, sports, his after-school job working for their neighbor's construction company, Nate had never felt as if his efforts were enough for his father.

They had fought most about college. His father, a tenured professor, researcher, scholar, had insisted Nate's future would be grim if he didn't graduate.

Nate probably would have done fine at university. There were times he regretted he didn't have a business degree, which would still come in handy these days.

His grades had only been average, from what he now knew was a combination of attention deficit disorder and undiagnosed slight dyslexia.

At the time, he had simply felt stupid and so very ready to be done with his educational journey. While he had weighed professional surfing, the military had seemed a more sensible choice.

Nate wanted to think he and his father had managed to attain some level of peace after he and Sophie moved back. Jack had never been anything but supportive as Nate faced the challenges of single parenthood.

His construction company, begun with only his meager savings and plenty of hard work, had taken off exponentially. His father must have seen what a better fit that had been for Nate than an academic track would have been.

By the time the damn cancer came for Jack, the two of them had healed those old wounds from his angry adolescence.

"I found something!" Sophie suddenly exclaimed from ahead of them. She scooped something up and brushed sand away while the dogs raced around them, sensing the excitement.

"Oh, what is it, darling?" Eleanor called. She rose from the bench for a closer look. "Did you find a stopper?"

"Better! It's a whole bottle. And there's a note in it! We found a message in a bottle!"

That was an even more thrilling discovery than a mere bottle stopper. The bottle Sophie held out was clear, sealed, about the size of a small ketchup bottle. He could clearly see a rolled note inside.

"I can't believe I found a message in a bottle. I've always wanted to! What do you think it says?"

"I think you'll have to open it to find out," Eleanor said. "Can you get it out?"

"I think so."

Sophie twisted off the stopper of the bottle. Her fingers were too large to fit inside but she shook the bottle and the rolled message came out just enough for her to grasp with her thumb and forefinger.

Sophie's eyes were wide, her color flushed. If he had known she would get this excited about a message in a bottle, he might have planted one on the beach ages ago for her to find.

Yeah, he knew that wouldn't have been the same as this discovery but it might have been worth it.

"What does it say?"

"I don't know. I can't read it very well."

"Is it old?" Jess asked. She also seemed to be caught up in the excitement.

"I don't know." Sophie frowned. "I don't think so. It's typed. It doesn't look like the old-fashioned type from a typewriter so I don't think it's *that* old."

She straightened it out. "It looks like Chinese or Japanese!"

"Oh dear." Eleanor looked disappointed. "Well, maybe we can find someone to translate."

"There's English, too," Sophie exclaimed. "It was sent in 2015! It says, 'We are students at Taku School in Japan, studying the ocean currents. We are dropping one hundred bottles into the ocean in April 2015. We would like to know where they travel.

Please respond to this email address with the date and the GPS location where you found this bottle so that we may add you to our study. In return, we will send you postcards and a small gift from Japan. Sincerely, Taku School students.'"

"How cool is that?" Jess said. "You can be part of a research study into ocean currents."

Sophie beamed. "Supercool. I mean, I kind of wish it was somebody on a deserted island who needed help or maybe a guy who wrote a letter to his dead girlfriend or something. But this is supercool, too."

"Are you going to answer?" Nate asked.

"Well, yeah."

"Wouldn't it be wonderful to receive some postcards from Japan? Maybe you can make a new pen pal."

"I'm going to send the email right now."

"Let's take some pictures of you finding it, then you can send those along with the location and your information," Nate suggested.

"Use my phone," she demanded.

He picked up her sparkly pink device and snapped a bunch of pictures of her with his mom and Jess.

"You should be in the picture," Jess said. "Let me take a few."

He handed her the phone and tried to ignore the little pulse of heat exchanged between the two of them.

He posed with his mother and Sophie, then Jess took one of just him and Sophie. He really wanted that pic. He would have to ask Sophie to text it to him or take it off her phone when it was charging every night in the kitchen.

"Okay, that's enough pictures. I want to send it now."

She took her phone, then her face fell. "Darn it. I always forget we can't get a good cell signal down here. Not enough bars to send photos, anyway."

"You can always send it later tonight."

"I don't want to wait. I'm going back up to the house."

"I'll come with you," Eleanor said. "This is so exciting. How many times have we hoped to find a message in a bottle? I gave up looking years ago!"

When he and Jess started to follow them, Eleanor waved them back. "Stay. Sunset will be in another twenty minutes or so and it looks like it will be spectacular from all the clouds we had earlier. Jess should have the chance to enjoy our gorgeous sunset displays here."

"I can walk back on my own," Jess protested.

"It's always better to have someone with you, especially when you're walking back after dusk. If I don't see you again tonight, good night. Thank you for all your help today."

"Come on, Gram," Sophie urged.

Eleanor laughed then followed her up the path, leaving the two of them alone.

8

Jess

JESS WATCHED ELEANOR AND SOPHIE CLIMB THE PATH up the hill toward Whitaker House, Sophie taking her grandmother's arm as the two chattered in excitement to each other.

"I think we've been ditched."

"Apparently." Nate looked bemused at how quickly the situation had shifted.

"You really don't have to stay with me," Jess assured him. "I don't mind walking up by myself. I spent two tours overseas and put about two hundred thousand miles on my truck for Transitions since I've been home. I think I can manage to walk a few hundred yards without any major catastrophes."

He smiled, teeth gleaming in the dying sunlight, and she felt that ridiculous shiver again. "I never thought otherwise. I'll go if you would prefer to be alone. Otherwise, I don't mind staying so I can let the dogs run off more energy."

She had forgotten all about the dogs. She shifted her gaze

from Eleanor and Sophie, almost to the top of the hill, toward the dogs, who were tussling over a piece of driftwood they had found.

The air had cooled a few degrees, making her grateful for her hoodie.

"I would hate to deprive the dogs of their fun."

By tacit agreement, they both headed for the bench his mother had just vacated. The dogs hurried over, Charlie the victor of the tug-of-war. The dog presented the stick to Nate, who picked it up and threw it in a long arc down the beach for both dogs to chase gleefully.

Given their contentious meeting the day before, Jess wouldn't have expected to find so much enjoyment in his company. Their conversation since they headed down the path to the cove had been funny, interesting, insightful.

She rather liked the man, which surprised her. It shouldn't, she supposed. She already adored his mother and was growing quite fond of his daughter.

All of the Whitakers were very hard to resist.

This time when the dogs came back, Cinder had the stick. The Lab disarmed her by bringing it straight to Jess and laying it in her lap.

"Thank you," she said.

"She doesn't always know when to stop," Nate said with a smile. "Now you're her hostage."

"I don't mind." She scratched the dog's head and chin, again wishing she could figure a way to have a dog of her own.

Her rambling life wasn't very conducive to caring for a pet who needed a yard and space to run. Maybe she could pick up a senior rescue who wouldn't need as much activity and might be more content spending long stretches of time in the trailer while she worked.

"How did things really go with my mother today?"

She sent him a sidelong look, wondering why he was asking.

She shrugged. "Progress is progress, right? We still have a long way to go but it's a good start."

He took the stick from Charlie and tossed it again, just shy of the surf.

"How is my mom handling everything?"

"Emotionally or physically?"

"Both. Either."

"She seems to get teary every so often over something we find that brings back memories. She has told me a few stories about your father as we work and it's clear they were deeply in love."

"Yes. These past six months have been hard on her." He paused. "You seem inordinately concerned about her health. Have you noticed anything unusual?"

She was reluctant to tell him, though she wasn't exactly sure why. She couldn't fault the man for being concerned over his mother's welfare.

"She had to stop to rest a few times. She said she was tired. But when she returned to help me, she seemed fine. Is there something I should know about her health?"

"I'm wondering the same thing. She doesn't tell me much. I think she doesn't want to worry me, probably because Dad's cancer was tough on all of us. She doesn't realize that I end up worrying *more* because my imagination goes in all directions."

"I can understand that."

"You'll tell me if you see anything you think I should worry about, right?"

"I...sure."

The dogs seemed to have lost track of the piece of driftwood they had been using to play catch. They started sniffing at something in the sand on the far side of the cove and Cinder let out a concerned bark.

"I'd better go see what they've found. It's probably a crab." Nate rose and headed toward the dogs.

The sun slipped down another notch and the colors seemed to intensify, oranges and ochre and purple.

Her phone suddenly buzzed with a text. Apparently her cell carrier had slightly better service here at the cove than Sophie's.

She thought about ignoring it then suddenly remembered she had meant to reach out to her sister that day and had completely forgotten. Guilt pinched at her like the crab the dogs were bothering.

So much for her intentions to spend more time with her sister and her nieces and nephew.

The message was indeed from Rachel.

Sorry. The day got away from me. I meant to text earlier. Want to catch dinner tomorrow? Cody can watch the tribe.

Did she? Her relationship with her sister was so layered with complication that the idea of a few hours of conversation, just the two of them, left her suddenly tense. At least when the kids were along, they provided a buffer of sorts.

No. She was a big girl. She could handle a few hours alone with her sister.

I can make that work. What time? I can pick you up.

I'll pick you up, Rachel replied. How about 7?
Sounds good, she answered. See you then.

She sent her answer and, wishing things could be different between them, she gave a heavy sigh as she shoved the phone back into the pocket of her hoodie.

Nate, returning to the bench, caught the tail end of it.

"That sounds serious. Everything okay?"

"My sister wants to meet for dinner tomorrow. We were working out details."

He raised an eyebrow, probably because her sigh had sounded anything but pleased at the prospect.

"My mother told me your sister is Rachel McBride. I'll admit, I was surprised. You're very different, aren't you?"

That echo of old pain resurged, regret that their lives had diverged so widely. "We have led quite different lives since our parents died."

"You took the military route while she seems pretty happy being a mom and social media influencer."

"Yes."

They had always been different, Rachel quieter, happy to have a good book and somewhere comfortable to read it while Jess always wanted to go on a hike, go swimming, ride her bike around the neighborhood. Something active and away from home.

Despite that, they had been best friends, only two years apart. Rachel had known the deepest thoughts inside her.

Shared trauma should have brought them even closer together. Instead, it had ended up driving a wedge they couldn't seem to bridge.

"I don't know how to ask this delicately so maybe I should just shut up."

"Ask what?"

She knew. His next question wasn't at all unexpected.

"I've known Rachel peripherally for years. I'm fairly certain she lived with Kurt and Jan Miller in high school. Their older daughter Shannon is a friend."

"That's right."

"Why weren't you together?"

That was a long and difficult answer that she wasn't prepared to share with Nate Whitaker right now, no matter how much she liked him. "We were both in the foster care system from the time we were teenagers, when our parents died. She ended up with the Millers and I…didn't."

Her life would have been so different if she had made other choices.

Due to those choices, Jess had ended up spending two years in a miserable, cheerless group home in Sacramento while Rachel had found a home here in Cape Sanctuary with the warm and loving Miller family.

"How did your parents die?" Nate asked.

She tensed. This was the question she always hated and the one she was certainly not prepared to tell Nate.

"Violently." The word came out hard, blunt, ugly.

"Sorry. That was rude and intrusive," he said after an awkward pause.

"Not rude. You're only curious. I just don't like to talk about it."

"Understood. I'm sorry I asked."

She wanted to tell him, an impulse that shocked her. She didn't, of course. She barely knew the man. Instead, they sat in companionable silence as the sun slid farther and farther down until it was swallowed by the vast sea.

She appreciated his silence. Too few people were comfortable with it, feeling compelled to fill every empty space with chatter. Nate didn't seem to mind it, which she found both surprising and refreshing.

The sunset was one of the most spectacular of her life, the sky a wild, colorful display reflected on the undulating waves. As gorgeous as it was, she was surprised at how quickly it was over.

"Wow," she said as the sun slipped below the horizon line in one last brilliant show. "That was unforgettable. I'm so glad we didn't go up with Sophie and Eleanor."

He smiled down at her, skin crinkling at the corners of his eyes. He was tanned, fit, gorgeous. And off-limits, she reminded herself. He was the son of her client and she was very careful not to mix business with personal. It never ended well.

Since she was working all the time and rarely had the chance to meet anyone outside of those circles, that meant her social life was basically nonexistent, unfortunately.

She wasn't going to change that with Nate Whitaker. What would be the point when she was moving on in a few weeks?

When he was the first to look away, whistling for the dogs, she told herself she was glad.

Cinder and Charlie bounded over with enthusiasm, the little furry Cavapoo in the lead.

"Thank you for staying with me."

"My pleasure. I don't take nearly enough opportunities to simply sit and think and enjoy the beautiful surroundings where I live. But it will be full dark in a few minutes and that path to the house can be treacherous if you can't see where you're going. I stupidly didn't bring a flashlight so we should probably go back."

She didn't want to leave this idyll but could only imagine how the rocks might trip a person up in the night.

They headed across the sand toward the path with the dogs in the lead, then Jess and Nate in the rear.

"Your shoelace is untied," he said after a moment. "You probably want to take care of that so you don't trip on the way up."

"Thanks."

His words were prophecy of what came next. Before she could stop to tie her lace, she stumbled on the root of a tree that grew across the path unevenly.

The epitome of grace and panache, as usual, she staggered slightly and would have face-planted onto the trail if Nate hadn't reached out both hands to catch her and pull her against him.

She could feel the heat of him scorching her from her neck to the curve of her back.

"Oh," she exclaimed. She looked over her shoulder and their gazes met, his suddenly hot, intense.

Her breath caught, the moment suspended between them. She thought she could feel each beat of her heart.

His gaze flickered to her mouth then quickly away.

Did he want to kiss her? Did he feel this heat that seemed to have exploded between them?

He set her on her feet and stepped away and she wondered if she had imagined the entire quicksilver episode.

"Are you okay?"

"Yes. Only clumsy. My dad used to say I could trip on painted lines on the road."

She bent down to tie her shoe snugly, grateful to steal a moment to collect her thoughts. She was glad he didn't kiss her. That was relief twisting through her, certainly not regret.

When they reached the top of the path, Nate walked her to the door of her Airstream, though she insisted he didn't need to.

"Thank you for a lovely evening," he said when they reached it.

"Thanks for staying with me to watch the sunset. I would have hated to miss it."

"You're welcome. And thank you for not holding a grudge over my rudeness yesterday."

She shrugged. "You were protective of your mother. How could I fault that?"

"And you'll let me know if you notice anything else unusual with her health?" he asked again. "Any more episodes where she seems to lose her energy?"

She didn't want to refuse but had to make it clear where her loyalties lay. "I don't want to be in the middle of you and your mother. Eleanor is my client, Nate. She's the one paying my bill. If you're concerned about her health, you should talk to her. I'm only the hired help."

"Fair enough," he said, his voice stiff.

Any softness she might have seen in his expression was gone now. That was a good thing, she told herself. It gave her the chance to rebuild her own barriers. What was the point in pretending, even for an instant, that kissing the man might be a good idea?

"Good night," he said abruptly.

He waited until she opened the door and stepped inside before he turned away to go back to his house.

Jess sank onto the sofa, her heart still pounding. What was *wrong* with her? All he had been doing was trying to keep her from tumbling down the path. She had been about half a second away from turning in his arms and kissing him.

Apparently Sunshine Cove was a dangerous place, giving people harmful ideas and unwanted desires. They ought to post a sign.

Okay. So she was attracted to Nate Whitaker, in a way she hadn't been to anyone in ages. Big deal. She could be attracted to the man without doing anything about it.

Anyway, other than that fleeting moment when she thought he wanted to kiss her, the man hadn't acted at all like he was attracted to her. End of story.

That was the way she wanted it, Jess told herself.

Her phone rang with a FaceTime call from Yvette right after she had changed into her most comfortable sleep shirt and picked up her book.

"Hey. Is everything okay?"

"I was about to ask you the same thing. You were supposed to check in and let me know you arrived safely yesterday in Cape Sanctuary and here I find you cuddled up in your jammies with a good book."

Even when her mouth was tight with annoyance, Yvette managed to look beautiful, with glossy black hair and perfectly applied makeup. Even when they were soldiers together, Yvette always insisted on looking good, no matter the circumstances.

That was two people she had failed to communicate with as she intended.

"I totally forgot to text you. I'm the worst! I'm sorry. I have no good excuse, other than the craziness of travel and talking to Rachel and starting the job today."

"How is Rachel? How's the house? How's Eleanor? I have all the questions."

"Rachel seems stressed. Her kids are a handful. Whitaker House is every bit as beautiful as the pictures and Eleanor is as delightful as she seemed in her correspondence."

"You get all the best clients, while I'm dealing with people who haven't cleaned out their refrigerator since 1970."

"As soon as I get a chance, I'm going to send you some pictures we took this afternoon of some vintage clothing. I think it could have value but as usual, I need your take on it."

"Sure thing."

"How's your job?"

"One word. Hoarder. How is it that you get the beautiful estate on the California coast and I get to deal with a hoarder in the middle of a Texas heat wave."

"I'm so sorry. Want to trade?"

"I'm good. I'm just messing with you. Not about the hoarder. That's a hundred percent genuine. But I wouldn't trade with you. You're right where God wants you to be."

Jess wasn't as certain as Yvette that there was some grand celestial design for her life. She certainly hadn't seen evidence of that yet.

"You said Rachel seems stressed?" Yvette asked. "How are those cute kids?"

Her friend seemed to know more about Jess's sister than *she* did. Though the two women had never met in person, they had an odd phone friendship. Also, Yvette followed Rachel on social media with an interest that bordered on obsession.

"I've only seen them all briefly for a few minutes yesterday but they seemed fine."

It wasn't strictly true. Rachel had seemed on the verge of a breakdown but Jess didn't feel right about sharing that with Yvette.

They talked mostly about business from that point on and the schedule of jobs each had coming up.

"I had better go," Yvette finally said after they had covered all the necessary topics. "I'm two hours later than you here and you know I need my beauty sleep."

"I hope your hoarder appreciates having someone who looks like she stepped off a magazine cover cleaning out her stacks of newspapers and dusty old tissue boxes."

"She better," Yvette said with a laugh. "Love you, baby. You be good to yourself, now."

"Same goes," Jess said as she ended the call, feeling much better about life than she had when she returned from the beach with Nate.

No, she might not have a man in her life right now and her relationship with her sister, her only remaining family, was strained at best.

But she had a job she loved, a business partner she loved even more and gorgeous sunsets to bring her joy. That was enough for now.

9

Rachel

"DINNER IS IN THE OVEN. I MADE TACO CASSEROLE. It should be done in about twenty minutes. When the timer goes off, take it out, add the chopped onions, tomatoes and corn chips and extra cheese and throw it back in for about a minute. Got that?"

Cody made a face. "I don't know. Maybe we should go through it again. You've only told me three times and written it down on that big yellow note card next to the oven."

She couldn't help it if she tended to overprepare. Cody didn't always pay attention when she told him things. The last time he had stayed with the kids while she attended a church women's meeting, he had gotten so busy building a fort out of blankets for them in the living room that he forgot to feed them dinner.

"The girls both need to wash their hair tonight. I need them for a product shoot tomorrow and I want to curl it in the morning, plus Ava got peanut butter in hers earlier when we were baking dog treats for Freckles."

Cody, holding Silas on his lap, nodded. "Rach. I've got this. We'll be fine. Go and have a good time with your sister."

She wanted to roll her eyes at that. She wasn't going to have a good time with Jess. Cody knew how messy their relationship could be. She had cried about it to him often enough.

Her heart was an open book when it came to her sister. She was like Freckles, following Jess around with her tongue hanging out, just waiting for a little affection.

She felt like she was always the one who reached out, who invited Jess for the holidays, who FaceTimed whenever the kids had a milestone.

Jess kept so much of herself closed off.

She hadn't always been that way. They had been so close once, sharing clothes and toys and secrets.

Her sister had become a polite stranger over the years since they had lived together. Rachel sometimes wondered why she even bothered pushing for them to stay connected.

What would they talk about during dinner? Their difficult history seemed to be off-limits and Jess never seemed to want to talk about her own personal life. Rachel didn't even know if she was seeing anybody.

She would probably end up babbling on for two hours about the kids and Cody while Jess sat across from her, trying not to yawn.

Was it too late to cancel?

"Don't forget Silas's antibiotic for his ear infection before bed and the drops after his bath. And you know he insists he has to have you read him the story about the purple dinosaur."

Cody smiled but she could sense his annoyance. "You wrote everything down. We'll be fine. I can call you if we have any problems. And it's not like you'll be in another time zone. You're only ten minutes away. Where are you eating?"

"The Fishwife."

"Always a good choice. Don't worry about us," he said again. "Go have a good time."

She wanted to cancel the whole thing. She couldn't feel good about leaving him with the kids, especially with the horrendous day she had just survived. Silas had been on a nonstop tantrum.

Nothing was right for him. The tags on his clothing bothered him until she cut them off, he ripped the pages out of a library book she had foolishly left within his reach, he didn't like the way she made his eggs so he threw them on the floor, to Freckles's delight.

The day had started out hard and had only grown worse. Now he seemed to be done with his difficult mood, content to sit on Cody's lap and play with his favorite fidget toy.

She couldn't help but resent the way Cody could just waltz in and calm things down, even though Rachel was the one dealing with Silas through most of the day.

She was exhausted, mentally and physically. She wanted to find a secluded beach somewhere, sink down in the sand and cry for the next year.

The only problem with that? Once she started, she probably would not be able to stop. The grief and worry she felt for her son's future always simmered beneath the surface but today it seemed to have boiled over several times.

The last thing she felt like doing right now was putting on a good show of determined cheerfulness for Jess, her sister, who was as hard to reach in her own way as Silas.

Rachel had invited her, though, and she couldn't back down. Might as well get this over with, right?

She put the spa channel on her car stereo as she drove to Whitaker House. The house was in such a striking location. Wouldn't it be something if Eleanor put it on the market? Not that she and Cody could afford it. They were doing okay. Not bad, actually, for two kids who had married right out of high school. The roofing company Cody ran with his brothers was always busy and she was starting to bring in decent ad revenue from her blog, YouTube videos and social media.

She was deeply grateful their years of struggle and grind were beginning to pay off. They did fine, but probably not the kind of fine that could afford a house like this, right on the water.

Someday, maybe.

When she pulled up to the house, she found Jess's Airstream gleaming in the fading sun, cute as ever, parked near the path that led down to Sunshine Cove. Her sister opened the door to the trailer the moment Rachel pulled up. Her clothes were casual and quite nondescript, merely jeans and a tailored white shirt. She didn't wear any jewelry but somehow Jess, lean and fit with their dad's honey-colored hair and their mother's green eyes, managed to look quietly gorgeous.

She rarely even wore much makeup, only lip color and mascara.

Rachel, who had spent more than an hour getting ready in between helping Grace with homework, prepping the casserole for them, and keeping Ava and Silas apart after Silas ruined his sister's block castle, tried not to be envious at Jess's effortless beauty. "Sorry I'm late. Things were crazy at home."

"No problem. I've been enjoying the night."

"How's Vera treating you?"

Jess made a face at the name her friend Yvette had given the Airstream. "Fine. As comfortable as ever."

"Have you made any other changes since you were here last? I know Yvette was talking about adding a few finishing touches."

"She made new cushions for the banquette."

"Ooh. Can I see?"

Jess hesitated, as if she didn't want to share even this small piece of herself with Rachel, but after a moment, she opened the door and gestured inside.

Rachel stepped inside and was charmed all over again at the

warm, comfortable interior of the trailer. "This is so fabulous. I should take some IG pictures. I could even do a YouTube video to show off your hard work. Yvette has done such an amazing job in here."

"She did. Though it was a team effort. We had some talented craftspeople work on the cabinets and the custom upholstery."

"Everyone did a stellar job. So can I feature it while you're here in town? I won't use your name or any identifying details. I can protect your precious privacy."

Jess didn't look thrilled at the idea but Rachel appreciated that at least she didn't completely dismiss it. "Sure, if we can find a time that works for both of us. You can come over during any day while I'm helping Eleanor, then I'll be out of the way."

"That might work. I'll let you know how my schedule is this week."

She wanted to stay here in this cozy little haven, close the curtains to block out the world and all its pain, and curl up on that bed. A rainstorm would be even better.

"Should we go?" Jess asked.

Oh. Right. She couldn't stay here, as much as she might want to. They had to get through dinner. "We probably should. We have a reservation in fifteen minutes."

"Where are we going?" Jess asked as they walked out of the trailer and headed toward Rachel's minivan.

"There's a place I love with excellent food and a nice outdoor space overlooking the sea. The Fishwife."

"Sounds good."

Just as they started to climb into her minivan, Rachel saw two people walking past on the way to Whitaker House.

"Hi, Rachel." Sophie Whitaker waved with enthusiasm. "Hi, Jess."

"Hello, Sophie the Fabulous," Rachel said with a bright smile for the girl who babysat for her sometimes. "Hi, Nate."

Nate Whitaker leaned in and kissed her cheek. He always

smelled good, with some kind of soap that held traces of juniper and sage.

She ought to ask him what he used and give some to Cody. But how did a woman come right out and ask a man what products he used so she could get them for her husband?

Cody smelled fine. She usually loved the way her husband smelled but a change couldn't hurt. Maybe if Cody used something new, Rachel could get back that tingle she used to have every time he walked into a room.

Oh, she missed those days, when she and Cody couldn't get enough of each other. They could have spent days, weeks, months in bed and never tired of each other.

They usually made love regularly but had been going through a dry spell lately.

She felt sometimes as if it was one more obligation at the end of the day. When was the last time she had actually craved sex, thought about it during the day, ached for her husband's touch?

Months, at least.

Silas, with his ongoing sensory and behavior issues, seemed to have exploded into their world like a hand grenade in the living room. Adding a son with autism to an already busy life, with two girls and two careers, was exhausting and overwhelming.

She felt guilty comparing the child she loved to an explosive device but it seemed exactly the appropriate metaphor. They were always aware of him, always careful, always afraid something would trigger a blast.

As a result, the hand grenade had taken center stage and everything else seemed to have shriveled in comparison. Including sex.

She loved her husband. He was a good man, a caring father, a wonderful provider. But by nightfall, after she had been wrestling three kids all day, she could barely keep her eyes open, even though she knew a good orgasm was a fabulous stress reducer.

She dragged herself back to the conversation to hear Nate and

Jess talking about how Jess and Eleanor had cleaned out another bedroom that day.

"Did you find any more cool retro clothes?" Sophie asked.

"No. But I sent my partner, Yvette, some pictures we took yesterday and she's pretty excited. She thinks she knows a good consignment shop where we can sell them."

"Cool," Sophie said. "I wore the dress we found yesterday to school today for Decade Day and it looked so good. I took some selfies. Want to see?"

"Sure." Jess smiled at Sophie with a warmth and kindness that shocked Rachel.

The girl scrolled through her phone then held it out to Jess.

"Nice. I like the necklace you're wearing with it."

"That's my friend McKenna's. Well, her mom's, anyway. I sent her a pic of the dress last night and she thought it would go perfectly."

"Can I see?" Rachel asked.

Sophie looked a little awestruck at that but handed over her phone. She was charmed by the picture of the teenager in a flapper-style '20s dress with fringe and a scalloped neckline. "Very nice. You found that in a closet?"

"Yeah," Sophie said. "And a bunch of other cool stuff."

"I'd like to know when you found time to coordinate accessories last night with your friend McKenna amid all the excitement over finding the bottle. Have you heard back on the message?"

"Not yet. But it didn't get autoreturned so I think it's probably still an active email account. We'll see what happens. It's pretty cool."

"You found a bottle?" Rachel tried to follow the conversation, still reeling at the ease and comfort with which her sister seemed to interact with Sophie. She also noticed a strange tension in the air between Nate and Jess. What was *that* all about?

"Yeah. A really cool one with a message inside from some

school in Japan studying ocean currents. They asked anybody finding one to email back. I can't wait to see if I get an answer."

"That's great! My kids are always looking for them!"

"We found it last night after dinner when we all went down to Sunshine Cove. So after Gram and I came back and left Jess and Dad down there, I sent the email to Japan and then sent the pic of the dress to McKenna, who showed it to her mom, who said she had the perfect necklace and earrings to go with it."

"It's nice," Jess said, apparently following that long-winded explanation. "I like the way the colors complement each other."

Somehow Rachel managed to keep her jaw from sagging. Was this really her former military truck–driving, no-nonsense sister talking about fashion?

"I can't believe you found such a great dress in a closet," Rachel said.

"Jess found a bunch of cool clothes. Lots of them fit me, too. Gram says I can keep whatever I want."

"Which seems to me just a way of moving Gram's clutter from Whitaker House to our place," Nate pointed out. "That hardly seems fair."

Jess shrugged. "My job is to help your mom clean out her place. You can't hold me responsible for the amount of clutter that migrates from her house to yours."

Nate laughed and Rachel could swear she saw Jess give a smile in return before her mouth straightened up again.

What in the world? Something was *definitely* up between the two of them.

"We were just about to grab dinner with my mom. You're both welcome to join us."

Rachel was almost tempted to call The Fishwife and cancel their reservations just so she could see if her initial instincts were right.

"Thanks, but we have reservations," Jess said. "And we should probably get going so we're not late."

"Too bad," Sophie said with a little pout.

"But totally understandable," Nate said. "Have a good evening."

"You, as well," Rachel said. "Give my love to your mom."

"I will."

They waved and headed on their way toward the house, and Rachel and Jess both climbed into her van.

"Nate is such a great guy," Rachel said as she started driving the short distance to downtown. "Half the women in town are in love with him and the other half are in lust."

"Including you?" Jess asked.

"No!" Rachel exclaimed. "I have Cody."

For now, anyway. Until he decided not to put up with his bitchy wife anymore. She felt that familiar tremor of fear, the helpless feeling that washed over her whenever she worried she wasn't doing enough to keep her marriage together.

She pushed it away for now, determined to try harder.

The Fishwife was busy, as always.

"Good thing I made a reservation," she said as she and Jess walked through the crowd of waiting people.

Inside, she greeted the hostess, Maria Sanchez, a college student whose mom went to spin class with Rachel.

"Your table isn't quite ready. I'm sorry. It's being bused now so should be soon. Would you like to wait in the bar?"

"The bar is great," she answered, though she was tired enough after her hard day to wish she could stretch out on the long bench out front and take a nap.

"You wanted the patio, right?"

"Sure. The weather is nice. That's good."

"It shouldn't be long now," the hostess said.

"Thank you," she said.

She and Jess both ordered the same drink, a classic mint mojito, which surprised her. That had been their mother's drink, she remembered. Veronica Clayton hadn't been a big drinker but when she did imbibe, she favored mojitos. She ached for her mother suddenly, for warm cookies after school and the smell of her vanilla musk perfume and a soft hand on her forehead when she didn't feel good.

"So. How are you, anyway?" Jess said, taking a sip of her drink.

"Fine." Rachel forced a smile. She didn't want to be here suddenly. She wanted to flee the restaurant, climb in her car and drive down the coast. Away. Just away.

Away from her failures and her fears and all the things she couldn't fix.

"Is everything okay?" Jess gave her a careful look.

No. Not really. My life is falling apart. But thanks for asking.

She couldn't say that, of course. She forced a smile, though she felt as if her face would crack with the effort. "Great. Just great. Couldn't be better."

10

Jess

SHE KNEW DAMN WELL HER SISTER WAS LYING.
Rachel *wasn't* great. For one thing, Jess could see the shadows under her eyes that concealer couldn't hide. For another, though her words were benign, the despair that trickled into her voice wasn't.

"What's going on?" she asked softly. She couldn't help remembering the little sister who always turned to Jess when she had a bad dream or when their father would go on a rampage.

They were best friends, united in all things to protect each other from the chaos of their home, until that terrible June night when everything changed.

Rachel took a healthy sip of her mojito. "Nothing. I'm perfectly fine. Couldn't be better."

"You're lying." She tilted her head, trying to see beneath her sister's facade. "Is it Silas?"

Rachel let out a short laugh. "Why would you think anything might be wrong? I'm only dealing with three kids under the age of seven, one of whom happens to be on the spectrum."

This time Rachel took an even healthier sip of her drink.

"I don't know how you're doing it," Jess said.

"What choice do I have?"

Jess blinked at the hard tone, one she hadn't ever heard from her sister.

Rachel immediately backtracked. "Sorry. That didn't come out the way I meant. I love my life. Cody, the girls, Silas. I am so lucky to have them all. I can't imagine my world without them. I don't *want* to imagine my world without them. Today was a hard day and you're on the tail end of my bad mood. Sorry."

Before Jess could respond and tell her sister what a wonderful mother she was and how she admired the way Rachel handled her challenges with grace and courage, the hostess returned.

"Your table is ready. I apologize for the wait."

"No problem," her sister chirped with another one of those fake smiles. She grabbed her purse in one hand and her drink in the other and followed the woman.

Jess didn't have any choice but to do the same, though she wished the hostess had waited five more moments so she could have told her sister how much she admired her.

It was a beautiful view, she had to admit. The Pacific stretched out in both directions. She could look down and see rock formations up and down the coast. She could even see Whitaker House, with its small protected cove.

The night was pleasant but cool, making Jess grateful for the sweater she had brought along and also for patio heaters that sent out a comforting warmth.

"Simone will be your server and Donnie will be helping her out," the hostess informed them with a polite smile as she set two menus in front of them. "Is there anything else I can do for you?"

"No. We're fine. Thanks," Rachel said. Her features were so

pleasant and controlled that Jess had to wonder if she had imagined that hint of despair.

"I can't wait to order. I'm starving," Rachel said as soon as the woman glided away. "They have the most amazing scallops here. The sauce is seriously to die for." Her sister then started chattering about some of the things going on in her life, talking about the PTA, her women's group, her garden, where the peas were already coming on.

Rachel hardly let Jess squeeze a word into the conversation and barely slowed down to let them both order when Simone came over.

Jess's day had been long and busy and she had hardly stopped long enough for lunch. She ended up ordering the scallops and a house salad.

For all the hype she had given, Rachel ended up ordering something completely different, a blackened salmon and strawberry salad she said was her second favorite thing on the menu.

After the server had taken their menus and walked away to put their orders into the system, Rachel sipped from her water glass then folded her hands together. "So. How are things going for you? You're helping Eleanor Whitaker clean out her house. That must be amazing. I've always wanted to have a day to spend just wandering through that place."

"It is beautiful."

"I still want to know if she's going to put the house up for sale. I always thought Nate would inherit it, that it had been in the Whitaker family too long to let it pass to someone else. But what do I know?"

"I don't know her plans," Jess said, in complete honesty. "Right now, we're just focusing on cleaning out the house and getting rid of some of her husband's things."

"Jack was such a great guy. I remember in high school he visited as a guest lecturer to my English class. I think he was friends with Stella Davenport, my teacher. He could really make Steinbeck come alive. His death was so tragic. I mean, cancer isn't uncommon but colon cancer is so brutal and painful. So sad."

"Yes."

"How did Eleanor hear about you?"

"She had a friend who used our services. And apparently you mentioned Transitions to her once, so that was another mark in my favor. Thanks for that."

One of the servers delivered a wooden bowl of sourdough bread to their table. Rachel instantly picked up a chunk and broke off a piece of crust to eat first.

She had always done that, Jess remembered. Jess had loved the inside and Rachel had loved the crusts. They had made the perfect pair.

"I don't remember that conversation at all but if she says I did, I believe her. I'm glad she listened to me."

"So am I," Jess said. "It's been a fun job so far."

"What about men in your life? Anything new there?"

For some ridiculous reason, Nate's image flashed into her brain. She frowned, annoyed with herself. "I'm taking a break right now from relationships. Work keeps me too busy to think about men much. Anyway, I'm never in one place long enough to form any serious connections."

"That's the way you like it, isn't it?"

Rachel's matter-of-fact tone held no condemnation but Jess instinctively wanted to protest anyway. How could she? Her sister was right. "Maybe. You know I'm not really on the happy-ever-after team."

"Only because you've tried hard to convince yourself of that. Everyone deserves a happy ending."

"Wouldn't you agree that happy-ever-after has a different definition for everyone? Finding someone you love enough to share your life with is only the first step on the journey. Then you have to figure out how to live with them to be truly happy. It's a marathon, not a sprint. Haven't you found that with Cody?"

For an instant, Jess thought she saw sadness in her sister's eyes but the server came with their salads and she couldn't be sure.

What was going on? Was Rachel's marriage in trouble? She had heard that having a child with special needs was one of the hardest challenges a couple could face together, that the divorce rate was higher than normal under those circumstances. Rachel and Cody had been in love since high school. She hated to think they might be struggling.

She wanted to ask but Rachel seemed determined to keep their conversation superficial, avoiding any of Jess's efforts to push more deeply.

She finally gave up. If Rachel didn't want to tell her, she couldn't make her. Still, Jess couldn't help but ache again for the close relationship they once had.

They opted to share dessert, a lemon cake so thick and luscious that Rachel had to pull out her phone and take pictures. Despite all the fuss, after she put away her phone, she only ate about two bites then set down her fork.

Fine. That just left more for Jess, she thought. When she had eaten as much as she could manage, she pushed away the cake and met her sister's gaze. Over the flickering candlelight, she saw another hint of that despair she had glimpsed earlier.

She sighed. She couldn't ignore it. This was Rachel. If she didn't push, her sister would never tell her.

"Okay. You've put on a good front for the entire dinner. I commend your efforts. Now, why don't you tell me the truth? What's really going on? How's Silas? You said today has been a hard day. Is it more than just today?"

She wasn't sure Rachel would answer. The silence dragged on for an uncomfortable moment, broken only by muted conversation and the chink of cutlery on china from nearby tables as well as the murmur of the sea below them.

After a long moment, Rachel curled her hand around her water goblet stem so tightly, Jess worried it would break.

"I hate complaining. It makes me feel like such a horrible mother. But the past few months have been *hard*. Silas has become really out of control lately."

"Out of control how?"

"Not napping. Not listening to anything I say. Not interacting with his sisters at all except to do exactly the things they don't want him to do. It's a lot to handle. My girls were both so sweet-natured at this age. Silas isn't and I'm at my wit's end, if you want the truth. There. Aren't you sorry you asked?"

"No. You shouldn't be carrying this by yourself. Have you talked to his pediatrician about it? Some of it might be his age."

"Not really. This is all pretty new. Within the past few months, anyway."

"Maybe you should call her."

Rachel sighed. "We're meeting with a team of specialists at an autism clinic next week in Sacramento. I hope I'll be up to the drive. Sometimes he can howl and bang his head on the seat the entire car ride. And other times he loves it. It's always a roll of the dice."

Jess had caught a glimpse of Silas's behavior issues the other day when she had dropped by unexpectedly and found the house in chaos. Was that the reason Rachel seemed so brittle? If she wasn't sleeping well and then had to wrestle with a challenging two-year-old all day, Jess couldn't blame her for being exhausted.

"Cody's going with you to help out, isn't he?"

"We both thought it would be better if he stayed with the girls to take Ava to preschool and then his mom's and get Grace off to school then be there when Grace gets home."

Rachel needed help. She couldn't drive all the way to Sacramento on her own with a difficult toddler. "I'll take care of the girls. I'm sure I can work out the schedule with Eleanor. I can probably even take Ava with me for the day."

"I can't ask that of you."

"You didn't ask. I offered. And I mean it. You and Cody are

in this together. As Silas's father, Cody should absolutely go with you to the clinic appointment."

Rachel appeared to be weakening as she considered the offer. "It *would* be nice to have him along. Silas does better in the car if one of us sits with him to keep him distracted from the sensory overload. It's an early-morning appointment, though. I have to leave at six to make it on time."

"You said this is Tuesday? Why don't you go the night before? I don't mind staying overnight with the girls. It will be fun. Like a slumber party. And maybe you and Cody can enjoy some time away together. You'll still have Silas, but not all three kids."

Rachel looked hopeful, as if the sun had slipped out from behind the clouds on an otherwise relentlessly stormy day. After a moment, she shook her head.

"It's too much. I can't ask that of you."

"We're family, Rachel. The main reason I took this job with Eleanor was to give me more time to be with the girls and Silas. This will be the perfect opportunity for me to hang with Ava and Grace. I'll feel even better, knowing I might be helping you out a little bit."

Rachel looked as if she didn't know what to say. "Let me talk to Cody and see if that might work with his schedule," she finally said. "We had basically decided he was going to stay with the girls. He might have scheduled a job for that day while Ava is with his mom."

"He can unschedule it," Jess replied bluntly.

She liked her brother-in-law very much, usually. Cody had always treated Rachel well, as far as she knew, and seemed to be a devoted dad to the girls and Silas. But she had to wonder if he had any idea the burden his wife shouldered all day, coping with three young children.

"I'm going to guess he's not too busy to go to an important clinic appointment with his wife and son. If he is, somebody should have a talk with him to remind him what his priorities ought to be."

"We are his priority." Rachel's voice took on a definite defensive note. "He just has a lot on his plate now with the roofing business."

"And you don't? Trying to manage Silas while you're busy with the girls, the house, not to mention your own work, too?"

"It's different. You know how it is."

Jess did not know how it was. All she knew about family dynamics was derived from her childhood, watching their father grind their mother's confidence down to nothing.

"Talk to Cody and let me know so I can arrange the time off with Eleanor. I know it won't be a problem."

"I'll talk to him. Thanks for thinking of it, Jess. Seriously."

Though Rachel put up a fuss, Jess insisted on paying for dinner. "My treat. Consider it a late birthday dinner."

They were on the way to Rachel's car when her sister suddenly stopped in her tracks and grabbed Jess's arm. "Speaking of birthdays. I completely forgot yours is coming up. Next week, isn't it?"

"I'm trying to forget about it. But yes."

She usually didn't mind birthdays but there was something about this one that had been wearing on her lately.

She was turning thirty. It was a number she still couldn't wrap her head around.

"We have to do something to celebrate! The kids and I would love to have dinner and make a cake for you. Can you put us on your calendar?"

The invitation touched her. How long had it been since she had spent her birthday with family? Probably fourteen years, since that last horrible summer.

"Considering you're among a very small group of people I know in town, it shouldn't be that hard to rearrange my busy social calendar. I'll plan on it." She paused. "I would enjoy that. Thank you."

"Great. I'll be in touch with details about that and about whether Cody thinks he can come with me. Thanks for offering. It's really sweet of you."

Rachel smiled and this time Jess was relieved to see it appeared genuine.

"I had better get you back to your cute trailer."

Rachel drove with the windows down in her minivan, the May night sweet with the scent of flowers and the sea.

"So what do you think about Nathaniel Whitaker?"

The question, coming out of nowhere, made her flush. Jess was grateful it was dark inside the vehicle and her sister couldn't see.

Had she given off some sort of signal that made Rachel somehow suspect her unwanted attraction?

"I haven't thought about him much at all," she lied. "He's Eleanor's son. He seems nice enough, I suppose, though I really haven't had much to do with him."

"Sad about his wife dying so young. Michelle is considered a hero in town, even though she and Nate never lived here together."

She didn't want to know this but didn't know how to tell her sister to stop talking without giving Rachel reason to wonder about her reaction.

"Is she?"

"Yes. I guess because he's a hometown boy and she was his wife, she gets the hero status by association. She was killed while she was deployed overseas when a soldier they were training went rogue and started firing on US soldiers. Michelle rushed him to try to stop him and was killed. Sophie was only a baby, I guess. I don't know if she even remembers her mom, poor thing."

Oh, how tragic for both of them. Jess fought the urge to press a hand to the sudden ache in her chest. Killed in action. She had lost friends of her own while she was deployed but it wasn't like losing a spouse.

"Maybe living through that kind of tragedy is what has made Nate such a great guy. You won't find anybody better. He's considered quite the catch around town, though he's really good at slipping through the net. If he dates anybody seriously, he doesn't do it here in town. At least not that I've heard."

"I'm not sure why you think I need to know this," Jess said stiffly.

Rachel shrugged as she pulled up next to Jess's Airstream. "I just figured you're working with his mom and he lives close to Eleanor. It never hurts to have some backstory."

Her sister was dead wrong. Jess didn't want backstory. What was the point, when she was leaving in a few weeks anyway? It was far easier to keep her guard up against him when she didn't know that kind of thing.

"Thanks again for dinner," Rachel said when Jess opened the door. "I'll be in touch about next week."

"I'm planning on staying with the girls," she said firmly. "I'll talk to Eleanor about it tomorrow. Cody really does need to go to the appointment with you and Silas."

"I'll see what his plans are. Regardless, it means a lot to me that you even offered. Bye, Jess."

Rachel looked as if she wanted to climb out and hug her. To Jess's vast relief, she didn't. She just smiled and waved then backed out of the driveway and headed away.

11

Nate

SOME MORNINGS JUST CALLED FOR CATCHING A FEW waves, even when he didn't really have time for this.

The sun wasn't quite up when Nate carried his board toward the trail down to the cove. Cinder came with him, barely visible in the gray predawn light.

As he passed the little Airstream, he saw a light glowing inside through the curtains but he couldn't glimpse any sign of movement inside.

He hadn't seen Jess Clayton in several days. He hadn't been looking, exactly, or at least that's what he told himself. Still, he was sorry their paths hadn't crossed.

The past several days had been crazy. His company had won the bid to build a new municipal library in Cape Sanctuary and bringing the project in under deadline was taking every available spare second.

Twice, Sophie had stayed overnight with Eleanor because

Nate knew it would be past midnight when he returned and he didn't like the idea of her staying at home by herself.

She didn't particularly agree. She thought thirteen years old was plenty mature enough to spend much of the night alone and that he was treating her like a child by making her stay with her grandmother.

Too bad. He was the parent and still got to make the rules.

Between the stress of the construction job and the angst of dealing with a moody teenage daughter, Nate needed an outlet. Surfing had always soothed the restlessness. The ocean calmed him.

He would be working late again that day. This might be his only purely self-indulgent interlude all month. He might as well enjoy the hell out of it.

A few hardy birds twittered in the coastal pine and manzanita as he started down the path.

Th sun came up above the mountains to the east just as he reached the shore.

Conditions were perfect, the waves easy and comfortable. He knew the break here as well as he knew his own face when he shaved.

He spent more time sitting on his board than chasing any huge curl, letting the waves rock him gently as he enjoyed the breaking day.

He loved the mornings when Sophie came with him. She was a good surfer, agile and unafraid. He had undoubtedly failed in many ways as a single father but Nate was proud that he had given her a love for the sea.

He had knocked on her bedroom door to ask if she wanted to join him that morning but she had only grunted a negative response.

Ah well. He had Cinder, at least. She swam beside him in her life jacket, gleeful to play in the waves like a sea otter.

Just as he was about to get out, he saw someone walking down the path. Maybe Sophie had decided to catch a few waves before school.

No. It was definitely a female but not Sophie. This person didn't have a board, for one thing. For another, she had short honey-streaked hair that gleamed in the morning sunlight.

Jess.

His heart pounded in a ridiculous way that annoyed him.

Cinder spotted her at the same moment and gave a bark of greeting before dog-paddling toward shore.

Nate watched as Jess greeted the dog with the delighted, generous affection he had only seen her give Eleanor and Sophie so far.

Why not him?

Oh, for crying out loud. Was he actually jealous of his dog?

Maybe.

He sighed, torn between talking to her again and staying out here in the water where he didn't run the risk of behaving like an idiot around her again.

He finally decided the benefits of talking to her outweighed the risks, and paddled the short distance toward shallow water where he could stand and walk out with his board.

"I saw someone surfing but didn't realize it was you until I reached the sand and saw Cinder," she said, approaching him as he toweled off. "You don't have to stop on my account."

He shrugged. "I was done anyway. I didn't have a lot of time this morning but the wave report was good so I didn't want to miss it."

"I wanted to beachcomb a bit, maybe see if I could find some sea glass for Sophie. The ocean is hard to resist in the morning."

This made him smile. "Agreed. Why do you think I'm here, even though I don't really have the time for it?"

"Well, I'm sorry to invade your solitude."

"You didn't. The beach is certainly big enough for both of us."

It wasn't precisely true. When she smiled like that, an aching hunger started in his gut and spread quickly. She crowded into his mental space and he didn't know what to do about it.

"How are things going at the house? I haven't seen you for a few days. My mom is pretty closemouthed."

"We're making progress, I think. Slow but steady."

"That's good. When she asked me to go through my dad's things a few months ago to take out what I wanted to keep, I struggled to decide. Culling is hard work. I was exhausted after only a few hours."

She laughed, a pure, lovely sound that slid over his skin like silky warm water.

"That's why people pay me the big money, so I can help them make those hard decisions. I usually tell people to keep in mind that most of their memories of a loved one are already stored in their heart. They're not tied to material things. Sometimes the clutter of those material things actually detracts from the memories and the joy."

Cinder snuggled up close to her and she petted the dog absently, gazing out to sea as the sunrise painted the waves a soft lavender.

His dog was a pretty good judge of character and obviously already adored Jess. So did his mother and Sophie.

He sat beside her on the bench, unable to resist stealing a few moments with a beautiful woman as day stole over the ocean.

"What room are you working on today?"

"The plan is to start in the hall closet and then start sorting through the books in your father's office."

"Good luck. Dad was definitely a bibliophile. My dad never met a bookstore he didn't like and was on a first-name basis with all the librarians in town. That gene skipped me but Sophie is the same way. She loves to read."

He did read, but usually nonfiction or long-form news articles. He had always wished he shared that passion with his father, that they could talk about literature and poetry and the other things that had interested Jack Whitaker.

"I wish I'd had the chance to know your father. He seems like he was a great guy."

"He left quite a legacy. Sometimes I think half my customers only accept my bid on a project because of my father's reputation around here."

"That must be nice," she said, with a wistful smile that made him wonder about her own family background.

Violently, she had answered when he had asked how her parents had died. He had so many questions but didn't think she would answer them.

"We'll be wrapping things up early today as I offered to stay with my nieces. Silas, Rachel's youngest, has a doctor appointment with a specialist early in the morning so Rachel and Cody are staying the night so they don't have to leave as early."

"Nice of you to step up."

"I don't know about that. I should have suggested that Cody's mom or sister could take the girls. I have no idea what I was thinking."

Her sudden panic at the idea of caring for her nieces made him smile, but he quickly hid it.

"Relax. They'll love spending time with their aunt. As long as you remember to feed them and don't let them play with rusty nails, you'll be fine."

"Those are your parenting tips? Don't let them play with rusty nails and remember to feed them?"

He shrugged. "Those are the basics."

"Easy for you to say. You've made it through thirteen years with Sophie."

"I panicked at first, too. Neither her mother nor I had the first idea how to raise a kid. The first few months were like being thrown into deep water without any idea how to swim.

And then Michelle was deployed when Sophie was barely three months old, leaving me paddling all by myself."

As soon as the words were out, hanging in the morning air between them, Nate wished he could swallow them back.

He didn't know why he had. Maybe it was the quiet peace of the morning that invited confidences.

"So young! That must have been so hard on all of you."

An understatement. If Michelle's unit hadn't been deployed or if she had applied to defer, maybe they could have worked out their issues. But she had been a decorated officer, on the fast track to becoming a colonel at the very least and had worried that deferring would sidetrack that advancement.

His goal had been to become a ranger and he had started the process of applying, but he had quickly realized after Sophie came along that they couldn't both pursue demanding military careers, even with good childcare.

When Michelle had been deployed, Nate realized he had to get out of the military and find something with more flexibility that would allow at least one of them to be the parent their baby needed. He had been making progress toward that goal when Michelle had been killed.

"Rachel told me your wife died overseas."

He nodded. Thinking about it still hurt but mostly for Sophie's sake.

"The irony is she was on the relative safety of base when someone she had trained, someone she considered a loyal asset, went rogue. Four soldiers were killed, including Michelle. I like to think she slowed the guy down long enough that others could stop him."

"I'm so sorry."

He had grieved for the woman he loved and for the future he had once hoped they could build together. "Thank you. It was twelve years ago. Sophie wasn't even a year when it happened and we already had moved back here to Cape Sanctuary so my parents could help me with her. She doesn't have any memories of Michelle, other than what my parents and I have told her. I'm not sure if that's a good thing or not."

"It's hard losing a parent, no matter your age or circumstances."

Violently.

He couldn't seem to get that word out of his head. How had her parents died?

"Anyway, enough about me. We were talking about you watching your nieces. You'll be fine. It's only one night and they're both old enough to tell you how their mom does things."

"I'm not sure that will be a good thing. I'm not anything like the amazing Rachel McBride."

"Just be yourself, Auntie Jess. I'm sure you'll all have a great time."

Her smile warmed him through the layers of his wet suit. "Thank you."

He wanted to kiss her.

The urge had hit him hard the other night but he had pushed it away. Now, in the fledgling morning light, the hunger was almost overpowering.

Almost.

"I should probably head up and start the day," he said, jumping to his feet and grabbing his board.

"Same here."

They walked together up the path with Cinder in the lead, racing ahead to explore something on the path and then returning for validation and affection.

"Would you like some breakfast?" Jess surprised him by asking when they reached her trailer. "I bought some fresh eggs at a roadside stand yesterday and have some veggies in the refrigerator. I could make a quick omelet."

"Sounds great but I better not. I need to get Sophie off to school. Thanks, though."

"Another time, then."

He liked that idea, of meeting her again down by the ocean and spending the morning together. Better yet, maybe they could spend the night together and could share breakfast the next morning...

No. She was leaving soon. He had to put that idea right out of his head.

"Good luck with everything on your plate today," she said.

She smiled again, eyes warm. She looked so lovely in the pure May morning that he couldn't seem to look away. Their gazes met and he saw something in her eyes, an answering heat that made him instantly aroused.

Walk away, a voice inside him cautioned. *Just grab your board and head home.*

He ignored it. He had no choice, did he? He set his board against her trailer and took a step forward.

To his shock, she met him halfway, her mouth warm in the cool morning air. She tasted of mint and coffee and he couldn't seem to get enough.

On some level, he was cognizant enough to know his wet suit would be cold, uncomfortable, so he purposely only touched her with his mouth.

It was enough.

Heat sparked between them, taking away any chill from the morning.

He had always thought surfing a few waves as the sun climbed the mountains was the best way to start the day. He was now prepared to reevaluate that. Kissing Jess Clayton, her mouth soft and willing beneath his, beat paddling in cold water any day of the week.

12

Jess

S HE HAD NEVER WANTED A SINGLE THING IN HER
life more than she wanted in that second to drag Nate
Whitaker into her Airstream, strip off his glossy black wet suit
and spend an entire week exploring all those luscious muscles.

What was *wrong* with her?

This wasn't the kind of thing she did, kissing a man she barely
knew.

The morning beside the sea had been magical, just the two
of them alone with the waves and the sky. Even before she had
known the early-morning surfer had been Nate, she had loved
watching him choose his break and then ride it to shore with
effortless ease.

And then they had sat together on Eleanor's bench, as they
had that night the previous week, and talked with the same kind
of comfortable affinity.

What was it about the cove that created this sense of intimacy?

So much for all her protestations to herself that she didn't become personally involved with her clients or their families. She couldn't get much more involved than tangling tongues with Eleanor's entirely too appealing son.

As his mouth explored hers, touching only there, hunger seemed to build between them. What would be the harm in dragging him inside?

She knew the answer to her own question. She didn't do quick and casual flings and that's all she could have with Nate, no matter how delicious she might find him.

She had to stop this. It couldn't go anywhere.

She was trying to find the strength of will when Cinder suddenly barked nearby.

Nate lifted his head and she saw a dazed sort of arousal there, which she found immensely gratifying, even though she knew she shouldn't.

"What is it?"

"Squirrel, I think."

She let out a shaky laugh. "Just as well."

He sighed, raking a hand through his still-damp hair. "Yeah. You're probably right. I don't quite know what happened there."

"One minute we were talking about omelets, the next you were kissing me."

"Breakfast doesn't usually turn me into a rampaging beast but I guess there's a first time for everything. I'm sorry."

She had wanted the kiss as much as he did. Maybe more. "It's no big deal, Nate. Really. You didn't do anything wrong."

"I don't like to make assumptions. I'm a big believer in asking a woman before I kiss her."

"I wanted you to kiss me," she admitted. "I probably would have kissed you if you hadn't started it first. Now we have it out of our systems and can forget it ever happened."

"Can we?" He raised an eyebrow, hair tousled and morning

stubble on his jawline, and it was all she could do not to go for another round. "I'm not sure it will be that easy."

"Well, we can try, anyway."

He smiled suddenly, his eyes warm and still aroused.

"I'm not looking for an affair, Nate," she said, though she wasn't sure if she was trying to warn him or remind herself. "It complicates everything, especially when I'm leaving as soon as the job is done."

"Fair enough. I don't disagree. I'm not looking for one either. Especially not with my impressionable teenage daughter sleeping a few hundred feet away."

"Good. Then we're on the same page."

"I suppose we are." He let out a breath that sounded like a sigh and his gaze flickered to her mouth one more time then away.

"I'll still have a tough time thinking about anything else all day. See you later, Jess Clayton."

He shook his head, picked up his surfboard and headed toward his house, his black Lab trotting along behind him.

After he left, Jess climbed into her trailer, closed the door carefully and sank onto the sofa.

Good Lord.

Her hands were actually trembling, from just a kiss.

Okay, not just a kiss.

One amazing kiss.

She supposed it had been inevitable. From the second she had walked down to the cove and watched him surfing, his body graceful and athletic, she had been fiercely aware of him.

If she were honest with herself, she had been aware of him since the day they met. Spending time with him this morning had been dangerously tempting.

What did it matter how attracted she might be to him? She wasn't the kind of woman who lost her head when a man paid her any attention. She had been careful her entire adult life to keep her relationships with men casual and fun.

Rachel had been right the other night when she said Jess didn't want a happy-ever-after.

Her mother had loved Doug Clayton with an all-consuming, obsessive love. She couldn't see anyone else but him. Even her children faded into insignificance when he was around.

The kind of hold Jess's father had on Veronica hadn't been healthy. Nor had it been easy to see. Roni could barely function without him.

Jess had vowed she would never let a man tangle her up like that. She would always be the one to set the parameters, would never lose her head in a relationship.

Her wild reaction to Nate Whitaker's kiss told her she wasn't as in control as she tried to tell herself. At least where this particular man was concerned.

She pressed a hand to her mouth, where she could still feel the heat of him, then caught herself.

Good thing she was only here a few weeks. Nate was the kind of man who would tempt a woman into throwing all caution into the ocean.

She would have to be careful not to lose control. The results would be disastrous and she couldn't afford it, professionally or personally.

Moving forward, she would simply have to keep their relationship friendly and casual so she could regain a little perspective.

No more early-morning kisses. That would be an excellent place to start.

Too bad.

13

Rachel

WHERE, IN THE NAME OF ALL THAT WAS HOLY, WAS her husband?

Rachel checked her watch for about the hundredth time in the past hour. Cody had promised he would be home by 2 p.m. so they could avoid the worst of the traffic and get to their hotel near UC Davis at a decent enough hour to get Silas settled for the night.

They had talked about ordering room service at the darling boutique hotel she had found. She had even called ahead to obtain the menu, hoping for a romantic and cozy evening with her husband after Silas was asleep.

All her plans would be for nothing if her blasted husband didn't come home soon.

"Don't worry. He probably got hung up at work. He'll be here."

Rachel didn't even want to meet Jess's gaze, afraid her sister would see into the depths of her frustration.

Grace wasn't home from school yet, Ava was watching TV and Silas was playing on the floor, not paying them any mind at all.

"I had everything all figured out so that Silas would nap and we could avoid the worst of the traffic. If Cody is much later, we're going to be stuck right in the middle of it and Silas will nap too late and then won't sleep tonight."

She could only imagine what a nightmare that would be with him screaming in a strange hotel room that probably had thin walls.

"I'm sure Cody has a good reason for being late," Jess said gently.

"He had better," she snapped. As soon as the words were out, she wanted to cringe at the bitchiness in her tone.

She couldn't seem to help it. No doubt Cody wouldn't have any viable explanation at all. He would simply say he'd been hung up at work, gotten busy at a job site, had a complication with a supplier. She'd heard every one of his excuses for working late over the past two months since Silas was diagnosed.

Cody seemed to be doing everything possible to avoid being home with her and their kids.

How could she blame him, when she was so miserable to be around right now?

"He'll be here. Don't worry," Jess said again. "Do you want me to go look for him."

Rachel frowned at her sister's light tone, doing her best to rein in her temper. Jess had no idea the high-wire act Rachel had to walk every single day, balancing the needs of the girls, Silas, Cody and her social media followers.

Her perfect life was slipping away, eroding bit by bit like the ocean working away at a sandbar.

"I might go find him myself if he doesn't get here soon," she said grimly.

A moment later, she heard his pickup in the driveway.

"Sounds like he's here," Jess said cheerfully.

Cody swept into the kitchen looking as sweaty and dirty as if he'd been rolling in the garden with the boys.

"I'm so sorry I'm late, babe." He gave the sheepish, apologetic smile she had come to know well over the past few months. "I had my day all planned but then Georgia Hayes asked me to bid on some roof repairs at her place. And you know how she likes to talk. I think it's gotten worse since old Walt died. She had me looking at every single thing that needs to be fixed at the house. Part of her porch has completely rotted away and I didn't want her falling through so I did a quick emergency repair while I was there. Took me longer than I'd planned."

Everything always took him longer than he'd planned.

She also knew the Widow Hayes had probably been desperate for company, especially a handsome contractor in a tool belt and tight T-shirt. And she knew Cody would probably underbid the job by a long shot and eat the cost of the labor to help the woman out.

She loved that about him at the same time it annoyed the hell out of her right now.

"We're going to be stuck in traffic. I don't see any way around it."

He shrugged, completely unconcerned about the havoc his good-guy helpfulness had wrought on her well-ordered plans.

"We'll still make it. If the traffic gets too bad, we can make a stop somewhere along the way for Si to run out some energy. Maybe we can grab dinner somewhere at McD's and have a picnic."

That was such a far cry from the quiet, romantic room service meal at the hotel that she wanted to cry suddenly.

"That sounds nice," Jess said.

"I want to have a picnic and play at the park," Ava complained, wandering in from the TV room. "Why does Si get all the fun?"

"I promise, you wouldn't think it was fun if you were the one who had to be poked and prodded by the doctors," Rachel told her daughter.

"But Silas gets to go stay in a hotel with you. Maybe they even have a pool."

"You get to have fun with your auntie Jess," Jess said. "Maybe we can pack our own picnic and go to a park nearby."

"Can we stay up past our bedtime?" Ava asked hopefully.

Rachel gave her sister a pointed look.

"Nope," Jess said. "Sorry, kiddo. We'll have a great time while of course following all your mom's rules."

Ava looked resigned but Rachel could tell she was already trying to figure out how to work around those rules as she headed back to watch her show.

"I am sorry I'm late." Cody headed in the direction of their bedroom. "Give me five minutes to shower the work stink off and throw a few things into a bag then I'll be ready to go."

"I've already packed for you. I've left clothes on the bed for you to wear on the drive, as well."

"Great. Then I should be ready in no time."

He smiled but she could see the hint of annoyance in his eyes. If he didn't like it when she micromanaged his life, maybe he shouldn't cut things so close.

When he left, Jess gave her a careful look. "I know you're going for a clinic appointment but I hope you guys can try to enjoy yourselves."

So far, they weren't getting off to the greatest start.

"Are you sure you're up to this tonight? It's not too late for me to ask Cody's mom or one of his sisters. Or Kurt and Jan love having them, too."

If she hadn't been paying attention, she might have missed

the way Jess's features tightened slightly at the mention of Rachel's foster parents, who had stayed close to her all these years.

"We're going to have a great time."

"There's a three-ring binder on the counter that has all the info you should need about their bedtime routine and house rules. I also left several possible healthy meals in the fridge you can choose to give them for dinner."

"Great. That should make things easy."

"Grace will be home in about an hour. She has school tomorrow and Ava has preschool in the morning. The addresses and drop-off instructions are listed in the binder."

"Efficient as always, Rach."

Rachel knew that was another way of calling her a control freak. Okay. Maybe she was. How else was she supposed to manage the chaos without everything completely falling apart?

Jess could mock all she liked. She was a single, carefree woman who didn't have to worry about one child's peanut allergy or another one's aversion to any food touching another food on her plate.

Jess didn't know the first thing about having to cope with a child who could have a meltdown at the slightest provocation, usually at the most public, inopportune moment.

"I only want to make things as easy as possible for you." Her voice sounded stiff, even to her.

"I know. And I appreciate that. You know I have no experience at this kind of thing. I have to admit, I was panicking earlier, afraid I couldn't handle it. Nate managed to talk me down."

Nate again. Was something going on between them? She wanted to ask but swallowed the question. She had enough to worry about right now without trying to micromanage her sister's love life, too.

"You'll be fine. The girls already love you. They have really been looking forward to having you stay."

"There you go. We'll all survive, right?"

"Sure," she answered with a tight smile as Silas came into the kitchen.

"Eat," he said. At four months shy of three years old, he could say six words now. *Eat, Mama, Dada, drink, yes* and *no*. Both of the girls had been early talkers. Ava, for one, hadn't stopped talking since she first put sentences together at about eighteen months. Speech was one area Silas needed help. She knew that was a big source of his frustration, when he couldn't communicate what he needed.

One of many areas.

She sighed and handed him a cheese stick, which he promptly devoured in about ten seconds, before returning to his toys just as Cody came back to the kitchen.

Rachel managed to avoid looking at her watch, just barely.

"That was fast," Jess said.

"I wouldn't want to mess up the schedule any more than I already have," Cody said with a smile that stopped at his mouth.

When was the last time she had seen a genuine smile on his face, at least one aimed at her?

She so desperately missed her husband.

Right now, he seemed farther away than ever. Any hope that they could spend at least a little time reconnecting on this trip seemed to shrink with every passing second. She was ruining everything.

"Are you sure you'll be okay?" she asked her sister one last time.

"We are going to be totally okay. Go. Focus on what you need to do and don't worry about us for a minute."

That was impossible. Sometimes Rachel felt as if her soul was shaped out of anxiety and inadequacy, stitched together with guilt.

"I can take the suitcases out to the van," Cody offered.

"I already did that earlier. Everything is ready."

His jaw tightened. Rachel gave an inward wince. Cody did love to help out. She should have left *something* for him to do.

"Grace's carpool will bring her home in about twenty minutes. I would like to stay to say goodbye but we really do need to go."

"You do," Jess said pointedly.

"Call me if you have any questions at all."

"I will absolutely do that," Jess claimed. "Now, go on. Get out of here. We're fine."

Rachel picked up her purse and the water bottles she had already filled with ice and filtered water for all three of them.

"Silas, want to go for a ride?" Cody asked.

She held her breath. If she suggested the same thing when Silas was in the middle of something else, it could sometimes be enough to trigger a meltdown.

Not when Cody suggested it. Everything seemed like an adventure coming from him.

Silas nodded and walked to his father with his arms up. Cody lifted him up easily.

"I want to go with you," Ava said again, her FOMO even more pronounced than usual.

"Not this time, honey. But I promise, you and I and Gracie will do something fun when we get back, just the three of us," Cody promised. "Come here and give me a hug."

Ava flew to her father and hugged his waist. He scooped her up in his other arm and squeezed both Ava and Silas. Ava giggled and even Silas gave the lopsided smile that was as close as he got to showing true joy.

Cody kissed Ava on the top of her head, spun her around a couple of times then set her back down.

Yes, he worked hard, but when he was here, Cody focused completely on the kids. He was a great father.

She knew plenty of women in town who would love to have a husband like Cody, who worked hard and adored his family.

No, he wasn't perfect, but he was doing his best.

She vowed that she would spend the next twenty-four hours trying to remember that, instead of focusing on all the areas that could use a little work.

14

Jess

SHE WATCHED THEM GO, RACHEL STILL STONY-FACED and Cody doing his best to entertain Silas.

Something was definitely wrong between Rachel and Cody. The tension in the room had been thick enough to drive a Humvee through.

Jess frowned, worried about them. At random moments, Rachel seemed desperately unhappy.

Rachel's problems were her own, Jess reminded herself. Her sister had made it plain over the years that she didn't need Jess interfering in her life.

Jess's only job right now was simply to enjoy herself with her nieces.

She spent the time until Grace came home from school going over the scarily efficient three-ring binder Rachel had left her while Ava finished her show.

Jess closed the binder just as Grace burst into the house, looking adorable with her hair in braids and her backpack almost as big as she was.

"Hi, Aunt Jess!" she exclaimed. She dropped her backpack and hugged her. Jess hugged her back, warmed by the spontaneous affection.

"Hi there. How was school today?"

"Good. I got to be the teacher's helper at recess today and make sure everybody got in line the right way when it was time to go inside. And we had a spelling bee in our class and I won."

"That's terrific. Congratulations!"

Jess had never been that kind of student. She had been mostly bored and uninterested, happiest at recess and when they could have free reading time.

After she gave the girls a Rachel-approved snack of oatmeal and raisin cookies and almond milk, she suddenly realized she had left her phone charger and her favorite pillow in the Airstream.

She *could* get by without them, but why stress about it when Whitaker House was only a mile or so away? "All right, girls. I've got to run to my place for a couple of things. Who wants to come?"

"Me!" Grace exclaimed.

"Me!" Ava echoed. "And Freckles does, too."

"Can we ride bikes? I love riding my new bike and I'm really good at it."

"That does sound like fun but I'm afraid I don't have a bike."

"Mommy has a bike," Ava said. "She rides her bike and Si and me and Freckles sit in the trailer. You could use that one."

She calculated that bike riding to her Airstream and back to the house would probably take them all the way to dinner. Exercise and fun at the same time. Seemed like a win-win.

"Good idea. Let's check it out. Is it in the garage?"

"You shouldn't borrow things without asking, though," Grace

said with a worried look. "Maybe you should text Mama and ask if you can use her bike."

Grace was definitely the rule-follower in the family. That was obvious. Jess supposed every family needed one but the girl was going to have some serious mental health issues later in life if she didn't relax a bit.

"I don't want to bother her right now while she and your dad are busy driving to your brother's appointment. I'm sure she won't mind a bit. Can you tell me where we can find bike helmets?"

Grace jumped on the chance to be helpful. "They're always hanging on the bike handlebars in the garage. I'll show you."

Soon after, she and the girls were on their way, the dog and Ava in the bike trailer already attached to Rachel's beach cruiser and Grace riding along on her cool-looking retro banana-seat bike.

"Are you okay riding up the hill?" she asked Grace as they started toward Whitaker House.

Her niece nodded, offering up her gap-toothed smile. "I have strong leg muscles from all the swimming we do. That's what Mama says."

Her sister was a good mother. These girls were lucky to have Rachel on their team. She would never put her own fulfillment, her own obsession, above their happiness.

Jess considered herself healthy. She ran, she lifted weights, she jumped rope. Not to mention that her job was usually physical, moving boxes, carrying out furniture, hauling bags of trash to the garbage.

When she was in the military, staying fit had been a necessity and she had carried many of those healthy habits with her after she left the service.

Still, pedaling a bicycle she wasn't accustomed to up a hill pulling a trailer containing a little mixed-breed rescue dog and a particularly adorable preschooler was harder than she might have expected. By the time she reached Eleanor's house, she was sweaty and her leg muscles ached.

Grace didn't seem at all fazed by the exertion. In fact, she kept up a running commentary about her school, about her friends, about the trip she wanted to take to Disneyland someday.

Her conversation was punctuated by Ava's occasional contributions, usually centered around when she saw a dog or a cat or a pretty bird at a house they passed.

Jess should have brought water along, but at least she had cold water in the Airstream.

"The ride down will be easier," Grace said cheerfully as they turned into the Whitaker House driveway. "We won't even have to pedal!"

Just as she pulled up to the Airstream, she spied a figure in a black wet suit walking toward the path down to the cove with a long, curved surfboard.

For a wild instant, she thought it might be Nate and her heart rate accelerated. All day, she hadn't been able to stop thinking about that incredible kiss.

As soon as she got a true glimpse of the surfer, she realized her mistake. It wasn't Nate, it was his daughter.

"Hey! That's my friend Sophie," Grace exclaimed. "Hi, Sophie!"

The girl paused at the top of the trail, her surfboard under one arm and her cell phone in her other hand.

"Hey there. What are you guys up to today?"

"This is our aunt Jess. She's our mom's sister. She's staying over with us tonight," Ava announced.

"Cool."

Something was wrong. Jess could see Sophie looked distracted and her eyes were edged with red, as if she had either been crying or trying to keep herself from crying. Had she been fighting with her dad again? And what was she doing heading down to the cove by herself?

"What about you?" she asked, trying for a gentle tone. "Are you waiting for someone?"

Sophie looked at her surfboard, down the path and then back at Jess. "Oh. Yeah. I was telling this kid at school, Tyler, about the waves we have here. He's a ninth grader. He just moved here a few months ago and hadn't heard about the cove and said he might come over after school to check it out. I guess he changed his mind, or something came up or something."

She spoke in a casual tone that didn't fool Jess for an instant. Sophie was interested in the boy. Did Eleanor or Nate know she had prearranged a surfing rendezvous with someone from school? And that he hadn't showed?

Was she planning to go down there by herself? That had to be against the rules. There were no lifeguards on what was virtually a private beach. During her time here in Cape Sanctuary, Jess had only seen three or four other people going down there besides the Whitakers, usually at low tide when people might be beachcombing. From what Eleanor had told her, there were better surf breaks in town, all of them more easily accessible.

What should she do? She was the adult here.

"Are you supposed to go surfing by yourself?" she finally said.

Sophie gave a nonchalant shrug. "Sure. I do it all the time."

Jess frowned but didn't know how to push the issue. If Nate and Eleanor let her go by herself, how could Jess argue that it couldn't be safe?

"Okay," she finally said. "Well, be careful."

"Maybe I'll wait up here for a while longer to see if Tyler shows up."

Disquieted, Jess parked the bike and helped Ava and Freckles out. "I need a drink. What about you?" she asked the girls.

"I'm so thirsty!" Ava exclaimed, with all the drama a five-year-old girl could muster.

"You didn't even do anything." Grace sounded outraged. "You sat in the trailer while Aunt Jess did all the work."

"I had to hold Freckles," Ava protested.

"We all worked hard to get here," Jess said to keep the peace. "We can all have a nice glass of water. I've got some in the refrigerator."

The girls were excited to visit her Airstream again, exclaiming over the desk and the mini-sized appliances. The whole time Jess poured them water and even found them a non-Rachel-approved Oreo for a treat from her secret stash, she fretted about Sophie.

She just didn't feel right about the girl surfing on her own and couldn't believe that Nate, who seemed so protective in so many other ways, would allow it.

Through the window, Jess watched Sophie look at her phone again, then down the street from town.

"Can we sleep here tonight?" Grace asked.

"Yes, can we?" Ava pressed. "It's so cute and little."

She gave them a distracted smile. "You have school and preschool tomorrow. You had both better sleep in your own bed. But before I leave, maybe you can come spend the night here, okay?"

"Promise?" Ava asked, looking so much like Rachel when she was that age that Jess couldn't help smiling.

"Promise."

She sensed movement outside and saw Sophie take a step down the path. Apparently, she had given up waiting for the boy she liked and was indeed going on her own.

"Hold on a minute, girls. Why don't you show Freckles my bed?"

Not waiting for a response, she opened the door to the Airstream.

"Your friend didn't make it?" she asked.

Sophie gave another shrug, not meeting her gaze. "I guess not. He wasn't sure if he would be able to come anyway. Guess he had something else."

Jess knew it wasn't her business. But how could she just stand

by and let Sophie risk her life? "I don't feel good about you surfing on your own."

"It's fine. My dad surfs alone all the time. He did it just this
morning. He wanted me to go but I didn't want to get out of
bed. If he can do it, why can't I?"

*Because you're thirteen? Because your dad has decades' more expe-
rience swimming and surfing in the ocean? Because of a hundred other
reasons.*

First, she said she did it all the time. Now she was giving a
completely different impression.

Jess knew she wouldn't be able to convince Sophie not to go.
She had been a teenage girl once, too, obstinate and determined.

She had a couple of options. She could let Sophie go and call
Eleanor, who wouldn't be able to make it down the path easily.

Alternately, Jess could let her go and call Nate, who might
be working across town for all she knew.

Or she could keep an eye on Sophie herself.

"Do you mind if the girls and I come down with you? We
were thinking about making a sandcastle," she lied. "We can
hang out on the beach while you surf."

Sophie looked surprised and, if Jess wasn't mistaken, a little
relieved.

"I guess that would be okay," she said after a long pause.

"Okay. Give me a minute to grab a few supplies. I could use
an extra pair of hands with my nieces."

She had no idea if this was a good idea. It was the best she
could come up with on short notice.

"Girls, how would you feel about going down to the beach
and building a sandcastle?"

"I'm really good at sandcastles," Grace informed her. "I know
just how to shape the towers so they stay together. Ava's always
fall apart."

"They do not," her sister protested.

"I'm sure you're both great. You're just the girls to help me out."

She quickly grabbed a few empty plastic containers for shaping sand and put them in a bucket, then added water bottles, a blanket and her supersize umbrella.

"I can take the umbrella," Sophie offered, reaching for it with the hand not holding her surfboard. Her phone was now in a dry bag around her neck, Jess noticed.

"Are you going to help us build a sandcastle?" Grace asked.

"Maybe. Or I might go surfing if my friend comes later."

The trip down the path was slightly more difficult than it had been this morning. This time she was holding Freckles's leash in one hand and Ava's hand with the other. Grace insisted on carrying the bucket of sand supplies down, which helped.

By the time they reached the cove, Sophie seemed to have forgotten all about the boy who had stood her up.

"Did I tell you I got an email back from the school in Japan? Finally. They were on a school break."

"That's terrific!"

"Yeah. No package yet with postcards or a gift, like they said in the letter, though."

"I'm sure it takes time to get mail from Japan, especially if they've been on a school break."

"What school in Japan?" Grace asked.

Sophie told both girls about finding the message in the bottle and the budding scientists in Japan who were studying ocean currents. By the time they reached the sand, both girls looked excited.

"Can we look for a bottle with a message?"

"Sure. But I've been looking like forever and only found one in all that time. You can look for other things, though. If you want."

Sophie seemed to have forgotten all about surfing as she

walked up and down the beach with the girls, pointing out agates and driftwood and the occasional sea-polished rock.

They didn't find much this time and quickly turned their attention to building a sandcastle.

"We should build the best sandcastle ever," Grace said. "Then we can take a picture and my mom can put it on her Instagram."

"Let's just do our best and see what we come up with," Jess said.

She left it to Grace and Sophie to strategize where to build the castle and how big they should go.

Soon they were all happily using the bucket to scoop seawater to mix with the sand for packing and creating.

Jess couldn't remember the last time she had done something like this. Maybe when she was Grace's age.

The castle came together quickly. In short order, it had a structure and form, with turrets and even a moat.

"So," Jess said to Sophie casually while her nieces had hurried to the shore to get more water in one of the containers, "tell me about this boy who didn't end up coming over to surf. Tyler. Is that what you said his name was?"

Sophie flashed her a quick look then returned her attention to the sand she was packing. "It's no big deal. He said he *might* come. I guess he was busy or something."

"I'm sorry."

"It's no big deal. It's not like he was my boyfriend or anything."

The girl's jaw tightened, which made Jess suspect she would have liked to have the kid for a boyfriend.

"Well, I'm glad things turned out this way. You're really good at this."

"I've built a lot of sand sculptures. My grandpa and I used to come down to Sunshine Cove all the time. We didn't make just sandcastles. We've done mermaids and ships and once a troll that was awesome. Gram even made a scrapbook with all the pictures of us in front of our sand sculptures. I can show you sometime."

She hadn't heard Sophie talk about Jack Whitaker before. The grief in her voice made Jess's heart ache. "I would love to see that."

The girls returned with water to add to their sand, Freckles trotting behind them.

"This is the best sandcastle ever," Grace declared as they carefully set the final turret in place.

"I wish we could live here," Grace said wistfully.

"I wish we could take it home so I could play with it in the backyard," Ava said. "Aunt Jess, can we build another one in our sandbox when we get home? I want to play with my princess toy in it."

"Our sandbox is too tiny for a castle like this," Grace informed her. "Plus Silas will only smash it the minute we build it. He smashes everything."

Jess didn't know how to answer that, sad all over again at the challenges her sister's family had to face.

"It really is a great sandcastle," Sophie said. "I haven't built a sand sculpture in a long time. Since my grandpa got sick, anyway. This was fun."

Better than surfing with a cute boy might have been? Jess highly doubted it.

"Thanks for helping us," she said.

"We should add some water to our moat," Grace said.

"Right. What good is a moat for keeping out invaders if it doesn't have any water in it?" Jess said with a smile.

The girls hurried to the ocean's edge again to scoop up more water.

Just as they finished, Jess spotted someone coming down the path. For a minute, she thought it might be Sophie's absentee friend, finally here, but this figure was too tall and didn't have a surfboard.

Nate.

He looked big, tough, gorgeous...and upset. His expression was tight, his eyes stormy.

"Sophie. Here you are! You scared us. I came home early and you weren't there. Your grandmother didn't have any idea where you might be and you didn't answer your phone, even though we both called and texted."

"I never got any calls or texts. I would have answered if I had. I probably didn't have cell service down here," she muttered, unrepentant.

"It's a good thing I thought to look in the garage and saw your board missing, though I can't believe you would come down here by yourself. You know the rules."

She looked annoyed at being called out. "I didn't even go into the water. We made a sandcastle instead."

"So why are you wearing a wet suit and why is your surfboard down here? Were you planning to go out on your own?"

She lifted her chin. "I'm thirteen. I'll be fourteen in five months. I've been surfing since I was younger than Grace. I'm old enough to go by myself. You do," she pointed out.

Nate frowned. "That's not the same thing at all. I have been surfing the cove for much longer than you have. Regardless of what a great surfer you are, the more important point is that we have a rule and you were going to break it."

"I wasn't going to be by myself. A kid from school was going to come check out the break at Sunshine Cove. I guess he couldn't come."

"Then you should have put your gear away when he didn't show up. If you're not responsible enough to follow that simple rule, maybe we need to go back to you staying with Grandma Eleanor after school instead of being on your own."

"I'm not a baby! When are you going to stop treating me like one?"

"I hate to state the obvious but maybe when you stop acting like one."

Sophie made a sound of deep frustration. "I didn't break any
rules. Maybe I thought about it but I changed my mind when
Jess asked me to build a sandcastle with her and the girls, okay?
I am so tired of you treating me like I'm some dumb baby all
the time. I *hate* you."

She grabbed her surfboard and marched up the path toward
home without another word, leaving a long, awkward silence
in her wake.

15

Nate

THERE IT WAS.

The *H* word.

How many times had he flung it at his own father when he was frustrated at some rule or other?

Raising a teenager was *hard*. He wasn't sure if he had the stamina to make it through another five years of Sophie flaunting the rules and then snapping at him when he called her on it.

Okay, maybe he had freaked out a little when he saw her surfboard gone and couldn't reach her, imagining all sorts of grim scenarios. It was just Sophie's bad luck that a college student had drowned just a few weeks earlier while surfing alone down the coast, leaving Nate slightly more paranoid than usual about water safety.

"Sorry," he said now to Jess. "We're having some boundary issues, if you couldn't tell. Namely that Sophie seems to be pushing against every single one of them."

"For what it's worth, she never did get in the water. I didn't want to let her come down alone so we decided to build a sand-castle as a diversionary tactic because I didn't know what else to do."

"Thank you for that. None of this is your fault."

"Do you like our sandcastle?" the smaller of the girls asked him.

"It's only the best sandcastle in the whole world," her older sister declared.

She reminded him of Sophie at that age, with her blond braids and gap-toothed smile. "It looks like a great one," he agreed. "I especially like the moat you've built there."

"I want to build another one at my house," the smaller one said, "only Grace says we don't have enough sand in our sand-box and our brother will smash it anyway."

"Brothers can be like that," he said. Their brother had some unique challenges, or so he had heard.

"Do you have a brother?" the youngest girl asked.

"Nope. I'm an only child."

"Our mom doesn't have brothers either," Grace informed him. "Only one sister. Aunt Jess. Our dad has two brothers, though, and one sister. Uncle Dallas and Uncle Wade. Uncle Wade has two kids and lives in the country and Uncle Dallas has one baby and lives by us."

He knew both men as they worked with Cody in the fam-ily roofing company, but didn't know how he was supposed to respond to this recitation of the family tree. To his relief, Jess stepped in.

"Let's take a picture of the sandcastle so we can send it to your mom, then we need to go find some dinner."

She took a few pictures of the girls beaming in front of their creation, teasing and smiling with them.

This was the first he had seen her since earlier that day when they had shared that incredible kiss. As he had told her, he hadn't been able to get it out of his head.

Every time he thought he was over it, that he could now simply move on, he remembered the way her mouth had softened beneath his, how her breath had come in sexy little gasps, how she had thrown her arms around his neck as if he had just rescued her from a thirty-foot swell.

As he watched her with her nieces, he was astonished at how different she seemed from the woman he had met over these past several days as she helped his mother.

There was a sweetness about her he didn't usually see, a gentleness that took his breath away.

She was a complicated woman, Jess Clayton. One minute she was tough, independent, bordering on prickly.

The next, she could be hamming it up for the camera as her older niece took a picture of Jess holding the younger girl.

She was beautiful, her eyes bright and amused as she posed for the camera, and it was hard to look away.

"Let me take a picture of all three of you. This grand castle was obviously a team effort."

"Too bad Sophie left already. She helped us a ton," Grace said.

"Why did she have to go?" Ava complained.

Good question. He had come down too hard on her. He knew it. Seeing that empty spot on the wall where her surfboard should have been had sent him into a panic, which was his only excuse.

He had calmed somewhat when he saw she was down at the cove with Jess and her nieces, instead of on her own as he had feared. Still, he found it concerning that she would even consider breaking the major family rule that she wasn't supposed to get into the ocean by herself.

Every time he wanted to have a real conversation with his child, she chose to escape rather than talk to him.

Maybe he hadn't picked the best venue here with an audience. He had been upset and worried about her, which might have made him respond more harshly than normal.

That didn't mean she had to stomp off every time he annoyed her.

He had to figure out a way to reach her, but not right now.

He took Jess's phone from her. "Turn this way so I can get the sun on your faces."

He didn't know much about photography. Not like her sister, Rachel, anyway. But he did like the way the sun hit them and the clear affection between the three of them.

"Thanks," she said when he handed her phone back to her. Their fingers brushed and he felt the electrical jolt down his spine. Did she? He couldn't tell for sure but was almost positive her breathing accelerated a notch.

Good. He liked knowing this attraction wasn't only one-sided.

Was she remembering their heated kiss, too?

"Let me take one with my phone so I can show Sophie."

He wanted to capture her like this, with her features open and happy. He took one of her and the girls but also one of Jess alone. She didn't have to know that, right?

"It really is a wonderful sandcastle."

"Can we come visit it tomorrow? I want to show Mommy," the younger McBride said.

"You can come anytime your parents want to bring you," he assured her and was rewarded with a wide smile.

"Thanks, mister."

"You can call me Nate, if you want."

"Thanks, Nate."

"Girls, should we go?" Jess said.

He could tell neither of them wanted to leave but they helped her gather up containers and slip them back into the bucket she had emptied.

She picked up her beach blanket and shook out the sand then folded it and slung it over her arm.

"What can I help you carry?"

"Maybe Ava."

"I can walk," the girl insisted.

"How about I hold your hand and help you up where the path gets steep?"

"Okay."

"I'll take your bucket and umbrella, too."

"Thanks."

She handed them over to him and then she and the older girl went ahead with the McBride family dog on a leash.

Ava was slow but cute. While she took each step one at a time, she chattered to him the whole way up, keeping up a steady stream of observations, stories, even a song or two during the five-minute walk.

A few times, he thought he caught Jess turning around to give him a sideways look, as if she couldn't quite figure him out.

What? He was good with kids. He had managed fine with Sophie so far—the past month notwithstanding.

"We're having a slumber party with our auntie Jess because our brother has a doctor appointment a long way away tomorrow," Ava informed him.

"I know. She told me. She's been looking forward to it." That might have been a stretch. She had mostly been in a panic about it but Ava didn't need to know that.

"She's our mom's sister but we don't see her that often."

"How fun that you can spend some time with her now."

"Yes. Can you do a cartwheel? I can. Want to see?"

"Not right now when we're on a hill like this. How about you show me when we get to the top and you have a flat area."

"Okay."

A minute later when they reached the top of the path, she broke away from him and did a cartwheel in the grass.

"Wow. Impressive."

"I can do one, too," Grace said. She took a little skipping run and then cartwheeled after her sister.

"You're both great," Jess said. "I had no idea you could do that."

"Mommy taught us," Ava said. "Can you do one, Aunt Jess?"

"Um. No. Sorry." She set the blanket onto the folding bistro table beside her trailer and took the bucket and umbrella from Nate, then started brushing the considerable sand off the girls.

Ava whispered something to Jess, who suddenly looked panic-stricken and handed the dog's leash to Grace.

"She has to use the bathroom. Watch Freckles, okay?"

Ava danced around as if on the brink of an accident and Jess lifted her up into the trailer and shut the door behind her.

"Do you want to see my new bike?" Grace asked eagerly. Only now did he notice the girl's bike and the adult bike and trailer, tucked behind her Airstream. So that's why he hadn't seen her truck when he hurried over looking for Sophie and why he hadn't realized she was at the cove with his daughter until he was about halfway down the path.

"That is a great-looking bike," he told the girl, admiring the retro banana seat and the tassels in the handlebars.

"Aunt Jess rode our mom's bike. She didn't ask before she borrowed it either."

"I'm sure your mom wouldn't mind."

"That's what Aunt Jess said."

Something seemed off on the bigger bike. He was giving it a closer look when Jess and Ava walked out of the Airstream looking much more relaxed now. The girl had apparently made it to the bathroom on time.

"Bad news," he said apologetically. "Your bike tire is flat. Looks like you ran over a nail."

She looked at it with dismay. "Oh no. Rachel will kill me."

"You should have asked her," Grace muttered, earning a dark look from her aunt.

"Not to worry. It's easily fixed."

"Sure. If you have the right tools and a new inner tube. Which I don't."

She looked at the girls and the dog and the bikes, and winced. "Looks like we'll have to walk back to my sister's place, get my truck and run to the bike store."

He suspected Ava would never make it, walking all the way to the McBrides'. The bike trailer was similar to one he'd had for Sophie that converted to a jogger stroller with the right accessories, but he suspected Jess didn't have those with her.

"How about this? We can load up the bikes into the back of my truck, run to the bike shop for a tube and have them fix it while we grab a pizza for dinner. It's the least I can do to thank you for watching over Sophie."

She looked shocked at the suggestion. "That's not necessary, really."

"Maybe not, but I would enjoy it. If you already have dinner plans, that's fine. I'll drive you home and pick up a tube on the way back, fix your bike and get it to you tomorrow."

"I would rather have pizza," Grace said.

"Pizza!" Ava exclaimed.

Even their dog seemed to agree, jumping around and giving happy little yips. He might have been picking up on the girls' excitement, though.

Jess looked uncertain, though he could see her beginning to weaken. "What about Sophie?"

"I'll go talk to her and tell her the plan."

"She wasn't very happy with you when she left. I'm not sure she'll be in the mood to hang out with us."

"Has it been longer than fifteen minutes?" he asked ruefully. "With the way her moods go lately, she's probably done being mad at me about the surfing thing and has moved on to something else completely."

She would still be mad at him, of course. That was a given. But maybe she would unbend long enough to enjoy more time with Jess and her nieces.

"I have to go talk to her anyway. If she doesn't want to help us with the bike, I can always bring her back some pizza, if it comes to that."

"How about this? If she wants to go along, we'll have pizza. If not, I'll just ask you to take us and the bikes back to Rachel and Cody's place, where I can look around for an inner tube or a patch kit."

"I'll see what I can do. I'll meet you back here in ten."

"Long enough for us to wash up. Thanks," she said, ushering the girls toward her Airstream steps as Nate headed for his place.

He found Sophie in the family room playing her favorite video game. She looked up when he entered but seemed too distracted by the game to glare at him. That was progress, at least.

"Hey there," he said with a smile. "I'm sorry I treated you like a baby. I was worried about you. I know you can take care of yourself in most situations but you know how unpredictable the ocean can be. You made the right choice in the end not to surf by yourself. I should have focused on that instead. I'm sorry."

She looked startled at the apology, which made Nate think maybe he didn't do enough of them.

"I should have texted Gram to let her know where I was. I do know the rules. I thought my friend would be with me."

He wanted to talk to her about this boy she had invited over after school but decided to pick his battles for now.

"Jess has a flat tire on her bike. We're going to run downtown to the bike shop and we're talking about getting a pizza. Want to come? You can get a personal-size with your own toppings, if you want."

Sophie had a long history of being picky when it came to her pizza toppings, which he had learned how to work around.

She appeared to consider the merits of staying home by herself with her video games or spending more time with Jess and the girls. They won.

"I guess," she said, saving and shutting down the game.

Nate figured he would take a shrug and an unenthusiastic response as a win in this case.

In the end, they decided to wait for the tire to be repaired at the bike shop, which didn't take long. They were done and ready to be on the road again in about twenty minutes.

All three of the guys working in the shop couldn't seem to take their gazes off Jess, each vying for her attention. She didn't seem to notice. Could she possibly be unaware of the attention she attracted?

"All done," Mike, the very married store owner, said with a flirtatious smile at Jess. She either didn't notice or had decided to ignore him.

"Thanks for doing it so quickly."

"Anytime."

She paid for the repair, which Nate would have liked to do, then she walked her sister's bike back outside the store to his truck.

"What a beautiful evening." She lifted her face to the sky and he fought the urge to kiss her again right there in the middle of downtown Cape Sanctuary.

"It really is." He looked around. "What's your pleasure? We can go to the pizza place or we could grab one to-go and eat it at the park."

"Good idea. Anything that will help me wear out the girls so they'll sleep well tonight gets a thumbs-up from me."

The best pizza in town was at a restaurant right next to Driftwood Park in the downtown area. Jess took Sophie and the girls to the park while he went inside and ordered for them.

He knew the owner of the restaurant, who offered to deliver the pizzas to them at the park so Nate didn't have to wait inside on such a lovely May evening.

They weren't the only people doing the same thing. As he walked back to the picnic table Jess had claimed, he greeted several other families he knew from town who were gathered around their al fresco meals.

Sophie was pushing the girls on the swings and laughing at something they had said when he slid onto the bench of the picnic table near Jess.

"The pizzas will be ready in about fifteen minutes."

"Perfect," she said. "This was a great idea."

Dinner with a lovely woman and some cute kids? He had to agree.

"They look like they're having fun."

"Sophie is great with them. She must do a lot of babysitting."

"Some. She's watched your nieces a few times to help out since their brother came along. She watched all three of them once a year or so ago but hasn't tended him for some time."

"Silas has some behavioral issues that make him somewhat, er, challenging for the average babysitter. I think Cody's mom usually watches him when Rachel needs help."

"How old is he now? Three?"

"Not quite. He'll be three in September."

"That can be a challenging age. Sophie used to hold her breath when she didn't get her own way. That certainly made life interesting. She grew out of it, eventually. Now she just snaps at me instead and storms off."

"She's a teenager. It's a tough time for every girl."

He suspected there was more to Sophie's anger at him than that but she had become very closemouthed and secretive lately and wouldn't open up.

When he pressed her, she just snapped even more, claiming she didn't know what he was talking about, that she wasn't acting any differently.

"So this appointment Rachel and Cody took Silas to. Is everything okay? Does it have to do with his autism?"

Jess gave him a surprised look. "You know about that?"

"I heard Rachel talking to my mom about it once when we bumped into them at the farmer's market."

"I don't know how public she's been with his diagnosis so I didn't want to say anything if you didn't know. Yes. They have an appointment with an autism clinic associated with UC Davis. It starts early in the morning and is supposed to last several hours."

"That's rough."

"The appointment or that Silas has autism?"

"Both, I guess."

"He's a sweet boy who just has some extra challenges to deal with right now. If anyone can handle it, it's Rachel and Cody."

"I completely agree. They're good people. And they have each other, which has to be a plus."

He saw a shadow briefly cross her expression but the delivery person from the restaurant found them before she could comment.

"I've got a medium cheese pizza, one with all veggies and a personal with only pepperoni and olives."

"Yes. That's right. Thanks, Aspen," Nate said. He tipped the girl, who was a few years older than Sophie and whose older brother worked for him during the summers when he was home between semesters at college.

They dug in while families played around them and the streetlights of town began to come on as the sun started to fade over the water.

This probably wasn't the best way to go about keeping his distance from Jess Clayton but right now he wouldn't trade this evening for anything.

16

Jess

IF THE AFTERNOON SPENT BUILDING SANDCASTLES on the shore of Sunshine Cove was enjoyable, the evening at the park was sheer perfection.

Jess didn't expect to enjoy it so much. Mainly, she had agreed because the girls were excited about the idea when Nate suggested it.

She enjoyed her own company and had no problem eating her meals alone. She had become so used to her solitary existence that she had almost forgotten how much she enjoyed fun conversation, delicious food and enjoyable companions.

The girls were hilarious. Ava and Grace were very different. Ava liked to be the center of attention, telling jokes and being silly, while Grace was more careful, concerned with propriety and following the rules.

Sophie did a wonderful job of entertaining both of them.

As for Nate, he was great with both of the little girls. Not to mention completely gorgeous. She couldn't stop thinking about how delicious his mouth tasted and how she really wanted him to kiss her again.

The long day of excitement was too much for the girls, though. Ava couldn't seem to stop yawning, even before she finished her pizza, and her older sister rubbed her eyes several times.

"This has been wonderful but I probably need to get these girls home. Their bedtime was a half hour ago and we still need to follow Rachel's ten-point schedule for a good night's sleep before I settle them down."

"I don't want to leave the park," Ava protested, over another big yawn. "This was so much fun."

"I know," Jess said. "But it will be dark soon and you have preschool tomorrow."

"Oh yeah. Plus Mommy and Daddy and Si will be home."

They all worked together to clean up after themselves and then walked back to Nate's pickup truck.

Like Ava, Jess didn't want the evening to end. It left her craving for something she hadn't known she wanted.

Connection.

Subtle and addictive. It left her feeling edgy and restless as Nate drove them home.

This was exactly the problem with letting herself get involved. She didn't need connection. She was just fine on her own. Things were better that way. Safer.

All these feelings zinging around left a person weakened, vulnerable to heartache and loss.

Better to stay on her solitary emotional island, fighting off anyone else who dared to come near, with whatever means necessary.

Ava, sandwiched between Sophie and Grace, fell asleep in the back seat of Nate's king cab pickup on the short drive to Rachel's house.

She didn't wake even after he pulled into the driveway, unloaded the bikes and put them in the storage area Grace pointed out in the garage.

"I'll carry her in," he offered.

Jess could do it. She lifted heavy boxes for a living. One little girl who couldn't weigh more than fifty pounds would be nothing. It seemed foolish to argue with him, though.

Something about the sight of the little sleeping girl nestled in his arms made Jess's knees feel wobbly.

Good grief. This was ridiculous.

She opened the door with the code Rachel had given her and led the way inside.

"Where am I going with her?" .

"Our bedroom is down the hall next to the bathroom," Grace informed him.

"Second door on the right," Jess said. "I'll show you."

She led the way down the hall to the girls' cute bedroom, decorated like an Instagram fantasy, with reading nooks and bookshelves and a glorious dollhouse she had yet to see the girls actually use.

"She needs a bath," Grace said. "We always have a bath before we go to bed."

"Well, this time I'm going to let her go to sleep and have a quick bath in the morning."

Rachel wouldn't be happy about it, but Jess was going with her instincts on this one. Waking up Ava and making her take a bath when she was exhausted seemed cruel.

Nate lowered her to the bed. Ava snuggled into her pillow, reaching to pull her comforter over her.

Letting her get by without a bath was one thing. Allowing her to sleep in the clothes she'd been wearing to play at the park and the beach was something else entirely. "I'll help her into PJs in a minute," she said softly. "Thank you for your help."

"My pleasure."

She walked him back to the door while Grace grabbed her pajamas and headed for the bathroom next to their room. "I'll be in to help you in a minute."

"I don't need help. I'm not a baby like Ava or Silas," Grace informed her haughtily.

"Leave the door unlocked anyway," Jess said. She didn't know what Rachel's rules were about that sort of thing but she wasn't taking any chances of leaving a child unattended around water.

Grace sighed and shut the bathroom door firmly. Soon after, Jess heard water running.

"At least she didn't slam it, like Sophie would have done." His daughter had opted to wait in the truck.

"Thank you for everything tonight. The bike tire, the ride, the pizza. It turned out to be a good evening, after all."

"I enjoyed it," he said, his voice gruff.

She walked him to the door, her mind suddenly filled with images from that morning when he had kissed her.

"You did great. See? Nothing to be nervous about."

"I'm still over my head, but so far we haven't had any broken bones or ER visits or other catastrophes. The night is still young, though."

He smiled. "Don't worry. If you do anything else wrong, I suspect Grace will be the first one to tell you."

She had to laugh at how accurately he had assessed her oldest niece. "I guess every family needs one who likes to follow the rules."

"I certainly wasn't that person and something tells me you weren't either."

How had he guessed that? "Not in the slightest," she answered.

"Yet we both joined the military, which is all about following the rules."

She was struck by the notion that they had far more in common than she might have thought.

Maybe that was why she was so fiercely drawn to him.

Not that it mattered. He wasn't for her, she reminded herself.

"Thanks again. You saved the day."

"I loved every minute of it," Nate said in a low voice. She caught her breath when he leaned forward. Was he going to kiss her again?

He did, but this time he only brushed his mouth to the side of hers with a gentleness that completely disarmed her.

"Good night. Try not to burn the house down."

She laughed a little raggedly. "I won't. I think we're safe for now. Thanks for the vote of confidence."

He smiled, waved and headed out the door, leaving her to watch after him and ache with longing for only a minute before she turned back to her nieces.

17

Rachel

AS RACHEL CLOSED THE DOOR INTO THE ADJOINING bedroom of their hotel suite, she wanted to collapse into a heap on the bed, pull the covers over her head and stay there for the next twenty-four hours.

The drive had been every bit the nightmare she had feared. Traffic had been backed up the whole way and then the GPS had led them the wrong way to the hotel, about twenty minutes out of their way to a similarly named hotel in a nearby community.

She had worried Silas would fall asleep on the drive and then not be able to sleep once they reached the hotel. By about thirty minutes into the drive, she was praying he *would* fall asleep.

She suspected he was carsick but he couldn't communicate that. Instead, he had cried and none of the usual soothing techniques seemed to be working.

Cody had suggested they pull over and trade places so she

could drive the remainder of the way to the hotel and he could try his hand with Silas.

She had ended up snapping that they were already late enough and she didn't want to waste time pulling over.

He was only trying to help. He wasn't trying to imply that he was better with their son than she was. She knew that but couldn't help feeling defensive. She was with Silas all day and knew him better than anybody did. She ought to be able to calm him, if anyone could.

Cody had been right. Silas had needed the distraction of his father sitting with him, not her. Instead, he grew increasingly irritable until they finally stopped at McDonald's to grab dinner for him in case he was hangry.

That had calmed him somewhat but they were all still upset with each other when they reached the hotel.

Nothing was going the way she had planned. So much for the romantic dinner she had planned. Cody had ended up buying something at McDonald's, too.

She could have told him she had prearranged a dinner once they arrived but by then she had been too worn-out to care.

Instead of bringing them together, she felt more distant than ever from her husband.

"Is he asleep?" Cody asked.

"Finally. I hope he stays that way."

She slumped into the armchair in the room, certain she looked as completely exhausted as she felt.

"You can't keep going on this way, Rach. You need help."

"I'm okay. It's just been a long day."

"Following a long week and a long month and a long two years and eight months. You're worn-out. I still think we should hire someone to help you. A nanny would take some of the burden off your shoulders."

And admit failure? She wasn't ready to do that. "We've talked about how much it would cost to have an autism-trained nanny come in. The expense would eat away all our savings, pushing back our plans to build our dream house by years."

"Do you think I care about any dream house? I just want my wife back."

His words and the edge of desperation in them made her guilty and defensive at the same time. "I haven't gone anywhere, Cody. I'm not the one who works sixteen-hour days so you don't have to come home and deal with your family."

Color rose in his face but he didn't deny that's what he was doing. "Why not? When I'm home, you don't seem to want or need me around. Everything I do is wrong."

She couldn't help that she had figured out the best way to do things after years of running their house. Every time she gently tried to explain why her way was better, he got mad and stormed off.

She was pushing him away. Why couldn't she just shut up and let him load the dishwasher wrong and add the wrong detergent to the white clothes?

Where the hell would her perfection get her when she didn't have a husband?

She didn't want to have this fight right now. Not in this cute boutique hotel with the bohemian decor and the tassels on the pillows. She had entertained all these fantasies about seducing her husband, sharing physical closeness, which usually led to at least some emotional closeness.

Right now sex was the last thing on her mind but maybe if she took a break from the situation she could come back more in the mood.

"I'm going to sit by the pool for a minute and call Jess to check on the girls."

"You don't have to leave. You can call from here."

"I've been sitting in the car for three hours. I need some air," she said.

He studied her, his blue eyes she loved so much suddenly

filled with a sadness that broke her heart. Could he feel their marriage slipping away, too?

"What about dinner? I ate at McD's but you didn't have anything. I can order room service for you. I could probably eat dessert."

"I'm not hungry," she said. "I'll take one of the protein shakes I packed down to the pool and drink that."

By the time she made it to the outdoor pool, surrounded by palm trees and lush landscaping, she felt even more horrible for her pissy mood.

What was wrong with her? She wasn't usually so negative. Ever since Silas's diagnosis, her temper was on a hair trigger.

She had taken everything out on Cody, who didn't deserve her constant bad mood.

She should drink her shake, call her sister, and then go back and have incredible makeup sex with her husband.

Jess didn't answer until after the fourth ring.

"Hi," she said, sounding breathless. "Sorry. I guess I left my phone down in the kitchen while I was reading a story to Grace. I barely heard it."

She suddenly yearned to be home with her girls with hugs and stories and the soft sweetness of bedtime.

"Is everything okay there?"

"Great. The kitchen fire was small and the firefighters were able to put it out quickly with almost no damage to the house."

"Jess." Sometimes her sister's sense of humor escaped her.

"I'm sorry. I'm teasing. We had a great afternoon and evening. We took a bike ride this afternoon, built an epic sandcastle, which I took pictures of, and ended up having pizza at the park with Nate Whitaker and Sophie. Ava is already asleep and Grace will probably be there by the time we end this phone call."

Nate again. Things there seemed more and more interesting.

"Thank you again for staying with them."

"It's been no problem at all." Jess spoke with a sincerity Rachel didn't usually hear from her sister, who tended to keep all her emotions tightly wrapped.

"They're great girls, Rachel. Funny and kind and smart. I can tell you're a good mom."

The quiet words of approval, so desperately needed, sent Rachel over the edge. Her throat tightened and tears burned her eyes.

She couldn't begin to tell Jess how much that meant to her. She wanted so much better for her children than she and her sister had for the first thirteen years of Rachel's life.

She wanted to give them confidence, curiosity, joy. She *didn't* want them to grow up in a war zone, with a perennially stressed mother trying desperately to achieve an impossible perfection.

"Thanks for saying that. I don't feel like it most of the time, but thanks."

"So according to your notes, I'm getting them off to school and preschool tomorrow then Cody's mom is picking up Ava when she gets out."

"Yes. And she'll get Grace from the bus and hang out with them at the house until whatever time we make it back in the evening."

"That works."

"Thank you again. I don't know how to make it up to you."

"No need. This is just what family does, Rachel."

"I'm still throwing you a big birthday party. I haven't forgotten. It's not every day my big sister turns the big three-oh. We have to celebrate!"

"We really don't," Jess began, but Rachel didn't let her finish.

"Yes. We haven't been together to celebrate your birthday in years. How long has it been? Probably before..." Her voice trailed off and silence fell between them like a cold, relentless rain.

"Right."

Rachel didn't want to think about that *before*. She had spent her entire adult life trying not to think about it.

"I'll arrange everything. I should invite Eleanor and Nate and Sophie! It will be terrific. Leave everything to me."

Jess sighed, clearly not excited about the party. Too bad. Rachel was doing it anyway.

She needed something good to focus on right now, something to take her mind off the chaos and mess of her life.

After they ended the call, she sat for a moment there beside the quiet pool, sipping her protein shake and watching a couple of kids play in the far end.

The fresh air soothed her, as it always did. She spent a lot of time working out in her garden or taking walks with Silas in his stroller for that very reason. She needed the peace and calm of nature to center her.

When she felt calm and relaxed, she returned to the hotel, prepared to apologize to Cody and see how much of their night away she could salvage.

She found all the lights out. Cody was stretched out on the bed, sound asleep, already snoring.

He had changed into the basketball shorts and T-shirt he liked to sleep in and had arranged the pillows the way he did at home.

So much for a romantic interlude. Rachel sighed.

Maybe this was their life together now. Two parents so exhausted by the efforts of keeping their family running that they grabbed sleep wherever they could find it.

Instead of the sexy negligee she had brought, she changed into her favorite sleep shirt that she had also tucked into her suitcase and slipped into bed beside her husband.

Cody made a sound, rolled over and wrapped an arm around her.

At least they had this, she thought, snuggling deeper into his heat. At least in sleep, he still turned toward her, even if he didn't seem to want to when they were both awake.

Maybe this could be enough for now.

18

Jess

AFTER ENDING THE CALL, JESS LOOKED AROUND AT the gleaming kitchen, wondering about the sister whose territory she stood in.

She had a deep, aching wish that they could be closer, as they once had been. She and Rachel always seemed to skim the surface of each other's lives. They could be cordial to each other, even loving, but never with the closeness they'd once had. She missed when Rachel had been her best friend, when they had turned to each other as a protection against the stress and trauma of their parents' ugliness.

Rachel was struggling. Jess didn't know if it was depression, anxiety or a combination of both. Either way, it was obvious her sister seemed deeply unhappy.

Jess didn't want or need a birthday party but if that would help Rachel through whatever dark time she was navigating, Jess would suffer through it.

★ ★ ★

After an uneventful night where she actually slept quite well on the family room sofa, the morning was far more hectic than it should have been.

Freckles ended up throwing up breakfast, which made Grace dry heave and almost lose *her* breakfast. Jess took time to give Ava a quick bath to make up for the night before. Ten minutes later, Ava spilled orange juice on the cute jumper her mother had thoughtfully set out for her, turning everything sticky.

By the time she cleaned up all the messes, changed Ava and got Grace off to school and Ava to preschool, Jess was exhausted. And her own workday hadn't started yet.

When she arrived at Eleanor's house, she found her employer in an odd mood, as if she knew a secret and was having a hard time keeping it.

"How did everything go with the girls yesterday?" Eleanor asked, eyes twinkling.

What did she know about the way Jess had spent her evening? Did she know about the impromptu pizza party with Nate and Sophie?

"Um. Great. We ended up building a great sandcastle down at the cove with Sophie in the afternoon."

"She told me. And Nathaniel showed me the picture. He's already printed one out for the album Sophie keeps of the sand creations she's made over the years."

"Oh. That's nice."

"She and her grandfather often built sandcastles together. Jack was always coming up with new things to create down there. It was one of their things."

"That's what she said."

"And then I understand you had a bike problem that Nathaniel helped you with and you three ended up having dinner with him and Sophie."

"Yes. They were kind enough to help me with a flat tire on

my sister's bike and then we had pizza at Driftwood Park. How was dinner with your friends?"

Eleanor had told her the day before an old friend and her husband were in town and they had plans to meet up.

"Oh lovely. It's always good to spend time with friends you haven't seen for a while. It's like picking up a book you love that you haven't read in a long time. I'm glad you had a good evening, as well. Sophie seemed to have enjoyed herself."

What about Nate? Had he said anything?

Jess frowned at herself. Good heavens. She wasn't in junior high school. She didn't need to ask his *mother*, of all people, if he had mentioned her.

"I'm glad my son offered to help you with your bike and the girls. He's a good man. I might be a little biased, of course, but I don't think so."

Jess was beginning to agree. In fact, she was finding him very hard to resist.

Maybe she needed to try harder.

"Which room would you like to start on today?"

They had finished the family room/den area, Jack Whitaker's office and several of the bedrooms. She would probably be able to wrap things up by Monday if they worked hard at it.

Usually at this stage in a job, she couldn't wait to finish and was already excited about helping someone else. This time, she was trying hard not to drag her feet.

"I don't know. I can't seem to make up my mind about anything these days."

The older woman looked pale in the morning light, Jess thought. Maybe she had had a few too many glasses of wine the night before. Or maybe she hadn't slept well. Jess knew Eleanor suffered from insomnia, probably missing the husband she had slept beside every night for more than forty years.

"What would you suggest?" Eleanor asked.

"We still have a few more closets, the outdoor shed, the

kitchen and your bedroom. Maybe we should start on Jack's side of your closet."

The two had a huge walk-in closet. So far, six months after Jack's death, all of his clothing still hung neatly in his half, gathering dust.

A spasm of deep grief creased Eleanor's features. "Not yet. I know I need to but…not yet. What about my craft room?" she suggested quickly. "I have projects in there from years ago and more material and yarn than I can ever use."

Jess didn't have the heart to push the matter. If Eleanor wasn't ready to clear out her husband's clothing, this last tangible link to the man she loved, Jess wouldn't force her. Yes, that might mean she had to leave part of her job here at Whitaker House undone. So be it.

Like the ocean, grief had its own timetable, its own rhythm and flow.

"The craft room it is. I was thinking maybe we could donate some of the supplies you don't want to the county women's shelter."

"Oh, what an excellent idea! Crafting and sewing can be so cathartic."

It turned into truly a delightful morning. Energized by the idea of helping out the shelter, Eleanor was witty and full of stories.

After a few hours, she started to flag but pulled over her craft chair and continued helping Jess sort through the bins and boxes in the room while telling her about the amazing trip she and Jack had taken through Europe the year before his cancer diagnosis.

"He really said that to the shopkeeper in Paris?"

"She was so rude to him. Accusing him of shoplifting, just because her perfume bottles weren't in perfect order! My husband was the most honest man you could ever meet. I wish you had been able to meet him. He would have simply adored you, just as the rest of us do."

She smiled, touched at Eleanor's open affection. The woman really was a dear. She would miss her so much when she left.

It wasn't as if she might never see her again. Unlike most of her clients, Eleanor lived in a town where Jess had family ties. When she came back to visit Cody and Rachel, she could always stop here at Whitaker House and visit Eleanor.

It wouldn't be the same as these long days they had enjoyed together since she came to town. Jess would be like Eleanor's old friend from out of town, meeting up with her for dinner or lunch when she made it to town for one of the holidays or one of the children's birthdays.

She tried not to let that realization sadden her.

They worked hard most of the morning and made a good start in the craft room. Jess was just about to suggest they take a break when she heard the kitchen door open.

"Hello?" a masculine voice called. Jess froze, her stomach doing idiotic backflips.

"Oh, that will be Nathaniel," Eleanor said with a smile. "Did I tell you I texted him earlier to ask if he can help carry my old sewing machine table and all the extra bins of material for the shelter to your truck?"

"Um, no. You didn't mention it."

"I thought some of those things might be too heavy for you to handle on your own, my dear. I wish I could be more help, but it's good I have a strong son to call upon."

Jess swallowed back her protest. Her entire job consisted of lifting heavy things by herself. She had been doing this for years and was much stronger than she looked, plus she knew the value of a good hand truck and the ramp she kept in the back of her pickup truck. Still, Eleanor was the boss.

"Great." Jess forced a smile. "I'm sure with Nate's help, we can make short work of it."

"We're in the craft room, darling," Eleanor called. A moment later, Nate poked his head through the doorway. He met her gaze first and for some ridiculous reason, Jess could feel her face heat. She had to hope neither he nor his mother noticed.

"How's it going in here?"

"We've made so much progress," Eleanor said cheerfully. "Well, Jess has made progress. I'm mostly sitting here like a lump and telling her what to do with things."

"It looks great."

"Thank you for coming over on your lunch hour. I know how busy you are," Eleanor said. "Here's an idea. Why don't you two load up Jess's truck with the sewing machine and the boxes while I make us all lunch."

Nate glanced at his watch. "I don't have a lot of time, Mom. I have to get back to the library job. I've got three different sub-contractors working there today."

Jess again wanted to tell both Whitakers she didn't really need help but that would sound churlish after he had made the time to drive home in the middle of the day.

"You have to eat," his mother said. "I can have a club sandwich for you by the time you come back in."

He looked resigned. "All right. Thanks. Where is the stuff we're taking?"

"The sewing machine and everything stacked to the right of the hallway is going to the women's shelter in Redding. Jess is driving it over today. They're thrilled with the donation."

"What a good idea."

"Isn't it?" His mother beamed. "I can't claim credit. It was Jess's idea. I never would have thought of it but it's genius. If there are things they don't want, they can sell it in their charity shop."

"I'll grab my hand truck. It shouldn't take us long." Jess hurried out to her pickup. By the time she returned, Nate was already on his way out of the house with his arms full of boxes.

"Am I loading them any particular way?"

"No. I'll make two trips. Goodwill can wait until tomorrow."

When he came back inside, she had just finished stacking boxes onto the hand truck.

"I can make another trip, if you want to go into the kitchen and visit with your mom."

"No worries. You're right, this won't take long."

It took them two more trips. He helped her stack the boxes in the back, return the hand truck and ramp, and close the tailgate, then they worked together to secure the whole thing with netting and bungee cords.

"This really is a lot of work for you. I guess I didn't think about the logistics of clearing everything out. Culling out the extra stuff is one thing but you still have to find something to do with it."

"Keep, donate, sell or bin. Those are the four options. I like this part of the job, actually. It's tangible progress. Probably like you feel watching a structure being framed. One minute there's nothing there, the next you have the bones of a house. In my case, the process is reversed in a way, clearing out the stuff to reveal those bones again."

"How did the night go with the girls?" he asked, leaning against her truck.

"We survived. No bad dreams, no bed-wetting. The morning wasn't terrific as we dealt with dog vomit but we survived that, too."

"Any word from Rachel about how the appointment went?"

"I think they're still there. It was supposed to last all day. I'm sure she'll text me when she's done."

"I had a good time last night. It's been a long time since I've had pizza in the park."

She smiled. "The girls did, too. Ava was still talking about Sophie's fun dad this morning."

He laughed. "I don't think Sophie would agree with that particular description right now."

"Is she still mad at you for laying down the law yesterday about surfing by herself?"

He sighed. "She's mad at me about something. I have no idea if it's something in particular I've done or just general discontent that she has me for a father."

"It's probably just a phase. Teenage girls can sometimes be moody. I know. I was one."

"I think this might be something more than that but she clams up whenever I try to ask. If she won't tell me what's wrong, though, I can't fix it."

"That must be tough." Jess gave him a sympathetic look. Nate was the kind of man who had to fix things. Find the answers. Solve the puzzle. That was in his nature. She understood him because she was the same, yet one more thing they had in common.

"Raising a daughter is not for the faint of heart," he said.

She had to smile at his heartfelt tone. "I'm sure when she's ready, she'll tell you what's wrong."

He didn't answer and she lifted her gaze, not sure why. He was looking down at her with an intent expression that made her toes curl.

She had always thought that was a stupid turn of phrase in books but now she totally understood what people meant by it.

He was gazing at her mouth, she realized, and she suddenly knew he was remembering their kiss the day before.

"I think we need a do-over," he said.

"Excuse me?"

"Yesterday wasn't a real kiss."

She blinked. "Funny. It felt quite real to me."

"It was mouths only. Does that really count?"

Oh, it counted all right. She'd never had a kiss that counted more.

"I wasn't aware we were keeping score."

"You said that kiss yesterday morning should work this attraction out of our systems. I don't know about you, but that certainly didn't happen on my part. I think we need a do-over. One where I don't have to worry about my damp wet suit making you cold."

"Oh," she exclaimed. "Is that why you didn't touch me?"

"Yes. And believe me, it wasn't easy, especially when I wanted to press you up against the wall of your trailer."

"Oh."

It was as if he had sucked all the oxygen out of the entire area. She was suddenly aware of nothing but him.

He took a step forward and she swallowed hard. "I don't think a mouths-only kiss was enough to get this out of our systems. I think we should try again when we can use hands."

She ought to make some glib comment and go back inside with Eleanor, where she would be safe.

She couldn't think of anything glib. She could only focus on the sudden aching hunger that seemed to have taken over all rational thought.

"That sounds fair."

Her words were barely out when he was reaching for her and pulling her against him, his mouth fierce and urgent on hers.

She kissed him back, all thought of caution completely escaping her brain.

He was right. She hadn't worked anything out of her system. Spending the evening with him and Sophie, seeing his sweetness to her nieces, had only increased her awareness of him.

The kiss the morning before had been delicious. This one, with her body pressed against his and his hands against her back and his hair beneath her fingers, was mind-bending.

She had spent more than twenty-four hours reminding herself of all the reasons why she couldn't have a fling with him. After thirty seconds in his arms, she forgot all about those reasons.

What would be the harm? They were both unattached adults.

He was a decent guy who cared about his family and was nice to kids.

She liked him very much and they certainly generated enough heat between them to burn down the surrounding forest.

Why not have a passionate affair for the remaining time she would be in Cape Sanctuary? That might be the only thing that would slake this all-consuming hunger.

It wouldn't.

She didn't know how she knew but something told her that even weeks or months or years wouldn't be enough, when it came to Nate Whitaker.

She froze in his arms, reality splashing over her like a cold rain.

She didn't want this kind of wild, frenzied desire that seemed to come out of nowhere. That she could feel this way toward a man she barely knew scared the hell out of her.

With great effort, she lowered her hands and managed to step away.

"I don't know about you, but that should do it for me," she said. It was a total lie and he had to know it. Her hands were trembling, for Pete's sake.

"Should it?" His voice was raspy, his gaze stunned.

"This can't go anywhere, Nate. You get that, right?"

He blew out a shaky-sounding breath. "Yeah. Of course. You're leaving town shortly. I get it."

"I'm not looking for a relationship. I like my life the way it is, where I'm free to pack up my trailer and move from place to place. I'm one of those people who is perfectly happy on my own."

"An admirable quality."

"It's not that I'm some kind of loner or don't like people. I do. I have friends. I just don't...put down stakes."

He studied her, his expression shuttered. "You don't owe me explanations, Jess. No is sufficient, I promise."

Most guys would have embraced the idea of a woman who didn't want anything serious. She found it rather refreshing that Nate didn't even try to persuade her he was that kind of guy.

"Okay. Thanks. I…hope this doesn't make things awkward between us."

He shrugged. "Why would it? You're leaving soon. I think I can manage to rein in my rampaging lust for you until you're gone."

She had to admit, her toes curled again at the idea that this entirely too appealing man could use the words *rampaging lust* about her, even in that dry tone. She also wasn't entirely sure she could do the same.

"We should go in," she said. "Your mom will probably be wondering where we are."

"I doubt that," he muttered. "I have a fairly good idea she suspects exactly what we're doing."

That did complicate things. Did Eleanor suspect her attraction to Nate? Oh, Jess hoped not. She wouldn't really be surprised, though. He was right. His mother was sharp and seemed to know everything that went on with those she cared about.

She sincerely liked the other woman and didn't want to dash any hopes she might have regarding Jess and her son.

"You go ahead. I, uh, need a minute."

She was confused for only a second, then could feel her face heat. He was obviously still aroused from their kiss, as she was, but it was much harder for a guy to conceal that, especially when he was walking into his mother's kitchen.

"Okay. I'll see you inside."

She hurried away, fighting with everything she had not to rush right back into his arms.

19

Nate

NATE WATCHED JESS WALK INTO THE HOUSE WITH her brisk, ground-covering gait he found so compelling.

Face it. He found everything about her compelling.

He took a deep breath of air scented with coastal pine and sand and salt water, willing his arousal to subside.

He felt like a damn teenage boy, so turned on by a kiss that he couldn't seem to think about anything else but chasing after Jess, pressing her against the nearest surface and kissing her again until she changed her mind.

He wouldn't, of course. But he wanted to.

He still wasn't sure how he had found the strength of will to let her walk away.

He couldn't remember a woman ever having this effect on him. What was it that drew him to her so fiercely?

He couldn't quite put a finger on it but thought it might have something to do with the complex mix of vulnerability and bravado he sensed in her, that hint that she had experienced deep pain but was doing her best not to let it define her.

It didn't matter. She was right. He might be wildly attracted to her but nothing could come of it.

He hadn't lived like a monk since Michelle died. He dated here and there. Not often and nothing serious. At first, he had been too busy surviving with a young daughter and trying to build his construction business to even have time to date.

About five years earlier, he had gone through a time when he had started thinking about remarrying. He'd had two semiserious relationships. One woman had ended up not getting along with Sophie—her fault totally, not Sophie's, who had adored her—and the other, for some weird reason, had resented his close relationship with his parents.

After those disasters, Nate had decided he would wait until Sophie was eighteen before he considered another serious relationship.

Jess was the kind of woman who tempted a man to forget all his best intentions. Her tough exterior fascinated him, especially as he suspected it was only a crackly veneer around a softness she didn't want people to see.

No matter. She had made her position clear. She didn't want a fling and she wasn't looking for a long-term relationship. That didn't leave a guy much room to work with.

Too bad for him.

After a few more minutes, he decided he was presentable enough to go inside.

He walked into his mother's kitchen to find Jess at the island eating a sandwich and his mother telling her about a cruise she and Jack had taken to the Norwegian fjords soon after his father was diagnosed.

Jess met his gaze, her color high, but quickly looked away. In that instant, Nate knew he couldn't sit there pretending he was anything but hungry for the delectable Jess Clayton. Especially not while his mother looked on.

He poured water from the filtered pitcher in the refrigerator and took a long swallow then gave his mom a look of apology.

"I need to head back to the job site. Will you forgive me if I grab one of your delicious sandwiches and eat it on the go?"

"Absolutely." Eleanor gave him a fond look. "Thank you so much for taking the time when you're so busy to help out."

"Glad to do it," he said, still avoiding Jess's gaze.

He didn't mind helping out but he should have resisted temptation and done without the kiss. The taste of Jess would linger on his mouth all afternoon.

Hell, maybe for the rest of his life.

"Thank you for the sandwich. I meant to ask, do you mind if I send Sophie over after school to hang out here?"

"Not at all. Not at all. We would love to have her, right, Jess?"

"Sure. We can always put her to work somewhere," she said with a slightly diabolical smile that somehow still made him want to kiss her senseless.

Yeah. He needed to get out of there before he did something stupid in front of his mother.

"Maybe she would like to go to Redding with you to help you drop things off at the shelter," Eleanor suggested. "Would that be okay with you, Nathaniel?"

It took him a minute to pick up the loose thread of the conversation and remember what she was talking about. "Sure. That's fine with me, if Sophie is up for it."

"We'll ask her and if she decides to go, I'll let you know," Eleanor said. "Let me wrap up your sandwich."

He couldn't spend another minute here. "No need. I'll take it on a paper plate. Thanks, Mom."

He kissed Eleanor's cheek, noting again that she had lost entirely too much weight since his father died.

Not trusting himself for even a casual cheek brush with Jess, he simply waved to her, picked up his plate and hurried out of the house.

20

Rachel

"I DON'T KNOW WHAT I WAS EXPECTING FROM AN all-day clinic, but that wasn't as bad as I feared it would be."

Rachel stared at her husband as he drove with his usual efficiency through Sacramento traffic.

Seriously? Had she and Cody been in the same exam rooms with specialist after specialist coming through to poke and prod and interrogate their child?

Silas had borne it much better than she had. All in all, he had been a trouper. He'd had only one meltdown, and they had managed to contain it after only about ten minutes.

He was sleeping now, looking so cherubic and adorable in his car seat, it was hard to imagine he could be so difficult sometimes. "I'm so glad we don't have to bring him back for a year."

"I really didn't mind it. They sure loaded us up with information. I feel like we've been hit with a fire hose of knowledge all at once."

"Everything you wanted to know about autism but were afraid to ask."

He smiled a little and reached for her hand. "You were terrific all day. So smart and organized. I could tell all the professionals were impressed at the therapies you're doing at home with him."

Rachel didn't feel like it would ever be enough. For every tiny bit of progress they made toward communication and socialization, she felt as if Silas took three or four steps back.

Still, she was grateful Cody would say so. "Thanks," she said.

"I know it was rough on you, but you were a champ. Next year, maybe I could get up to speed better and take him to the clinic myself, if you really hated it."

She couldn't say she hated it. The experts obviously knew what they were doing. She was excited about trying some of the behavior modification techniques they had suggested.

The day had been long and arduous, though. She still wasn't sure how they made it through as well as they did.

Yes. She did. It would have been impossible to keep Silas patient and relatively happy all day without Cody's help. He had been wonderful with their son, patient, loving, calm. All the areas where she felt she failed.

So why was it so hard for her to tell him so?

She had to try. They were in this together. That truth had been reinforced throughout the day. Raising a child with autism or other challenges was so much easier when parents could work as a team.

She gathered the words and finally blurted them out. "Thank you for taking time off work to be here. I know it wasn't easy for you and I just want you to know I'm grateful."

A look of surprise flashed across his strong features briefly, then he reached over and took her hand. The physical contact, so badly needed, made her shiver. "You don't have to carry everything by yourself. I wish I could convince you of that."

She knew he was right. Somehow it was a lesson she seemed to need over and over again.

She had spent her childhood in a terrible situation, with a cruel father and a mentally ill mother. She wanted to create a perfect life for her own children, though she knew that was not only impossible but not healthy for them. Children needed to learn resiliency, which they could only do by facing and overcoming hard things…or watching their parents do the same.

"I'm so sorry I fell asleep last night," he said gruffly. "I was looking forward to spending a little time with you."

She flushed, knowing he wasn't talking about ordering room service and chatting all night.

"You work long hard days and then had to drive in that crazy traffic. It's understandable. Anyway, we don't need a hotel room to, um, spend time together."

"True."

The lanes ahead were changing from three lanes to two for construction so he had to pull his hand away and focus on driving.

When they were past the merge, he spoke again. "How did Jess say things went with the girls?"

Rachel had called her sister while Cody and Silas had gone to the restroom at the clinic.

"She said they had a good night. Freckles threw up this morning but seemed fine when she and the girls left the house. Jess checked on her during the day and so did your mom and Ava and I guess she seemed normal."

"I'm glad Jess was in town so she could hang out with Grace and Ava. How much longer will she be around?"

"I think she's leaving next week. It's her birthday Thursday. The big three-oh. I thought we should have a party for her."

"Good idea. But she doesn't really know anyone in town except us."

"She knows Eleanor and her family. She knows Kurt and Jan, of course, and your mom and dad."

"That's true. Except your foster parents are still on their church mission. As for my parents, she's met them maybe three or four times, besides our wedding. I wouldn't say they're close, would you?"

"Fine. I won't invite your family. I just thought it might be more fun to have a big family dinner."

"More fun for who? If the party is really for Jess, you know she doesn't exactly love big crowds."

She hated when he was so reasonable. He was right. Jess wasn't an introvert but she didn't love making small talk with people she didn't know well.

Funny that they could turn out so differently. Rachel loved social situations that forced her to talk to strangers.

"It would be fine with just us and the Whitakers. I think Jess would enjoy that. But I'm sure whatever you decide to do will be terrific," Cody said diplomatically. "You've never thrown a bad party yet."

"It's true. My parties are pretty epic."

He smiled and she wished he could hold her hand again.

As they drove back to Cape Sanctuary and their girls, Rachel allowed herself to simply savor the time together.

Their life might not be as perfect as she had once dreamed. Silas and his challenges seemed insurmountably hard sometimes. But she had three wonderful children, a caring, hardworking husband and a fulfilling career she enjoyed.

She resolved to focus on those things instead of all the things she couldn't control.

21

Jess

"THANKS AGAIN FOR COMING ALONG WITH ME," Jess said to Sophie as they headed away from Whitaker House. "It's nice to have company."

She *could* handle the delivery of craft supplies to the women's shelter by herself. But she genuinely liked Sophie and figured it would be good for the girl to help her.

"No problem. I can't believe Gram said she would come with us and then backed out at the last minute. You must really be wearing her out. I don't remember her ever taking so many naps before."

Jess frowned, worried all over again at her friend's health. Eleanor seemed to be fine one second, then pale and exhausted the next. Before she left, she intended to suggest that Eleanor have a complete medical checkup. What was the good of organizing and cleaning out Whitaker House if the woman was too ill to enjoy it?

"So. What ever happened with your friend Tyler? Did you ever find out why he didn't show yesterday?"

Sophie made a face. "Maybe he was too busy making out with Ana Hernandez. I guess she's his girlfriend now. They were all over each other in the halls. PDAs are so lame."

Jess cleared her throat, grateful Sophie hadn't been around to see her own heated kiss with Nate earlier that day.

"I mean, we all get that you like each other, right?" Sophie went on. "You don't have to throw it in everyone's face all the time. So lame."

"True enough." Jess paused, giving her a careful look. "I'm sorry."

Sophie shrugged. "I'm not. He probably would have been a bad surfer anyway. Hey, do you care if we listen to music?"

At least she didn't seem particularly heartbroken, mostly annoyed that she had wasted her time on someone who didn't deserve her.

Good. Jess hoped she kept that attitude in all of her relationships moving forward, this girl on the brink of womanhood. "No. Go ahead."

Sophie played around with the stereo until she found a song she apparently liked. She started singing along, bobbing her head and shifting in her seat.

Jess tried to remember what music she had liked when she was thirteen and couldn't. Probably something emo.

They had been living in Texas, she remembered. Her dad had been at Fort Hood. School had been hard, home had been harder. She had wanted a dog desperately to ease some of the loneliness but of course her father wouldn't allow it.

She pushed away the memories she didn't want.

"How was the rest of school today?" She waited until the song was over to pose the obligatory question adults always seemed to ask.

Sophie shrugged. "This time of year is such a waste. I wish

we were having summer vacation right now instead of in two more weeks. We've already done testing. We're basically just wasting time until the end of the year."

"What are you going to do this summer?"

"I don't know. Probably hang out with my friends. Surf some. Go to the pool in town. And I'm on a softball team, so I'll be busy with that. I wish I wasn't too young to get a job somewhere."

"You do a lot of babysitting, right?"

"When I can. I wish I could do it more regularly."

Rachel ought to hire her to nanny for her during the summer. It would help on many levels and she knew Sophie would love it. She already had a case of hero worship over Rachel's social media influencer status.

As soon as the idea took root, Jess thought it was brilliant and resolved to suggest it to her sister while she was in town.

Not that Rachel seemed to want to listen to much that Jess had to say.

"Is there something you could do to help your grandmother?" she offered as a backup idea.

Sophie shrugged. "I mow the lawn and she pays me for that. It can take half a day, even on a riding lawn mower. Sometimes I help her with cleaning the house in between the weeks her cleaners come."

"Sounds like you'll be plenty busy."

Sophie chattered about some of the other things she wanted to do over the summer until they reached the shelter.

"Looks like we're here."

"This is just a thrift store." Sophie looked confused.

"The shelter doesn't take donations directly, they go through their charity shop. For the protection of those using the shelter, they have to try to keep their location private."

Sophie seemed struck by the implications of that. Had anyone ever discussed domestic abuse with her? Jess wasn't sure it was her place. On the other hand, teenage girls needed to know the warning signs of an abusive relationship so they could protect themselves.

If someone had told Roni Clayton, so much pain could have been avoided.

The director of the thrift store was thrilled over the donations of yarn and material and the sewing machine.

"Our clients can definitely use this," she said. "Thank you so much."

Sophie was quiet on the drive back to Cape Sanctuary.

"That was a nice thing Gram did. Giving them her extra craft stuff," she said.

"Your grandmother is pretty special," Jess said. She gave the girl a careful look. "So is your dad."

If she hoped she could get Sophie to confide in her, she was doomed to disappointment. The girl's jaw jutted out. "Sure. Except he's a liar."

"A liar?" Nate? She had a hard time believing that. "What did your dad lie to you about?"

"I would rather not talk about it," Sophie said. Her mouth was tight and she folded her arms across her chest.

"That's fine. But you should probably talk to your dad about it. I'm sure you misunderstood something he said."

"I didn't. I heard him loud and clear."

This must be the reason she was angry at her father. She had heard him lie about something.

Whatever it was, Sophie didn't want to talk about it and Jess didn't push. For one thing, it wasn't her business. For another, even if Sophie did confide in her, she couldn't turn around and betray that confidence by telling Nate.

She changed the subject and they spent the rest of the drive talking about books Sophie loved.

She would miss the girl, too, when she left Cape Sanctuary.

Sophie was funny and clever, with a stylish flair and her grandmother's kind heart.

Somehow all the Whitakers had managed to squeeze their way into her heart and Jess had no idea how she was going to push them all back out.

22

Nate

"THANK YOU FOR DINNER. IT WAS GOOD."

His spaghetti was never anything to write home about, just bottled sauce, frozen meatballs and pasta. But he appreciated any positivity from Sophie these days.

"You're welcome."

She had been quiet all through dinner and he wondered if it had anything to do with the trip she had made with Jess to the women's shelter earlier that day.

"Everything okay?" he finally asked.

"Yeah. Fine." She scraped her leftover food into the trash. "Actually, I wanted to ask you something."

He held his breath. "Go ahead."

She gave him a sidelong look, as if trying to figure out the words. Finally, she blurted it out.

"I was wondering if you would be upset if I gave my dollhouse away."

Of all the things he might have expected her to bring up, the elaborate Victorian dollhouse wouldn't have made the list right now. He had forgotten about the thing, truth be told.

"I thought you loved that dollhouse. We worked on it for weeks."

He had cherished memories of sanding the custom tiles for the roof, of wallpapering bedrooms, and helping her figure out how to create furniture out of scraps and items from the recycling bin.

From the time she was about six or seven, the dollhouse had always been her favorite toy. As her own personal style evolved, she had redecorated the rooms several times.

To him, that dollhouse symbolized her childhood.

"I did love it," she said. "But I'm thirteen, Dad. Don't you think I'm too old for dollhouses?"

No. He would never think that. She could play with it forever, as far as he was concerned.

"It's going to waste in a corner of my room, which is pretty sad. Right now, it's mostly taking up space."

Taking up space. Kind of like he felt he was doing in her life these days.

"It's a great dollhouse and there are probably other kids who would have fun playing with it."

"What other kids did you have in mind?"

"I was thinking maybe the shelter where Gram gave her craft supplies today. Jess was telling me that sometimes women go there with their kids when they're in a bad situation at home and need to stay somewhere safe. I bet those kids are scared. A dollhouse might help them feel better."

"Oh. That's a really great idea."

She smiled at him. After weeks of tension, his daughter actually smiled at him. "I thought so, too. I was trying to think about what I could do to help and that's the first thing that came into my head."

"Maybe we could take it over one night this week."

"Okay. Not Thursday, though. That's Jess's birthday party."

Jess, who would be leaving soon. "Right. We can't miss that."

"After we take the dollhouse out of my room, do you think maybe we could hang a swing in its place?"

"What kind of swing?"

"I was thinking maybe one of those cool hammock-type things. I've always wanted one in my bedroom. A place I can read and do my homework and stuff."

That was the first he had ever heard of that. Still, he would do all he could to encourage her anytime she actually asked for his help and seemed willing to carry on a halfway decent conversation.

"Sure. We can go to the Harper Hill garden store this weekend if you want. They've got a good selection of hammocks. Meanwhile, you can start researching what hardware we'll need for it. You'll want a swivel hook so it doesn't tangle and we'll probably have to find a joist to hang it from."

"Where would we find a swivel hook?"

"The hardware store can set us up. This will be fun."

"Yay! Thanks, Dad. I can't wait! I'm going online to see if I can find the style I want before we go to the garden store."

To his surprise, she gave him a quick hug and hurried out of the kitchen to her room.

He watched after her, feeling a curious mix of pride and sadness. She was growing up and he wasn't ready.

Still, the conversation had been cordial and even warm, the first one in weeks that hadn't been underscored by her moodiness.

He decided to focus on the positive and work a little harder to figure out what he had done to make her mad in the first place.

23

Jess

"HAPPY BIRTHDAY, MY DEAR." ELEANOR BEAMED at her as Jess walked into Whitaker House on Thursday morning.

"Thank you." She hadn't given her birthday much thought, though she had treated herself to an early-morning walk down to Sunshine Cove, where she had enjoyed the dawn by herself.

"I think we should take today off so you can do something fun just for yourself."

She smiled. "What are you talking about? This is fun for me. I love my job. Why would I need to take time off when I'm doing exactly what I love to do?"

She considered herself extraordinarily lucky to have found a job she enjoyed so much.

"But work is still work, no matter how fun it is. You deserve some time off."

"I'm good. I think we need to finally tackle Jack's side of the closet today."

She could tell by Eleanor's sudden tension that the other woman wasn't thrilled at that idea.

"But it's your birthday!"

What did that have to do with taking care of the one thing Eleanor seemed to be avoiding?

Anyway, her thirtieth birthday really wasn't a huge cause for celebration. It was just another day.

She wasn't worried about growing older. She saw each year as a time of growth, an opportunity for reassessment and re-adjustments. Birthdays were fine but she was a grown woman. She didn't need party hats and piñatas.

"Why don't we start with the kitchen today instead?" Eleanor suggested. "I was looking at it this morning when I had breakfast and thinking we could clear out all those old plastic containers I've saved through the years and never use. Plus, I have so many old cookbooks that are gathering dust now, since Sophie helped me digitize my favorites when she was home from school last summer."

Jess knew exactly what the other woman was doing. While it made her smile to picture Sophie poring through old cookbooks while helping her grandmother organize her kitchen, she knew they couldn't continue avoiding the central job she had been hired to tackle.

"We have to start clearing out his clothes at some point, Eleanor," she said gently.

"I know. And we will. Just not yet. Let's work on the kitchen today. And we still have to do the bathrooms, right? And we haven't even started the garage."

Her time here at Whitaker House would be wrapping up soon as they had already worked their way through most of the house.

She truly would be sorry to leave. Jess had never enjoyed a job as much as this one.

"All right. The kitchen it is."

"Once we clear out the kitchen, I need to mess it up again, just a little, while I make my favorite pasta salad for the party. I told Rachel I would take that."

Jess shifted, wondering if it was too late to call off her sister's grand party. No. She couldn't do that to Rachel. Her excitement had come through loud and clear the night after Jess had stayed with the girls, when her sister had called to thank her again and to confirm arrangements for Jess's birthday.

Rachel wanted to do this. She loved throwing parties. How could Jess deprive her of her fun?

She would simply smile and be gracious and try to enjoy herself.

For now, she could legitimately enjoy herself doing what she did best, cleaning out her client's kitchen.

Several hours later, Jess studied the stacks of cookbooks arrayed across the kitchen table with admiration. They had already worked their way through several cabinets and had finally reached the dusty cookbooks.

Eleanor had not been exaggerating about her collection. She had at least a hundred, most dotted with dog-eared and marked pages, in addition to the dozen most-cherished volumes she was keeping for Sophie.

"I can't imagine how many meals have been prepared using these."

"The best parts are the handwritten notes in some of them. That's why I'm keeping those few for Sophie. It's a link to her grandmother and her great-grandmother. I don't know if she'll want them someday but I'm going to let her decide that. As for the rest, I have no idea what to do with them. Do you think Goodwill would even want them? Some were in Whitaker House when I moved in here. They were probably here when my mother-in-law moved in here."

"You would be surprised. There's a healthy market for vintage cookbooks."

"I always thought I would hand the entire collection down to my daughter someday but I ended up only having a son who isn't much interested in cooking."

At the mention of Nate, Jess could feel her face heat. Though she hadn't seen him since Tuesday, when he had kissed her beside her truck, she felt like she hadn't stopped thinking of him.

It was hard to avoid the topic when she worked alongside his mother every day, especially when Eleanor had so much good to say about him.

How was she supposed to resist him when his mother, apparently his biggest cheerleader, told her story after story that only made him more appealing?

If she didn't know better, she would almost think Eleanor had set out on a well-organized campaign to make Jess fall for him.

She wouldn't, no matter how hard Eleanor tried.

Or at least that's what she told herself.

"Do you want to set all the cookbooks aside for Sophie? We could find somewhere in storage for them where we could protect them."

"No. I think I'll stick to giving her the best of the bunch. With that and the few recipes out of the others that I've saved, she should have more than enough."

"Wise decision. As to the rest, I'll box them up and ship them to a used bookstore we've worked with before in the Bay area. They'll give you a fair price before their markup."

Eleanor waved her hand. "Whatever you think. You definitely know best, as I've learned over the past week and a half."

Did she? Jess wasn't so sure. Her usual common sense seemed to have tumbled down into the ocean since she had arrived in Cape Sanctuary.

Eleanor surveyed the kitchen. "This house will feel so empty without all my treasures."

Jess nudged her with her shoulder. "Think of all the dusting you won't have to do now."

"I know. I know. And especially all the rubbish Nate and Sophie won't have to sort through after I'm gone."

"Which won't be for a long, long time," Jess said firmly.

Eleanor wore a distant look as she gazed at the cookbooks, as if seeing all the previous generations of women who had thumbed through them, seeking an answer to the eternal and relentless question of what to fix their families for dinner.

"I'm committed to cleaning out this house for Nate and Sophie's sake," she said. "I have no need to hold on to things I don't use any longer and I don't want them to have to deal with it later. Still, knowing all that, why do I find it so hard to let go of things?"

"Most tangible things are associated with good memories of a place or a moment. It's completely natural to want to hold on to that."

"Thank you for being so understanding. You're a dear. I think your job must be equal parts cleaning and therapy."

Jess had to smile, charmed by the description. "I hope both are helping."

"More than you will ever know. I've felt better these past ten days than I have since Jack died. Thank you for putting up with me."

"It's been my pleasure," she said, and meant every word.

Eleanor looked around her kitchen, which looked fresh and new, almost as if they had applied a coat of paint.

"This looks like a new room. I honestly don't know how you managed it."

"*We* managed it. You're the one making the final decisions."

"You're helping me every step of the way. What would I have done without you, my dear?"

"I should run this next load to Goodwill."

"They must cringe when they see you coming. Here comes that nice girl with all of Eleanor Whitaker's junk again."

"I doubt that. Just because you don't want it anymore doesn't mean your things don't have value. Someone else might have been looking for that mismatched china you've decided you don't need."

"I hope so. I always hated that china. But thank you again for working so hard on your birthday. Do something special to treat yourself this afternoon. You have more than earned it."

How about sleep with your son?

The totally inappropriate thought made her blush. She could only be grateful Eleanor, as sharp as she was, couldn't read her mind.

"I'll see you this evening at your sister's house."

She was not sleeping with Nate, she told herself sternly. Even if it was her birthday and Eleanor told her she deserved a treat.

"I'll see you there."

She kissed the older woman on the cheek, thinking how dear she was. Of all the clients Jess had worked with over the past five years, Eleanor had quickly become her favorite. She was sharp, kind, funny, generous. She had embraced Jess from their first interaction, treating her with warmth and welcome.

Jess would miss her when she left Cape Sanctuary.

And Nate. And Sophie.

All of them had impacted her life. This job would leave its mark.

She frowned as she carried the box of mismatched china to her truck.

That wasn't the plan. She was supposed to be the impersonal hired help who swept into town, took care of business, and then hooked up her Airstream and moved on to the next job.

She didn't need or want to make connections. Connections only led to heartbreak. That lesson had been imprinted on her psyche after years as a military brat, moving bases and schools just as she started to form one or two solid friendships.

It had always seemed more intuitive for Rachel, somehow. She always loved easily, gathering friends around her like Eleanor collected cookbooks.

Jess struggled to say goodbye each and every time, until she decided when she was about twelve or thirteen that she was done trying. She had Rachel. She didn't need other friends.

And then Rachel had betrayed her, too.

The ugly thought poked up like a noxious weed.

She didn't like thinking about that time, how lost and alone she had been after Rachel chose to remain here in Cape Sanctuary with her new foster family instead of coming to live with her once Jess turned eighteen and aged out of the system.

Intellectually, she knew her sister had made the right choice. Rachel had bloomed like never before when she finally found a home with Kurt and Jan Miller. She had been thriving in school, had friends, played the flute in the marching band. She even had a boyfriend, Cody, whom she would later marry.

The Millers had been wonderful to Jess's sister, giving her a safe, supportive home to finish high school. They loved Rachel and she loved them.

Even after she married Cody, Rachel had stayed part of their family. Jess knew Rachel's children considered them their grandparents and wrote to them weekly on their church mission working at a South American orphanage.

She couldn't blame her sister for making the mature choice to stay in a stable home here in Cape Sanctuary instead of leaving it all behind to live in a crappy studio apartment in a bad neighborhood in Sacramento.

Any sane person would do the same.

It still hurt.

When they had been separated after that first miserable foster care experience, Rachel had sobbed and sobbed, worse than the night their parents had died. Jess had vowed she would figure out a way for them to be together again as soon as possible.

She had worked two jobs in fast food after school and on weekends, scrimping and saving for first and last months' rent on an apartment. All along, through emails and phone calls and texts, she and Rachel had talked about moving in together, just as they had always planned.

Things hadn't worked out that way. Jess had stayed in the group home a few weeks after turning eighteen, until her June high school graduation, then she had packed up her few belongings and moved to her new apartment. She had paid a kid at school a hundred bucks to borrow his broken-down car so she could drive here to Cape Sanctuary and get Rachel and her things.

They had a plan, one they had talked about for more than a year. They would be together, finally. The two Clayton sisters against the world.

They had the small inheritance from their parents' life insurance policies and Jess planned to work however she had to so she could support them while Rachel finished high school.

She planned to take online classes at the local community college, then they would both use their military benefits inherited from their father to go to college together.

It had been the only thing keeping her going that long, lonely last year of high school by herself at the group home.

Instead, the day she had shown up here in Cape Sanctuary, Rachel had finally confessed that her bags weren't packed because she wasn't coming with her.

Rachel had looked awful, Jess remembered. Shadows under her eyes, her hair a tangled mess. She told Jess she hadn't slept in two nights, trying to figure out how to tell her that Rachel felt like she should stay in Cape Sanctuary.

She wanted to be with Jess but this was the best place for her right now, she had tearfully said. Things were finally good for her. She was happy.

That day—that horrible day—was permanently engraved in her memory. She had felt as if the entire world had crashed in on her. Her beloved sister, the one constant Jess had left, had chosen another life, another family.

She had been completely gutted. The worst part had been trying to pretend to Rachel that she wasn't. If Rachel had any idea how wrecked Jess had felt, she would have marched inside and packed her bags, even knowing it was the wrong choice for herself.

Jess couldn't do that to her. For her sister's sake, she had to pretend she supported Rachel's decision, that she understood completely and wanted this happy, rosy world for her. Jess had smiled until her cheeks hurt, all while inside she feared she would crumble apart.

Shattered.

Rachel still probably had no idea how completely lost Jess had been. Instead of driving back to Sacramento with her sister as she had so eagerly anticipated, chattering about starting the rest of their lives together, she had driven her borrowed car straight to the nearest recruiting office. Why not? What did she have to lose now? She knew all about the military life from her childhood. At least in the army, she wouldn't have to scramble to survive. She would have food, housing, somewhere to go.

Rachel had made the best choice for her life. Jess knew that and couldn't fault her sister for choosing stability and a family over chaos and uncertainty.

In return, Rachel certainly couldn't fault Jess now for protecting herself from the devastation of broken dreams.

24

Rachel

SHE DIDN'T KNOW HOW SHE PULLED IT OFF, BUT EV-
erything was turning out better than she could have imagined.

The steak and chicken thigh pieces were on skewers along
with fresh pineapple, ready to be grilled after soaking all day
in a teriyaki marinade she had found on Pinterest. The coco-
nut rice smelled delicious, keeping warm in her electric pressure cooker. She had bacon-wrapped shrimp appetizers ready on
a pineapple-shaped platter and she was especially proud of the
spinach dip with veggies served up in cute individual baguettes.

She had to admit, her absolute favorite part was the birthday
cake, a white-and-raspberry drip cake that was truly her best
work. She had created colorful tropical flowers out of fondant
that looked too real to be edible.

She was fiercely tempted to post it to Instagram right now but
she didn't want to spoil the surprise for Jess. She had no idea if

her sister even followed her, but she couldn't take any chances. Instead, she would photograph it today and then post tomorrow and watch her feed explode.

Rachel snapped another picture of the exquisite birthday cake, hoping Jess would love it as much as she did.

This had all been a labor of love. The decorations she and the girls had put up that afternoon, the little pineapple tea lights hanging in the trees, the leis they had made out of paper and straws.

It had been entirely too long since she had spent Jess's birthday with her and Rachel wanted this one to be unforgettable.

She was just finishing the fruit salad she was serving up inside a cut watermelon when the slider to the patio opened.

"Um. I think we're going to have to change."

"You don't have to change," she told Grace absently without looking up from rearranging fruit for best effect. "You guys look adorable in those Hawaiian dresses, especially with the plumeria in your hair."

"Not anymore," her oldest said.

Something in the gravitas of her tone made Rachel lift her head from the salad and she could only stare in horror.

No.

Impossible.

"What have you done!" she exclaimed.

All three of her children stood inside the kitchen looking like creatures emerging from a mud bog. The girls' hair, which she had spent an hour curling, now hung lank and wet and their darling matching muumuus she had sewn herself the day before were all but unrecognizable now.

If possible, Silas looked even worse. He was utterly drenched and had mud in his hair as well as across his face.

Ava was grinning from ear to ear, though Grace looked worried. As usual, she couldn't read Silas's expression but thought he looked…happy.

"What happened?" Rachel wailed.

Cody came in behind them, his drenched Hawaiian shirt sticking to his chest and shoulders. He had a big wet spot across the crotch of his shorts.

"It's totally my fault, babe. I'm so sorry."

"How did this happen? You were only outside for fifteen minutes! Oh! You're tracking mud everywhere."

"Everybody stop where you are," Cody ordered. "Come out into the mudroom and strip down. I'll carry you into the bathroom to clean off."

How could he do this to her, twenty minutes before her sister's birthday party? He knew how important this was to her. She wanted to cry, to scream, to throw the whole damn fruit salad in his face.

"Tell me what happened! You were supposed to just set up the table for the food and get the cooler for the drinks! I told you exactly what needed to be done. Nowhere in those instructions did I tell you to make a total disaster of the night!"

His mouth tightened. "I'm sorry. We were trying to help. A couple of the lawn chairs were dirty from the last rainstorm so we thought we would rinse them off with the hose. I went to turn it on but Silas grabbed the end with the power nozzle when I wasn't paying attention and ended up spraying everyone. The girls started shrieking and ran through the garden and he thought it was hilarious and chased after them with the hose. You should have seen him smiling. I think he might have even laughed."

Under other circumstances, she might have found this funny. She loved the times Silas acted like any other boy, teasing his sisters and learning if/then consequences.

Not now. Not when her sister was coming over to celebrate her thirtieth birthday any minute now, along with three dinner guests Rachel cared about and wanted to impress.

Cody picked up a wriggling Silas before he could run through the house and spread the mud. "I'm afraid he sprayed the table, too," he said, looking abashed. "I'm so sorry. Let me clean everybody up, then we'll see what we can do to salvage the decorations."

Now she really wanted to cry. Rachel and the girls had worked so hard to arrange the table with place settings, chargers, her favorite china. It had looked magical, if she did say so herself.

"What were you thinking to let him anywhere near the garden hose? What did you imagine would happen?"

"It was an accident."

"It always is. You didn't think because you never do. Silas needs to be watched every single second! I don't know how to get that through your head. I asked you to do one simple thing and look what happened! This was so important to me and now it's ruined. Completely ruined."

Cody's mouth tightened. "It's not ruined. The food will still be delicious. The cake is still epic. I'll clean up the mess. Maybe it won't be as perfect as you wanted but it will still be a great party."

"How can it be? Look at you all! I don't have backup Hawaiian clothes for the kids, Cody. What kind of a miracle worker do you think I am? It's a good thing I snapped a picture of them earlier that I can use on Instagram tomorrow."

She thought she saw annoyance flicker in his eyes but it disappeared before she could be sure. "So they can wear something else. They all have plenty of cute clothes."

"It won't be the same. You have no idea how hard I've worked for the past two days to make everything perfect for Jess."

"Jess doesn't need perfect. She'll know that you tried and she'll love you anyway for the effort."

"That's easy for you to say, especially now that you've ruined everything," she snapped. "Like usual."

Oh. She shouldn't have added that. She didn't mean it. Why did the worst things gush out of her when she was angry?

He didn't say anything but she could see the hurt in his eyes and she hated herself.

"Girls, go in and take a quick shower," Cody said quietly. "Grace, can you help Ava get the mud out of her hair? Once you're clean, find your prettiest matching dresses, the ones you wore in that family picture your mom had us take a few weeks ago."

"Okay, Daddy. Come on, Ava."

She dragged her sister away. As soon as they were gone Cody turned on Rachel.

"We were only trying to help. I'm sorry things didn't go the way you wanted. I wanted things to be perfect, too. I screwed up and I'm sorry. But it was an accident."

She didn't trust herself to speak, knowing her anger was completely out of proportion but unable to help it.

"Life doesn't always go the way we want it," Cody went on, his voice low and intense.

"You certainly don't have to tell me that," she said, her voice just as impassioned.

He jerked his head back as if she had slapped him. As he stood there holding their mud-spattered, beautiful little boy who faced so many challenges in his life and who had found a moment of joy in playing with a water hose, Rachel despised herself all over again.

Cody had been trying to help, not least of all by taking Silas off her hands for a minute. She knew how hard it was to wrestle him and get anything done. She spent all day, every day, trying to keep him out of one disaster after another.

She had taken a bad situation and made it so much worse. "I know I'm overreacting. I know. I'm sorry. I haven't spent a birthday with Jess in forever and I just wanted everything to be perfect."

There was that stupid word again. This time, her voice broke on it and to her dismay, Rachel felt hot tears begin to slide down.

Cody looked helpless. She knew he wanted to hug her but he was covered in mud and holding their son, also covered in mud, who was now cuddled up to him in a rare show of affection.

"We can choose to focus on what others might consider imperfection. Or we can choose to focus on the joy. Our decision, Rachel."

She hated when he was right. Which was most of the time. She wiped at her eyes, hoping her mascara wasn't running.

"Go clean up the two of you. I'll see what I can do to salvage things outside."

"I'll be out to help as soon as I can."

"Don't worry about it. I can do it."

He sighed and headed for the stairs, just as the doorbell rang. "I can get it," she said, walking to the entry.

"We're already here." He opened the door and suddenly there was Jess. She took one look at the mud-splattered Cody and Silas before her gaze shifted to Rachel's eyes, which she knew were probably red-rimmed.

"Obviously this is a bad time."

"Not a bad time," Cody assured her. "Just a messy situation. We had an accident with the water hose. Hi, Jess. Happy birthday. I would kiss you but Rachel would kill me if I got you muddy on your big day."

"I wouldn't mind. Hi, Silas."

He ignored her, busy playing with the button on Cody's golf shirt collar. Jess's smile never faltered.

"We need to run and change. As soon as I take care of that, I'll come and clean up the table out there. I think we can salvage most of the decorations."

Rachel highly doubted it but didn't want to argue with him in front of Jess. "Go change. I'll check it out."

"What can I do to help?" Jess asked after Cody left.

"Nothing. It's your birthday party. You can sit down and relax while I go see what I need to fix out there."

"Or I can come out and help you," Jess said with her usual stubbornness.

Rachel sighed. "Okay. But I'm afraid it's going to be ugly."

"Sounds like it's been a rough afternoon," Jess said as they made their way back to the patio off the kitchen.

"Cody was supposed to be home an hour ago to help me but got tied up on a job site, as usual. Silas has been on a rampage all day. Cody took the kids outside to do a few things while I finished up in here and apparently Silas discovered how fun it can be to spray his sisters and father with the garden hose."

"Who wouldn't enjoy that?" Jess teased.

"Me. Apparently I'm the party pooper because all I can think about are the ruined decorations."

"Like Cody said, it's probably not as bad as that. Let's go see."

When they walked to the patio, Rachel wanted to cry. The big tissue flowers she had made so carefully were soaked, their colors running onto the soaked tablecloth. The place settings were wet. The live palm tree she had bought at the garden center still looked good, at least.

"We can fix this."

"Not by the time Eleanor and her family get here," Rachel wailed.

"First of all, they won't care. Trust me. Second of all, I can help."

"It's your birthday. Your only job is to enjoy yourself. I wanted it to be perfect for you."

"I appreciate that. And the perfect birthday for me would be one where you let me help you fix this."

How did Jess always manage to turn things around so she ended up with her own way?

"Fine. Help me clear these dishes off and take them inside. We can't do anything about the flowers, but I'll figure something out. Meanwhile, I don't want to serve food on dishes that have been sprayed with the garden hose so we'll have to use the everyday dishes. Fortunately, they're white and will go with anything."

"Sounds like a plan. Operation Party Repair. Let's do this."

She and Jess hurriedly cleared off the cutlery, glasses and plates and carried them into the sink, then Rachel went to her linen closet. She could only be grateful she kept it organized enough that she could quickly find a pale green tablecloth of the right size.

Working quickly, she and Jess reset the table. She ended up taking a few of the extra leis that she and the girls had made and artfully arranging them along with some shells from a basket she kept in the living room.

"Beautiful," Jess declared.

It wasn't close to as gorgeous as the original table had been, but it would do in a pinch.

At least the night was lovely, warmer than usual with a soft, sea-scented breeze. And she had to admit, it was nice to work with Jess, united in a common cause. When they returned to the kitchen, slightly breathless from the frenzied repair job, Cody was coming down with all of the kids in tow.

Rachel mourned the girls' hairdos, which were now damp ponytails, but had to approve of the flowered dresses they wore.

"Will this work?" Cody asked.

She wanted to say something about how the little matching muumuus would have been better. She swallowed the urge and nodded instead. "It's good."

"What do we need to do?"

"Start the kebabs," she told him. "We've cleaned up out there. The Whitakers should be here any minute."

"I'll go check the coals and then come back for the meat."

"I'll bring it out."

She saw that Jess was currently entertaining all three of the kids, having them give her a tour of the elaborate, though still unfinished, playhouse Cody had been working on.

When Rachel carried the platters of meat out to the grill, Cody grabbed her for a quick hug. He smelled so good right after he showered. She had bought a new soap on Etsy, scented with cedarwood and sage and citrus. It made her want to just stand and inhale his neck.

"You fixed it out here. It looks great."

Not as good as it was but it would do. "Jess helped."

"I am sorry, babe."

After a minute, she stepped away. "It wasn't your fault. Silas is quick."

"He didn't understand what he did wrong. I know it was a disaster but I really do wish you could have seen him laughing as he sprayed everything in sight. He was just like any other kid, up to mischief."

"But he's not like any other kid, right? You have to watch him every single second. He could have pulled the hot barbecue grill over on him."

"I only had my back turned for a second. I might not be the world's greatest dad, but I know how to keep an eye on my kids."

The defeat in his voice made her want to hug him and tell him he was a wonderful father, but the doorbell rang, announcing the Whitakers, and the moment was gone.

25

Nate

FROM THE INSTANT HE WALKED INTO THE MCBRIDES' lovely backyard overflowing with flowers, Nate sensed a subtle tension in the air.

He couldn't quite figure out the source and wondered if he was imagining it. Everyone was cheerful enough, welcoming him and his family. The cute little McBride girls ran up and hugged Sophie, who seemed to lap up their attention. To his surprise, the youngest girl, Ava, then hugged him, too.

"Hi, Mr. Nate," she said. Apparently, they had bonded during the evening he spent with them and their aunt.

"Hi there, Ava."

"Guess what? Freckles is going to have puppies!"

"That's fun."

"Yeah. And I hope we can keep every single one of them."

"We can't," Rachel said, which was obviously a position she

had taken before and would probably have to reinforce over and over until after the puppies had a new home.

"Hey, want to see our playhouse?" Grace asked Sophie. "We got a new table in there. Our dad made it."

"Sure. Let's see it. Come with us, Silas." She reached for the boy's hand and he let her take him toward the playhouse with his sisters.

Sophie had always loved kids. She was so good with them. A complete natural. She must have inherited that skill from his mother.

As soon as the children were gone, Eleanor immediately turned to Rachel. "Where would you like my salad? Over on the long table?"

"Yes. That works. Thank you."

"How can I help?"

"Everything is ready. We just have to get things on the grill, which shouldn't take long," Rachel said with a smile that seemed not quite genuine.

"I can help with that," Nate said, heading in Cody's direction.

"Sure. I would appreciate the company," the other man said.

The two of them talked about the various construction sites they were working on while the three women brought out salads and appetizers.

It was a beautiful evening on the coast, one of those perfect, seaside spring nights. Though the McBrides' yard did not have a view of the ocean, he could hear it ever present, murmuring somewhere not far away.

Jess seemed slightly restless, as if uncomfortable at being the center of attention. Even as she smiled and made conversation, Nate somehow had the feeling she wanted to be somewhere else.

His mother was the complete opposite. She seemed in her element. She helped Rachel with the food, she entertained the children, she held Silas on her lap when he was about to throw what looked like an epic tantrum during dinner and distracted him by folding her napkin into a paper airplane.

What was the story between Rachel and Jess? Though it was clear they cared about each other, he sensed an uneasy edge between them.

"Thank you, everyone, for coming to this special celebration," Rachel said after they finished the delicious meal of tender grilled chicken and juicy, flavorful steak kebabs.

"Everything was so good," Eleanor said. "You have to give me your marinade recipe."

"I'll email it to you," Rachel promised.

"Is it time for cake yet?" Ava asked eagerly. "I can't wait. I'm starving."

"You just had two chicken kebabs and tons of fruit salad. You're not starving."

"But chicken and fruit salad aren't cake. I'm starving for *cake*," she said.

He couldn't fault her logic and had to smile. Jess smiled, too, her face looking bright and amused in the flickering garden lights. He didn't want to look away.

"I guess we should get to the cake so I can get you three to bed, since you girls have school tomorrow. Ava and Grace, why don't you come into the kitchen with me to help me light the candles for your auntie Jess's birthday cake."

"Cake," Silas said from his spot in a high chair next to Cody.

"Did you hear that? Did he say 'cake'?" Cody stared at his son.

"It sounded like *cake* to me," Jess said, beaming over at the toddler with a soft light in her eyes.

"Say it again, sweetheart. Tell Mommy what you want," Rachel urged.

"Cake," he said clearly.

Judging by everyone's excitement, he gathered Silas didn't have much to say most of the time.

"Good job, kiddo," Cody said gruffly.

"I should have known one of his first words besides the basics would be *cake*," Rachel said, rolling her eyes.

"Count your blessings, I suppose. It could be something worse. Nate's first word was *poop*," Eleanor said.

The girls giggled and looked at him with wide eyes while Sophie groaned with disgust.

"Thank you for sharing that, Mom," he said dryly.

She gave him an angelic smile. "You're welcome, darling."

Rachel took Ava and Grace inside, and a few moments later, they came back out carrying Jess's birthday cake, a lovely concoction covered with tropical flowers. On top were two candles, one the number three and the other a zero.

"Oh wow. It's so gorgeous," Jess said. "Thank you. It looks too pretty to eat."

"Guess what?" Ava said. "You can even eat the flowers! Mama made them out of frosting. They're really good. I ate one of the leftovers."

"That's beautiful," Eleanor said. "You are so talented, my dear."

"I didn't get a leftover flower," Grace complained.

"You were in school," Rachel told her. "I'll make sure you have a flower on the piece I cut for you. Should we sing to your aunt?"

Jess again seemed uncomfortable when all the focus shifted to her, though she smiled while the children cheerfully sang the birthday song at the tops of their respective voices.

"Thank you."

"What are you going to wish for?" Ava said.

To Nate's astonishment, Jess's gaze flickered to him and then quickly away, so quickly he didn't think anyone else even noticed.

"After this perfect night, I don't think there's anything else I could ever need."

"You have to wish for something," Grace insisted. "That's the rule."

"But she's not supposed to tell or it won't come true," Sophie said.

"That's right," Rachel said. "And you can wish for whatever you want. Go ahead and blow out the candles."

"Cake," Silas said again, which made everyone marvel again.

"Cake coming right up, young man," Jess said. She quickly blew out the candles.

The cake was delicious, white with raspberry layers.

But for some reason, Jess only ate a few bites. Rachel must have noticed, too. "Is something wrong with the cake?" she asked, sounding defensive.

Jess blinked, looking down at her plate as if she had only just remembered the cake was there. "No. It's delicious."

"So why are you only eating a tiny bite at a time?"

"Maybe I want to savor every bite."

Rachel frowned, clearly not believing her. "Is it the raspberries? I always thought you liked them."

"I do. The cake is fabulous." She took another bite, bigger this time, and made a big show of eating it then scooping up another bite.

"I should have called you first to find out what kind of cake you wanted," Rachel said. She blinked rapidly, as if trying not to cry.

"Rach. It's a fantastic cake," Cody said. "One of your absolute best."

"Everything has been perfect," Jess said. "I could not have asked for more, honestly. I'll remember turning thirty for a long, long time."

"I'm glad we could share it with you," Cody said gruffly.

Again, Nate had the sense that all wasn't perfect between Rachel and Jess...or between Cody and Rachel, for that matter.

He wanted to fix it for her. Whatever was wrong, he wanted to sweep in and make it all better.

He remembered that moment when he was almost certain she had looked at him.

What are you going to wish for?

The low ache of hunger that seemed to have taken up permanent residence inside him since she came to town seemed to sharpen.

Unfortunately, Nate knew even the best-tasting cake in the world wouldn't assuage it. Only one thing would do that and Jess had made it clear they would never be together.

26

Jess

WHY DID SHE FEEL AS IF SHE ALWAYS HAD TO WALK on eggshells around her sister?

Maybe because Rachel right now seemed as fragile as an entire bushel of eggs.

Her sister was obviously still upset about the mess Silas had made with the garden hose. Though Rachel tried to be bubbly and happy with the Whitakers, Jess still knew her sister well enough to see it was an act. Beneath that crackly facade, Rachel was on the edge of tears.

Her sister seemed desperately unhappy and she didn't know how to fix it.

After the cake, Rachel insisted everyone leave the dishes for now so Jess could open presents.

She didn't want gifts but loved them all anyway. Cody had made a beautiful wooden frame lined with magnets to go on her refrigerator and the girls had each drawn pictures of themselves that she could hang in it.

"I love it. Thank you so much."

She hugged her nieces and nephew. The girls hugged her back while Silas mostly tolerated it.

"You're welcome. Hopefully, it will help you remember you have a family while you're on the road," Rachel said.

"Thanks," Jess said cheerfully.

"We kind of had a similar idea," Eleanor said. Jess unwrapped their gift and was astonished to find a small watercolor she had admired at Whitaker House.

It had been painted by a friend of Jack Whitaker's years ago and was an overview of Cape Sanctuary, with Sunshine Cove in the distance.

"I can't accept this. It's an original."

"Nate and I both want you to have it. Don't we, darling?"

Her son nodded. "Absolutely."

"We want you to have something to remember us by after you leave. I thought it was small enough you could hang it inside your trailer so you have a little piece of Cape Sanctuary with you wherever you go."

She was immeasurably touched by everything. "Thank you. I'll treasure all of these gifts."

The Whitakers stayed for a while longer as Sophie and the children were enjoying an impromptu soccer game on the grass.

After helping to clear the dishes from the patio, they then said their goodbyes with a flurry of hugs.

"I'll take care of bedtime then come down and help you clean up the dishes," Cody said after they were gone. He started corralling the kids up the stairs toward their rooms.

"That's a great guy you have there," Jess said.

"Sometimes."

A glimpse of that unhappiness flashed across Rachel's expression before she turned away and headed into the kitchen.

Jess followed her and started filling the sink with soapy water.

"It's your birthday. You don't have to help me clean up. I am perfectly capable of cleaning my own kitchen," Rachel snapped.

"I never said you weren't," Jess said carefully. "I don't mind helping. It's the least I can do to pay you back for such a great party."

"You don't have to repay me. That's the whole point. There's no scorecard in families. And anyway, you hated the party. You don't have to lie to me, now that we're alone."

She tensed. "Why would you say that?"

"Admit it. You didn't want a party in the first place. I forced you to have it. If you had your way, you'd be holed up in your trailer by yourself."

Had it been that obvious? She thought she had done a pretty decent job of hiding it.

Jess shoved her hands in the soapy water and scrubbed vigorously at a salad bowl. "I'm sorry I'm not a big fan of birthday parties. I told you I didn't need one. That doesn't mean I'm not grateful for all your hard work and didn't enjoy the result."

"I don't think it's birthday parties you don't like. I think it's me."

Jess did *not* want to get into this right now. Or ever. "You know that's not true."

"I don't. That's the only thing I can figure out."

"Why would you say that?"

"What else am I supposed to think? You rarely come to visit and when you do, you act like you can't wait to leave. You're always halfway out the door, just like Dad was."

"I am not like Dad at *all*," she said, her careful hold on her temper beginning to fray. Why did Rachel have to ruin what had been a lovely evening by bringing their parents into things?

"You might not be an abusive jerk. But you're as closed off as he always was. I never know what's going through your head. And I feel like I'm the one putting all the work into this relationship, just like Mom did with theirs. More often than not, I'm the one who texts or calls you and invites you to things. And most of the time, you can't be bothered. I'm really tired of being an afterthought in your life."

Jess gave up any pretense of washing dishes and faced her sister, trying not to let her see her hands tremble. "You're not an afterthought. I love you. I love the kids. What do you want from me, Rachel?"

"I just want to know we matter to you."

"Of course you matter. I only took this job in Cape Sanctuary because it meant I could be closer to you and the kids."

"Right. Because this setup is just the way you like it. You can stop for a minute, keep everything superficial, then move on to your next job. You've created your life so that you have no close connections, except maybe Yvette. Even your bond with her is over the phone. That's not normal, Jess."

Rachel's words stung, mostly because Jess knew she was right. She didn't consciously push people away, but Jess knew that was the net impact.

Because it hurt so much, she reacted defensively by lashing out.

"And you're doing just great, right? No problems here. You're just throwing away a great marriage to a kind, caring man because you're unhappy that your perfect Instagram life isn't the beautiful picture you've always dreamed about."

She shouldn't have said it. As soon as the words were out, Jess regretted them, especially when Rachel seemed to pale and take a step back.

"Leave my marriage out of this." Rachel's voice quivered with emotion. "You don't know what the hell you're talking about. How could you? You've never even had a relationship that lasted more than a week because you're so screwed up about what happened with our parents that you're afraid to let anybody get close to you."

A second deadly but accurate uppercut. Jess was going to be dangling on the ropes in a minute. She drew in a ragged breath, not wanting Rachel to see the fresh wounds.

She had to get out of there before she said or did something she wouldn't be able to take back.

"You're right. I was out of line. Thank you for the birthday party. I appreciate all the effort that went into it, even though it wasn't really for me, was it? Give my love to Cody and the kids."

She grabbed the bag containing her birthday gifts—the ones she wasn't sure she would ever be able to look at now without remembering the pain of this moment—and walked out of her sister's house.

27

Rachel

HER HEART WAS POUNDING AND SHE FELT HOT AND cold at the same time.

Was she having a heart attack? She checked her heart rate on her smartwatch and saw it was about the same as when she was doing sprints uphill on the treadmill.

Not a heart attack but maybe a broken one. She closed her eyes, trying to breathe slowly to calm herself. She didn't know when she had last been so angry or so hurt.

Jess could be so *difficult*. She always kept part of herself out of reach.

She never used to be that way but their experience in foster care had changed her. They always used to share everything. Hopes, frustrations, fears. She didn't know her sister anymore. Not really. She felt the loss of that tight bond with a physical ache.

Still. Her sister seemed to see Rachel with painful clarity.

You're throwing away a great marriage to a kind, caring man because you're unhappy that your perfect Instagram life isn't the beautiful picture you've always dreamed about.

With every passing second, those harsh words seemed to echo around and around her kitchen, getting louder by the second.

You're throwing away a great marriage.

She thought of her ridiculous out-of-proportion anger at the garden hose accident and how terrible she had been to Cody, when he really had been trying to help.

Jess was absolutely right. She was going to lose her marriage if she didn't figure out how to get her stuff together, if she didn't find a better way to deal with her sadness and worry for Silas than taking everything out on Cody.

He was a good man. The best man she knew. He didn't deserve the kind of wife she had been to him, a woman who was so damaged by the trauma of her past that she couldn't embrace all the joy of her present.

28

Jess

SHE HAD LITTLE MEMORY OF THE SHORT DRIVE between Rachel and Cody's place and Eleanor's house.

The confrontation with Rachel seemed to have opened the box she kept padlocked inside her, where she had stored all the memories of that horrible night.

Now they seemed to swirl inside and around her, ugly and dark and hateful. Somehow, she made it to her trailer parked beside the path to Sunshine Cove, her own private sanctuary that had become more of a home to her than any place she could remember.

She sat in her truck. For the first time in longer than she could remember, she didn't want to go inside the Airstream, afraid the thin aluminum walls wouldn't keep out the mass of emotions that wanted to crowd in.

She needed to move. A good, hard run would do the trick.

Or she could make her way down to the beach and try to find calm where she could.

Driven to action, any action, she hurried inside and quickly grabbed a flashlight and hoodie then started down the trail toward the beach.

The ocean beckoned her.

She stumbled a little going down the path but managed to catch herself and didn't fall.

At the water's edge, she immediately went to Eleanor's bench and sank down, already feeling the ocean's calming effect.

The tide was going out, she could see with a quick sweep of the flashlight. Stars spilled across the sky and the moon's reflection danced along the surface of the water, dancing on the waves.

Her sister's words seemed to replay over and over in her head.

You've never even had a relationship that lasted more than a week because you're so screwed up about what happened with our parents that you're afraid to let anybody get close to you.

Rachel was exactly right. Jess sucked at close relationships and inevitably pushed everyone away before they could really know the heart of her.

It seemed that in every relationship, romantic or otherwise, she struggled to find her way. She was either afraid of becoming abusive and controlling like her father or needy and subservient like her mother. Jess had no idea how to find a healthy way through those two dynamics that had surrounded her as a child. As a result, she didn't even try.

She was lonely.

Bitterly lonely.

Most of the time she told herself she was happy with her independent, no-strings lifestyle. And maybe most of the time she was. But every once in a while, like tonight on this day she had turned another decade older, she wondered if she could endure a lifetime of this.

She didn't know how long she sat there trying to find peace

in the low murmur of the sea. Sometime later, she caught a glimmer of light out of the corner of her eye and finally looked away from the waves to find a flashlight coming toward her.

So much for her solitude. Was it a late-night beachcomber? Or maybe kids coming down to make out on this isolated beach.

She saw a dark shape bounding toward her, dragging a leash, and recognized Cinder, Nate's black Lab.

In the moonlight, the dog wagged her tail, looking thrilled to find her there as Jess reached out to pet her.

"Sorry," Nate called. "She got away from me."

"No problem," she answered, wishing she could figure out a way to have a dog so she would feel a little less alone in the world.

"Are you all right?" he asked as he approached the bench. "I saw you drive up and sit in your truck for a while then rush straight down here."

"Are you worried turning thirty has me so distraught I'm going to walk into the ocean and you'll be stuck having to clean out the rest of your mother's house by yourself?"

Nate sat beside her on the bench. He was big and warm and she had a sudden, completely irrational urge to nestle against him.

"No. I'm just worried about *you*. Everything okay?"

She laughed humorlessly. "Not really."

"Want to talk about it?"

Did she? Or did she want to wallow here in her angst?

"Rachel and I had a fight. I said things I wish I hadn't. And she said things I wish *she* hadn't, but things I probably needed to hear."

"I've never had a sibling. I can't imagine it's always easy."

"No. They see the worst in you and usually know all your darkest moments."

That was an understatement of epic proportions. Rachel

had been there, too, both of them helpless to stop the events of that day.

One would think that enduring something like that would have created an unshakable bond between them. Instead, they were virtual strangers who kicked out at each other instead of finding solace together.

"What are your darkest moments?" he asked.

She didn't want to tell him. She rarely told anyone. Yvette knew, of course. Other than that, she liked keeping that box locked up tightly.

It was open now, the memories seething restlessly. There was something about the kindness she could see in his eyes, even in the dim moonlight, that made her want to lower her guard. All those memories swirled faster, until they threatened to pull her down with them. The fight with Rachel made everything seem so vivid.

"It's ugly. So ugly."

"Is this about your parents?" he guessed.

She nodded, not trusting herself to speak.

"You don't have to tell me if you would rather not," he said quietly. "I know you're a private person and I understand and respect that."

She sighed, petting Cinder. She found comfort and an odd sort of strength in the dog's heat and the soft fur under her hands.

She would prefer to forget the whole thing but the box was open now. Perhaps the telling of it would help her gather all those memories and stuff them back where they belonged.

She released a shaky breath, twisting her hands in Cinder's fur. "My parents married when my mother was only seventeen. My father was twenty-six."

"A wide age difference."

"Yes. Disproportionate in every way. They had a horrible relationship. My father was in the army and his favorite assignment was drill sergeant. He was the worst kind, cruel bordering on sadistic, and he ran our house just like his troops."

"I know the type. I'm sorry."

The compassion in his voice told her he understood exactly what she was talking about. "Our mom, Roni, adored him. She wouldn't listen to a word against him. Even when he ground her self-confidence to nothing, she loved him."

"Did he…abuse her?"

"Physically, no. At least not that we ever saw. In every other possible way, yes. He cheated on her, verbally abused her, made her feel like nothing. And basically did the same to me and Rachel."

The darkness seemed to surround her and she was grateful for his presence, solid and reassuring. Not that she couldn't fight off the memories herself but sometimes it was nice to have someone else there to give her strength.

"Your mother didn't try to protect you?"

"All she ever saw was our father." Jess had figured out even at a young age that their mother wasn't healthy, either mentally or emotionally. Her complete, unquestioning loyalty to her husband, no matter how he treated her or their children, was wrong on every single level.

"I don't want you to think it was all horrible. He was deployed for long stretches at a time, which was great. We could all relax for a time. And Rachel and I always had each other. We talked about how we were going to move out as soon as we could, just the two of us, and get a place together. We were going to go to college together. She was going to be a schoolteacher and I was going to be a veterinarian."

She was silent, remembering nights in whatever base housing they currently called home when she and Rachel had talked long past midnight about what they would do when they were free of the tension inside their family.

Those dreams seemed so far away now. Another lifetime.

"I told you Doug cheated on Roni. He always made sure she knew, just to twist the knife. What would she do? Leave him? He knew she wouldn't. He knew just how much she loved him, how far he could push her, and he used her love to control and manipulate. Looking back, I think it was a game to him. He was a sociopath at the least, more likely a psychopath."

Her father had taken Roni's love and twisted it to his own ends. It had been horrible to watch as an impressionable young girl. Even then, she had known it was wrong.

Her mother had loved him so much and Jess would have been surprised if Doug gave his wife and family even a passing thought throughout his day.

She was silent for a long time, listening to the wind and the waves and the dog's soft breathing. She didn't want to tell him the rest. How could she stop now, though?

"When I was fifteen and Rachel thirteen, he…pushed her past the breaking point. He threatened to leave, which of course was nothing new. I can't count the times he had done it before. Something felt different this time and I think…I think she felt it, too. He started packing his bags, telling our mother the whole time about the other woman he was leaving her for. Her name was Susie. She was younger than Roni. Prettier. Smarter. Everything my mother had once been but that he had ground out of her over the years."

Once upon a time, her mother had been soft, loving. Jess had flashes of memory of Roni reading to them, of her making cookies, of her playing dolls with them.

Sometimes it shocked her to remember her mother had been seventeen when she had Jess and would have only been a few years older than Jess was now when she died.

"This was apparently her breaking point. As he walked out into the living room with his suitcase, Mom followed him, begging him not to go. When he…when he laughed at her, she pulled out his own handgun that he kept stashed by their bed and, without saying a word, shot him three times in the heart."

He inhaled sharply. "Oh, Jess."

"A lot of that night is a blur. I do remember that Rachel and I both screamed. It went on and on. That seemed to wake Mom out of whatever trance or spell or whatever she had slipped into. She stared at us then she stared down at our father, who I think was dead before the second gunshot."

This was the worst part, the part that had replayed over and over in her head for many years after that night. Sometimes she still woke up from dreaming about it, shaking and nauseous.

"Roni…our mother looked at us both one more time for maybe five seconds and then without another word, not even an 'I'm sorry,' she lifted the gun to her own head and squeezed the trigger."

29

Nate

S HE HAD TOLD HIM IT WAS UGLY. NATE DIDN'T KNOW what he had been braced to hear but a murder-suicide where her mother had been the murderer probably wouldn't have made the list.

He could feel her trembling, barely imperceptible shudders that broke his heart. He wasn't sure she would welcome his touch but he couldn't sit beside her and let her shake without at least trying to offer comfort.

Without asking permission, he eased an arm around her shoulders. After a frozen moment when he held his breath, thinking she would shove him onto the sand, she sagged against him, nestling in like a tiny bird finding safe shelter in a hailstorm.

"That's what haunts me most," she said after a long pause, speaking as if from some distant place. "Roni knew damn well we were there. She looked at us. It was like she didn't even see us, like we didn't matter one iota. I'm not sure she even spared a thought for us, for the carnage she was leaving behind in our lives. She didn't care."

Her voice wobbled a little, breaking his heart. "She knew and she didn't care."

Her trembling intensified and he sensed she was fighting back sobs. He wanted to tell her to let them go. She deserved to weep and cry and rail at the world. "I'm sorry. So damn sorry, Jess."

She nodded against his chest but said nothing, just held him while she continued to shake.

He had to wonder how long it had been since she had let all this out. Had she ever?

He held her while the surf crashed into the shore and an owl hooted somewhere above them and the moon danced on the waves.

After a long time, her trembling began to ease. He wanted to think he had provided comfort. Given what he had learned about Jess Clayton during her time in Cape Sanctuary, he guessed she had simply won the battle against her emotions.

"So there you have the whole ugly story," she said, sliding away from him and regaining control. "Our parents died in a murder-suicide when Rachel and I were teenagers."

Violently.

That was how she had told him their parents died.

He had never dreamed the truth behind that single word would carry so much pain.

"How did you and Rachel end up separated?"

Her heavy sigh was filled with sadness, regret, pain. "After our parents died, we were immediately put into an emergency foster home. It wasn't the greatest situation. I…acted out."

"Acted out how?"

"I was in a fight with another girl. She had targeted Rachel, for some reason. She was the tough girl in the group home, the top dog, and I think she mistook Rachel's sweet nature for weakness and pounced on it. I wasn't sweet. Or weak."

"I hope you kicked her ass."

"Yeah," she said simply. "I was unhappy and angry and wanted everyone there to know you didn't mess with either of the Clayton sisters. But she told the staff I attacked her for no reason and they believed her, which meant I had an immediate black mark against me."

She was quiet, absently petting Cinder, who was being shockingly well-behaved.

"After maybe six months in the group home, a spot opened up here in Cape Sanctuary with the Millers but they could only take one foster kid. Our social worker thought it would be a good fit for Rachel and I knew she needed to get out of the group home. So she came here and I stayed."

It would have killed Jess to be separated from the sister she loved and adored, the one she had fought to protect.

She had lost everything.

"That must have been hard for you."

She looked out to the vast darkness of the sea, her features tense in profile. "It worked out for the best, didn't it? She loved it here. She met Cody, fell in love, worked hard to get good grades. Everything I would have wanted for her."

"What about you?"

She shrugged and met his gaze. "I survived."

That told him everything. His heart ached in his chest and he wanted to gather her against him again, to whisper that she was amazing and brave and she had done far more than just survive. She had thrived, under the weight of pain that would have made most people buckle at the knees.

"When did you join the army?"

"Right after high school. I needed direction, purpose. I figured at least I would have a place to sleep and three solid meals a day."

"Not the first soldier to enlist for those reasons."

"I also knew not every soldier was like my father. Most are

good women and men wanting to serve their country. It turned out to be a good decision. I became a driver and loved it. I learned how to drive anything and everything, made it through two tours overseas and discovered important life lessons about myself and the world. That should be on a recruiting poster, right?"

He smiled, enchanted by this woman who could still crack jokes after sharing such a heartbreaking story about her past.

"How amazing that you came through it as strong and loving as you are. Both of you did. Rachel is terrific. I never would have guessed she had been through so much."

"She is pretty amazing." Jess was quiet. "I want her to have the perfect life she deserves. She's struggling right now but I wish she could see that doesn't change the fact that she's a good mom who loves her kids. She would never in a million years think about abandoning them without a word."

She was talking about her mother, he realized. Somehow he knew that abandonment, her mother's decision first not to protect them then to leave her daughters to fend for themselves, hurt worse than all the years of emotional abuse handed down by her father.

Nate didn't take the chance to tell his own mother how much he loved her often enough. He vowed right then he would do it every day until she died.

"So now you know the whole sordid story."

"Thank you for telling me. Probably not the way you wanted to spend your thirtieth birthday, rehashing such tragic history."

"I don't like thinking about it, much less talking about it. But my fight with Rachel tonight kind of opened the door to all those memories. You were unfortunate enough to be here when I walked through."

"Not unfortunate," he said gruffly. "I'm honored you felt you could trust me enough to tell me."

She sent him a sidelong look. "I'm still not completely sure why I did."

He smiled. "My charming personality and overall good-guy demeanor."

She gave a short laugh. "Yes. That must have been it. Also, I happen to adore your mother. She has become one of my favorite people. You might be benefitting—or suffering, depending on how you look at things—by association."

"I'll take it. And she adores you right back. So does Sophie."

He had a hard time remembering his suspicions of Jess Clayton when she'd first come to Whitaker House. How had she become so entwined in all of their lives?

He was well on his way to falling in love with her.

The thought should have terrified him. He wasn't interested in love again. Not now, anyway, when he was struggling to navigate through Sophie's teenage years.

He hadn't been looking for it but how could he help falling for Jess? She was everything he admired in a person. Tough and kind at the same time, with a deep core of sweetness he didn't think she even recognized in herself.

Wasn't it just his luck, to fall in love for the first time since Michelle with a woman who would be leaving in a matter of days?

He didn't want to say goodbye.

"I can't believe I'm saying this, but I feel better after telling you."

"I'm glad."

She continued to pet the dog. "It just occurred to me that Rachel might not appreciate that you know," she said after a few minutes. "She seems to have put everything about our past and our parents behind her here in Cape Sanctuary. I'm not sure who knows and who doesn't."

"I won't say anything," he promised.

"Thank you."

They sat together for several more moments while that owl

hooted again above the murmur of the sea. Clouds were gathering. He could see them beginning to build and the air had a wet, expectant feel to it that told him rain would be coming soon.

She finally shifted to face him. "Do you know what I really wanted for my thirtieth birthday?"

"Let me guess. A bigger Airstream?"

She smiled. "Vera is perfect as she is."

Clouds drifted past the moon, lighting up the scene a little more and making her eyes sparkle as she studied him "No," she whispered. "I wanted to kiss you again."

Her words instantly stirred up all those feelings he had been trying to tamp down, the wild hunger growling to life again.

"Jess."

He didn't know what he intended to say but she shook her head slightly. "I know we shouldn't. One more kiss won't hurt, will it?"

Something told him it would. He would hate seeing her walk away in a few days.

How could any sane man resist such a soft entreaty?

He eased his mouth to hers and she seemed to sigh a welcome that shivered down his spine.

Her mouth tasted like raspberries and vanilla from her cake. Rich, luscious, addictive. He wasn't sure exactly how but he miraculously managed to shove down the urge to kiss her fiercely, hungrily, with all the wild desire surging through him.

Instead, he instinctively knew this night, this kiss, required gentleness. He kissed her slowly, softly, exploring each delicious inch of her mouth.

She wrapped her arms around his neck, pressing against him, and he wanted this kiss to last forever.

Tenderness for her, this brave, tough, wounded woman, curled through him.

He wanted to make love to her. To lay her down onto the sand and spend the night trying to ease her pain however he could.

He couldn't do that, as tempting as he found the idea. For one thing, he would be an ass to take advantage of her in such a vulnerable, exposed moment. She had confided in him, something he knew she likely didn't do often. That she had trusted him with this difficult part of her past humbled and amazed him.

How could he turn around and betray that trust by pushing her to do things she already had made it clear she didn't want?

For another thing, it was starting to rain. He could feel small, misty drops on his head, trickling down his neck.

Ending the kiss was the last thing he wanted to do but concern for her well-being beat out his profound desire to stay exactly where they were.

He suspected the sky would unleash a downpour on them in another few minutes.

Calling on all his self-control, he lifted his head. She blinked, skin immediately dewy with rain.

"Oh. It's raining," she murmured. He probably shouldn't find it so intensely, powerfully seductive that she hadn't even noticed.

"Yes." He eased a little farther away. "We should go. The path can be slippery enough when it isn't raining, especially the steep parts."

She sighed, looking a little lost. "I wish we didn't have to. I wish we could stay right here."

"So do I," he said gruffly. "But I would hate for you to catch pneumonia on your birthday."

With another sigh, she rose and wiped off sand from the bench. He grabbed Cinder's leash and his flashlight in one hand and her hand in the other and they made their way to the path.

He really should build some sort of shelter down there. A gazebo or even a shed where they could store the boards, kayaks and other water equipment. His dad had never wanted anything down there, concerned it would mar the view.

Your grandfather never wanted anything that shows the hand of man down there, Jack used to say. *I feel the same. When I'm in the cove, I like to believe I'm alone with the sea and the sky and nothing else.*

His father had relented enough to put in the bench for Eleanor. Nate regretted now that he had never followed through with building a structure, so they could have had a dry place to wait out the storm.

The rain started in earnest when they were about halfway back to her trailer, pouring in sheets that obscured his vision.

By the time they reached her Airstream, a silvery, sleek refuge from the rain, they were both drenched.

"Do you…want to come in and dry off?" she asked, her face a pale blur in the darkness as she stood under her awning.

Saying no was just about the hardest thing he had ever done.

"I want you more than I've ever wanted anything else in my life. More than I want to breathe. But I don't want either of us to regret it. Though I hate like hell having to say this, I don't think this is the right moment. Not when you're still upset after the fight with your sister."

She didn't say anything for several seconds. Finally, she nodded. "You're probably right."

She leaned in to kiss him softly. "Thank you for listening."

He lifted a hand to gently brush her cheekbone. "You don't need to carry the weight of the world by yourself, Jess. It's okay to put it down once in a while and let someone else help you."

"I do feel better. Thank you."

"You're welcome. Happy birthday."

"So far thirty is terrific," she said dryly. "I can't wait to see what the rest of the year brings."

He smiled at her sarcasm, kissed her one last time, then he and Cinder slipped away through the rain toward his house, yearning with everything inside him that he could stay.

30

Jess

SHE STOOD UNDER THE AWNING, DRENCHED AND chilled, as she watched Nate and his dog hurry away until they were out of view.

She shivered from more than just the wind blowing through her wet clothes.

She didn't want him to go. She wanted to call after him and drag him inside her cozy trailer and make love all night long, safe and dry in his arms while the rain pounded the aluminum skin.

Oh, this was bad.

She couldn't believe she had told him about that last horrible night with Roni and Doug. The words had spilled out of her like rainwater carving a channel to the sea.

Right there under her awning, Jess stripped out of her wet clothes to her bra and panties and draped them over the bistro chairs so they wouldn't drip all over the trailer then hurried inside.

She grabbed a towel first and wrapped it around her, then turned on her propane heater to warm the space.

One of the few things she *didn't* like about living in these close quarters were the bathing facilities. She loved glorious, luxuriant showers but the water capacity was severely limited in the Airstream.

Sometimes on the road, she checked into a hotel room for a night simply so she could indulge and take a long, hot shower where she didn't have to worry about the water running out.

Still, she made do as best she could then slipped into her favorite warm sweats and thick socks. Jess knew she ought to climb into bed. The day had been long and she felt wrung out from the wild emotions of the past few hours.

Her mind was racing too much to sleep, jumping between Rachel, Cody, her parents.

Nate.

She was relieved he hadn't accepted her invitation to come inside. It had been a spontaneous thing, spurred by the hunger that had only been growing stronger since the first time they kissed and by the security and safety she felt in his arms down at the cove.

He was right. She would have regretted it in the relentlessly harsh light of morning.

Jess had friends who could sleep with any person who caught their eye. Sometimes Jess wished she could do the same. That casual approach fit so much better with her own personal narrative, the persona she tried to portray of someone who hurried into town, took care of what needed to be done and then moved on.

How much easier would it be to keep everyone from getting too close if she were the sort of woman who could invite a desirable man into her bed at night, take what she wanted from him and kick him out in the morning without a second thought?

Over the years, she had learned that the price for a few hours of intimacy was simply too steep. She ended up feeling more alone than ever.

Too bad.

Right now, with the rain drumming against the Airstream and her body still quivering from Nate's touch, she wanted so much more.

No. It was for the best. She already felt closer to him than any man she could remember, even the few she had dated for more than a few weeks.

She had never told either of those guys about her parents. She had just said they died when she was a teenager and neither had pressed.

Why had she spilled everything to Nate?

She still didn't know.

All in all, it was probably a good thing she planned to leave the following week. A few more moonlit meetups with Nate and she would be so tangled up with him, she wouldn't be able to extricate herself.

Would that be so horrible?

Yes. She knew the answer to that. Nate was the sort of man who would never be content with a casual relationship and she simply didn't know if she had anything more to offer.

A text came through just as Jess was finally slipping into bed.

Hey, beautiful birthday girl. How was the par-tay?

She smiled, wondering how Yvette's simple texts sounded so clearly like her friend.

She texted back a pic she had taken of the girls in their cute little flowery sundresses holding her birthday cake. Gorgeous cake, Yvette texted back. And then a second later.

Dayam, girl. Who's the hottie?

She looked at the photo again and saw that Nate was standing in the background. He was smiling at the scene and looked big and dark and luscious.

Eleanor's son, she answered back. He and his daughter came to the party.

You been holding out on me. Too bad you're almost done there. Maybe I should still fly out to help you finish up. I'd like a taste of that.

She almost texted back, Nate's mine. That wasn't true, of course. She just wanted it to be.

You know I always have a pullout couch ready for you, she texted.

Yvette sent her the thinking emoji, which made her smile.

Yvette was someone else who had never taken no for an answer. When they met during basic training, Jess had put up all the usual back-off signals. Yvette had shoved them all out of the way with her characteristic style and insisted they were fated to be friends. Jess had been helpless in the face of such blatant confidence.

Their bond had been cemented through their initial training and had only been reinforced when they served together in Iraq.

They had worked perfectly together building Transitions. Each had strengths that complemented the other.

She wasn't alone, Jess reminded herself. She had a sister she loved, nieces, a nephew. She had Yvette, an interesting job, a tiny house that was just right for her, barring the unfortunate showering limitations.

So she didn't have a man in her life. That was her choice. The smartest choice for her situation right now—even if a rainy, cold night like this one made her wish she could make a different one.

31

Jess

SHE WAS FINISHING HER COFFEE AND SOME AVOCADO toast the next morning before heading over to Eleanor's when someone knocked rather tentatively on the door of her Airstream.

For one wild moment, she wondered if it might be Nate, if he might have come to pick up where they had left off the night before.

Butterflies immediately swarmed in her stomach and her heartbeat edged up. No. It couldn't be Nate. He was probably getting Sophie off to school and heading off himself to a job site. Anyway, something told her his knock would have been more forceful.

With all the heat they seemed to generate between them, maybe he wouldn't have even bothered to knock, just would have forced the door open and swept her into his arms.

She swallowed hard and warily opened the door.

It wasn't Nate. Instead, her sister stood on the other side. For once, Rachel didn't look Insta-polished, her makeup flawless and her hair styled.

She had circles under her eyes, no makeup as far as Jess could tell and her hair was swept back into a messy bun with a few strands hanging out. She looked as if she had been up all night.

The memory of their fight the night before and the hard words they had flung at each other seemed to swirl around them like mist in the morning air.

"Rachel. Hi." She looked over her sister's head to her empty minivan parked next to Jess's own pickup. "Where are the kids?"

"Cody had an issue with a supplier so had the morning off. He offered to get the girls to school and hang out with Silas while he makes some phone calls at home so that I could come talk to you."

"Okay."

What else did they have to say to each other? Her stomach burned a little, but she told herself it was only because she'd had too much coffee and not enough toast.

There wasn't much room inside her trailer for both of them, especially not with these big feelings between them.

Since the morning was beautiful, the ocean gleaming in the sunshine after the rain, she gestured to her turquoise bistro set, grateful she had taken her still-damp clothing inside to dry in the shower now that she was ready for the day.

"Do you want some coffee? I was just eating breakfast. Can I make you some avocado toast?"

Rachel shook her head but slid into one of the chairs. "I'm not hungry. And I really don't need more caffeine."

"What do you need?"

"To talk to you."

More than a little wary now, Jess grabbed her own breakfast and sat down across from her sister. She was still feeling vaguely queasy from the emotional turmoil of the night before. She wasn't sure she was up to more today.

"I ruined your party," Rachel said, her voice quivering slightly. "I wanted it to be perfect and then I...I ruined it."

Rachel met her gaze and Jess saw that her sister looked wretched.

"You didn't ruin anything."

"I did. And the worst part is, I have no idea why. I have all the best intentions and then all these awful things come gushing out."

As Jess feared, her sister started to cry, big tears dripping down her cheeks. Her nose started to run and she looked around rather wildly, as if Jess would have a box of tissue always at the ready.

Not sure what else to do, she handed over the napkin she hadn't used yet and Rachel wiped at her nose and her eyes.

"I'm a hot mess," Rachel sniffled. "You were absolutely right. I don't know how to fix it. I keep thinking I'm doing okay and then something sets me off. And I'm losing my husband."

The tears finally became one sob then another and another. Jess didn't know what to do. She hated tears in herself and really hated them in her sister. She wanted to run inside the Airstream and close the door tightly behind her. But Rachel was being vulnerable with her. She couldn't just stand by and stare.

She rose and hugged her sister, wishing the gesture that had once been so routine between them felt a little more natural and a little less forced.

Rachel didn't seem to mind. She rested her head against Jess's chest and held tight to her waist, letting the tears flow.

"You're not losing your husband. I shouldn't have said that yesterday. Cody adores you."

"How can he? You were right. Everything you said last night."

"I'm the last one to offer marital advice, sis. You know that. The only experience I have was being a witness along with you to our parents' train wreck of a marriage. It might not have been the worst marriage ever but it would surely have a place of honor in the Bad Marriage Hall of Fame."

Rachel eased away, wiping at her eyes with the bedraggled napkin. "Yes. If there were such a thing."

"Yours doesn't belong anywhere near there. You love Cody, right?"

"So much." Rachel gave a watery smile. "Since the moment I met him when I was a scared fourteen-year-old foster kid. He was so kind to me. We had gym class together and you know I wasn't athletic at all. He worked with me after school for a week, trying to teach me how to shoot a free throw so I wouldn't humiliate myself by shooting air ball after air ball in my new school."

"You never told me that."

Rachel shrugged. "There are a lot of things I didn't tell you. I didn't want you to think I was a weakling. You were my tough, fearless, invulnerable sister."

"Ha. That's so not true. You know it's not."

"You became a soldier, Jess. Two deployments to the Middle East. You've always been a badass. Which is why I didn't want to bother you with my dumb problems. You had bigger things to worry about. But Cody helped out. I'm actually really great at free throws now. You should see me."

She brushed a strand of Rachel's hair out of her face. "Cody helped you with that. He can help you deal with Silas, too, but you have to let him."

She remembered Nate's words to her and decided to repurpose them for her sister. "You can't carry everything by yourself, Rachel. I don't know why you feel like you have to."

To her dismay, this seemed to set off the tears again. More dripped down her sister's cheeks, so many that the poor napkin wasn't going to cut it. Jess jumped up and reached into her trailer for the box of tissues she kept in the cabinet next to the door.

"I know." Rachel sniffled. "It's just that Mom was helpless

about everything. She wouldn't make a decision about changing toilet paper brands without Dad's say-so. I don't want to be like that."

"It seems to me that you've gone in the exact opposite direction. You don't want to rely on Cody for *anything*, even when your life feels completely overwhelming."

"It does. It's so hard. There are days I want to get in my car and just drive and drive and drive and never look back. I can never tell Cody that. It would break his heart."

She buried her face in her hands. "I love our family. I do. I just…wish things could go back to the way they were when Silas was a quiet, easy baby, before he was diagnosed. Before I had pages and pages of books to read about how to handle him, before we had daylong doctor appointments, before the future became so uncertain and so damn scary for my child." She sobbed again. "I don't know if I'm strong enough to do this."

Her shoulders shook with her sobs and Jess had never felt more helpless. How could she offer comfort to her sister? She had never had a child at all, let alone one with a serious, potentially life-changing disability. She didn't have any words to make this better. Nothing she said would change Rachel and Cody's reality anyway.

She picked her words carefully. "You are an amazing mother, Rachel. Every time I see you with the kids, I'm impressed all over again at how you make it look so effortless."

Rachel scoffed. "I wish."

"You do. The one night I stayed with the girls was one of the hardest things I ever did. And I didn't have Silas that night, just Grace and Ava, who are basically self-sufficient. Everything the girls told me about their daily routine just reinforced what a good mother you are."

She gripped Rachel's hand. "The amazing thing to me about it is that you're completely self-taught. We didn't get any guidance from Roni. But the girls told me that every day you make them come home and report about a good deed they have done that day. They showed me the shelves full of books in their room and the reading nook you created and told me you read to them every single night."

"I've always loved books."

"I know. And you're teaching your children to love books, too. Even Silas. Yesterday at my party, he sat on Eleanor's lap for a long time while they looked through picture books. That's all coming from you."

Rachel sighed. "I don't feel like anything I do is enough."

"That's the first thing you should stop right now. Stop comparing yourself to everyone else. I know social media is your business and that you're great at it but somehow you have to stop looking at how everyone else defines a good mother. Give yourself a freaking break, Rachel."

Her sister gave another watery laugh. "Is that an order, Staff Sergeant Clayton?"

"Sure. If that's what it takes."

She squeezed her sister's hand again. "I also think you need to start taking time for yourself without feeling guilty about it. When was the last time you spent a few hours doing exactly what you wanted, not for a blog post or an Instagram story. Just for your mental health?"

Rachel looked pensive. "I don't know. I honestly can't remember."

"There you go. Take Silas to your mother-in-law's house while the girls are at school. She raised Cody and his siblings. Four kids born within six years, right? She can handle one two-year-old."

"Silas is harder to handle than your average two-year-old. He can be so difficult sometimes."

"And you'll be the only one who can ever care for him unless you let others step in once in a while and try to figure it out. It will be good for him to spend some time with Grandma, and you can go to yoga class or something. Or better yet, put on some sexy lingerie and text Cody that you fixed lunch for him at home."

Rachel blushed and gave a breathy laugh, but Jess thought she also looked intrigued by the idea.

"I could maybe do that."

"You should. It will be good for you and for Cody. Don't forget that he's still your hero who taught you how to shoot free throws. You've loved him since you were fourteen."

"I have. Silly, isn't it?"

"No. It's beautiful. And, Rach. If you're the best mom I know, Cody is the best dad. The girls and Silas clearly adore him. You two make a fantastic team. You've just lost sight of that somewhere along the way and think you have to make all the free throws by yourself. What's the good of being an ace shot if you won't let anybody else on the court with you?"

Rachel laughed and shook her head. "I can't believe you're using a basketball analogy."

"If that's what it takes," Jess said again.

Her sister rose and hugged her again. It felt so much like the old days, the Clayton sisters against the world, that Jess's throat thickened and *she* almost started crying, too.

"Thank you. I came here to apologize for the way I ruined your party and the terrible things I said."

"You didn't ruin anything," Jess assured her. "It was a wonderful party. I've never seen such a gorgeous birthday cake. I'll never forget all the trouble you went to in order to make it special for me."

"We should get together again before you go home. What do you think about driving up to the Redwoods? It's not that far."

"I would like that. I'm probably leaving Monday. Maybe we could go Sunday."

Rachel's face fell. "I wish you could stay longer."

"I do, too," she said, and was slightly shocked to realize she meant it.

"Maybe we could meet up somewhere during the summer," Jess suggested on a whim, without really thinking it through. "In late June, I've got two jobs in a row lined up in the San Diego area. The kids might like to come down and enjoy Southern California. I have a week on either end. Maybe we could find a vacation rental together and do all the touristy stuff. Lego-land, the San Diego Zoo, Disneyland, Universal Studios. I don't know if Cody could take the whole week away from work, but maybe he could fly down for a few days."

It wasn't her idea of a relaxing vacation, but it would be fun to spend more time with her nieces and Silas, and she knew planning the trip would be Rachel's idea of paradise.

As she expected, her sister immediately lit up. "That would be fantastic! Oh, Jess. I would love it. Especially being with you."

"Good. Talk to Cody and let me know."

"I will," she promised.

Rachel hugged her tightly and Jess closed her eyes, feeling as if a small bruised corner of her heart had begun to heal.

"I love you, Jessica Marie," her sister said.

She had to smile. How long had it been since someone called her by her full name? "And I love you, Rachel Elizabeth. You're going to be okay."

"I hope so."

"I know you will. You called me a badass. As far as I'm concerned, what you're doing as a mom to those three precious kids requires next-level badassery."

Rachel laughed. "I might have to make a bumper sticker out of that. Motherhood. Next-level Badassery."

"It's got a ring."

Rachel smiled, waved at her and climbed into her minivan, looking a hundred times better than she had when she showed up.

As she watched her drive away, Jess felt as if they had turned a corner in their relationship. She and Rachel had been pulled apart by life and circumstances. She wanted to think maybe this time in Cape Sanctuary had helped them begin the process of finding their way back together.

Now on to her next challenge: persuading Eleanor to let Jess tackle what the other woman had actually hired her to do.

32

Rachel

AS RACHEL DROVE AWAY FROM WHITAKER HOUSE, the entire day seemed more beautiful, somehow. The sun seemed to shine more vividly on the water and the sky was a pure porcelain blue, with only a few puffy clouds above the mountains to the east.

On impulse, Rachel pulled into one of her favorite spots in Cape Sanctuary, a pull-out along the cliffs overlooking the water and downtown.

She didn't do this enough. She was always rushing off somewhere and didn't take time to stop and breathe and think.

Maybe it was the good hard cry that, like the rain of the night before, had cleansed the sadness out of her system, leaving room for her to remember the joy. She felt a renewed sense of optimism about so many things.

She loved and admired her sister. The strain between them over these past years had felt like another loss. That Jess had suggested a trip together, especially one with a theme park itinerary Rachel knew perfectly well her sister would *never* choose on her own, meant the world.

It would be so much fun to spend that time with her sister. Rachel loved planning trips and couldn't wait to get started on this one, though she planned to factor in plenty of downtime for all of them. Pool time at the hotel, walks along the beach for just her and Jess to talk.

She couldn't wait.

How would Silas do on a trip like that? She would do everything in her power to make sure he had a good time. Jess, Cody and the girls would help. All the pressure didn't need to rest on her shoulders alone.

She had to remember that lesson, moving forward. Yes, Silas still faced an uncertain journey. But Jess had been right. She and Cody made an excellent team. She had to remember they were in this together, fighting to give their son the best possible future.

She stepped outside her van, letting the sea air wash through her and the morning sun warm her shoulders.

She loved the life she had created here. Why did she allow herself to get so caught up in the day-to-day rush that she forgot? She should make a date with herself monthly to come right here to this spot to recalibrate her soul.

After a few more deep breaths, she felt more refreshed than she had in months. She even sang along to the car stereo as she drove through town.

When she arrived home, the peace of the morning was broken by hammering, coming from the backyard. She followed the sound around the house and had to stop short.

Apparently, Cody had decided to use his limited free time to finish the shutters on the kids' playhouse, a job they had talked about a few days earlier. He was wearing his tool belt, the one she always told him looked sexy.

And next to him was Silas, wearing an adorable little matching tool belt she hadn't seen before.

Her heart seemed to melt. Cody must have bought it for Silas, without telling her, just as he had bought one for each of the girls when they were about this age.

"Okay, it's your turn to hammer again," Cody was telling their son. "I've got a nail started for you right there. Here you go."

Silas grabbed the child-size hammer with both hands and started whacking at the nail his father had pointed out. He missed more times than he made contact with the nail, leaving divots in the soft pine, but Cody didn't seem to care. He just beamed at the boy, sunlight gleaming off the lighter strands in his hair.

"That's the way. Good job, kiddo. Keep going."

Silas looked at his father with all the trust in the world and continued hammering with far more enthusiasm than skill.

"That was our last one," Cody said. "Look how nice they look. Now we just have to clean up before Mommy gets back."

"Mama," Silas said. He had spotted Rachel before his father did and came toward her, hammer still in his hand.

"I'll take this," Cody said quickly, grabbing it away.

He gave Rachel that sheepish smile that made her insides quiver.

She loved this man. The man who had patiently and lovingly taught his toddler son with autism to use a hammer was the same one who had helped a fourteen-year-old girl learn how to shoot free throws so she wouldn't embarrass herself at a new school.

He was the best husband and father she could ever wish to find and she loved him with all her heart.

She picked up Silas and went to Cody. With her free hand, she touched his face and then kissed her husband with all the fierce tenderness burning through her.

"Down," Silas said, using yet another new word. Apparently,

he wasn't a fan of his parents' public displays of affection. She lowered him and he immediately went to his sandbox and started playing with his trucks, which left her free to kiss Cody again, this one more lingering and tender.

"What was that for?" Cody somehow managed to look both confused and aroused.

"Because you're amazing. Because I'm the luckiest woman in the world. Because I love you more than life itself."

His expression blazed with heat and an answering tenderness that slid through her like healing balm. He wrapped her tightly in his arms and kissed her with so much love that Rachel felt tears rise again.

These were happy tears. Cleansing tears. How had she forgotten how much safety and peace she found in her husband's arms?

"Any chance your mom could watch Silas for an hour or so?"

He looked a little dazed. "Probably. Why?"

"Oh, I'm sure we could find something to do."

"I'll check." He stepped away and whipped out his phone so quickly she almost laughed.

He texted his mother and she responded almost instantly.

"She said she would love to watch him. She didn't ask why."

"Tell her I need your help with a project that requires both of our undivided attention."

He grinned, looking so much like the sixteen-year-old boy she fell in love with that everything inside her seemed to sigh with happiness.

While he and Silas left, Rachel went inside to shower and change into some sexy lingerie she bought a long time ago and hadn't worn yet.

This was an important part of their life together and both of them had neglected each other for too long.

Her joy seemed to bubble over. She loved her husband. She loved their children, she loved their home, she loved the life they were building together.

Like the children's playhouse that now had hammer-sized indentations on the shutters, it might not be Instagram perfect. But it was as close to it as she could ever need.

33

Jess

"WE'VE CLEANED OUT EVERY OTHER SPACE IN the house, Eleanor. I'll be leaving in only a few days so I can move on to my next job."

The older woman's mouth drooped. "Oh, don't remind me. I don't want you to go. I have so loved having you here."

"I'm sorry. You know I can't stay here indefinitely, though."

"I know. You have other obligations. You're a busy woman."

This was Friday. If she and Eleanor worked hard that day and Saturday, they could finish. That would give her Sunday to spend with Rachel, Cody and the kids before she drove south Monday.

Technically, her next job wasn't scheduled to start until a week from Monday, but she had planned to spend a few days at her long-neglected apartment, catching up on paperwork and doing some strategic planning with Yvette.

They needed to make a decision about adding another person

to their team. She and Yvette had more work than the two of them could handle and she hated turning down clients.

That was a worry for another day. Right now, she needed to focus on finishing *this* job.

"Eleanor. Today's the day. We've put it off long enough. It's time to start going through Jack's clothing."

She tried to use the gentlest tone she could manage, but Eleanor still tensed.

"Today? I don't know if I'm up to it today."

Jess frowned. "That is your decision, of course. You can leave things like they are, with his things taking up half your closet and an entire chest of drawers. If you want my help, I'm afraid we're running out of time."

Eleanor pressed a hand to her heart, as if the gesture could ease the ache there at missing her husband. "I know. It's just so hard to think about boxing up his things for the last time. Not being able to stand in the closet and smell him. It makes everything feel so...final."

"I understand. We don't have to do it at all. I told you that. If you would rather tackle the job on your own once I'm gone, that's totally fine. It's your choice."

Eleanor sighed. "Without you to push me, I would probably leave his clothes in there forever."

"If that would make you happy, there's nothing wrong with keeping his things close to you."

Eleanor gazed off into space, her lined face etched with vast grief. After a moment, she shook her head. "No. It's only his clothing. It's not him. I won't forget him. I don't need some dusty old sweaters to remind me how much I miss my husband. He's with me constantly, right here."

Again, she pressed her heart.

"Are you sure?"

"Yes. Let's do it. Though I confess, I'm not sure I can watch."

"Then you don't have to," Jess declared. "As you and Nate

have already taken out the things you want to keep, the rest is simply sorting through what should go to the charity shop and what they likely won't take. It shouldn't take long at all. Why don't you go to your craft room and work on your knitting and watch the sea? I think another storm might be coming and I know how much you enjoy watching them."

Eleanor looked tempted, then shook her head. "I can't abandon you like that."

In some respects, the job would be easier, the decisions more clear-cut if she didn't have Eleanor standing over her shoulder.

"I don't mind. But you could also sit in your chair by the window there and knit. You still would have a view and could offer input if I need help. But that way you wouldn't have to be as hands-on."

"That would work."

Eleanor left the room. When she didn't return immediately, Jess started folding up clothing and sorting items into piles. Some for the charity shop, some for a consignment store Yvette liked to use and a few for the rag pile.

When Eleanor returned after about fifteen minutes, she carried her knitting bag and her eyes appeared suspiciously red-rimmed.

Oh, poor dear. Eleanor was torn between needing to move forward with her life and wanting to hold tight to the past and the memories and these tangible things that represented Jack Whitaker's life.

If she died, who would mourn her like this? Rachel would miss her, certainly. And Yvette would be sad, as well. But not with this bone-deep grief.

Jess wasn't that important to anyone.

A sobering thought the day after her thirtieth birthday.

"Which do you prefer? Being closer to the closet so you can see what I'm doing or sitting out here by the window?"

"Closer to you, I think."

Jess moved Eleanor's favorite ergonomic recliner and footrest from its usual spot looking out to sea to the other side of her bed. Fortunately, it wasn't heavy. "There you go."

"Oh, thank you, my dear. You're so thoughtful."

She didn't necessarily agree but appreciated Eleanor's opinion.

They slowly worked their way through Jack's side of the closet. Like his book collection, Jack had many items of clothing, some more worn than others. He didn't seem to have discarded many things over the years. The wardrobe spanned several different decades.

After a few hours of work, they still had most of the large walk-in closet to go.

Jess pulled out a suit with wide pinstripes and even wider lapels. "Wow. This is very cool. This looks like it's from the '40s."

"That suit belonged to Jack's father, who was quite a dapper fellow in his day. Jack couldn't part with it, though I begged him. He said it was a part of his father, one of the few he had left."

She gave a distant sort of smile. "They were much the same size and Jack would wear that for certain occasions. He looked great it in, let me tell you. So handsome. Like a more distinguished James Dean. One year for Halloween he wore it and dressed like a gangster. I went as his moll. I had the whole fancy outfit, including a fake derringer in my garter."

Jess had to smile. "I wish I could have seen that."

"I've got pictures somewhere. Maybe I'll look through them this afternoon and see if I can find one. We were something."

"I bet."

Eleanor pressed a hand to her chest again, which made Jess frown. Did the other woman have any idea how often she did that? Was it only because of her emotional heartache or was something physical going on?

"I used to love to go out dancing with Jack. There was a place down the coast that had live music—the big band stuff, not rock and roll, though we liked that, too. We used to dance all night.

That was before our Nathaniel came along, of course. He was such a miracle that I didn't like to leave him, even for an evening, especially at first."

"A miracle?" She had to ask.

"Completely. We tried for ten years to have a child. It was our greatest sorrow. Jack and I were so happy together and we knew a child would only add to our joy."

Jess listened, fascinated, while she folded and boxed clothing they had sorted into piles.

"I had three miscarriages before Nathaniel came along and also one late-term miscarriage that was considered a stillbirth. I lost a baby girl at twenty-four weeks. She was perfectly formed in every way and doctors never knew why she didn't survive. We named her Jennifer."

"Oh, Eleanor. I'm so sorry."

This woman had endured so much sorrow and loss in her life, yet she was still warm and gracious to those within her orbit. She made Jess feel small and petty in comparison.

"Doctors warned us I shouldn't get pregnant again, that it would probably end the same way." She continued knitting, not breaking the flow of her work while she spoke. "Jack didn't want to try again. He wanted to start the process of adopting and I finally agreed. I knew I would love any child, whether or not I gave birth to him or her. We were only just beginning to fill out the paperwork and had decided to stop trying ourselves to get pregnant."

She chuckled. "Would you believe that after all those years of infertility, the minute we stopped trying, I got pregnant within the month?"

"Wow. That's amazing!"

"Right? Wouldn't you call that a miracle? And the pregnancy was easy the entire nine months. No morning sickness, no early contractions. He was just a joyful baby."

Was that the reason Jack and Eleanor's love had been so strong, because it had been forged through shared heartbreak? It must have taken so much faith for them to try again after multiple pregnancy losses.

"I guess Nate made up for being an easy baby in his difficult teen years."

Eleanor looked surprised. "Did he tell you about that?"

"He mentioned he sometimes clashed with his father when he was younger."

"They wanted very different things. Jack wanted Nathaniel to go to college. Maybe even graduate school. He was so good at engineering and math and could have done great things. But he wanted to build things. I think he got that from my side of the family. My father was a builder and Nathaniel adored his grandfather. And he was always puttering around here."

She shrugged. "Jack had his own ideas for his future. They fought bitterly about it, month after month. Nathaniel finally ended the argument by enlisting after high school. He only told us about it after it was a done deal."

That must have taken great courage, for Nate to leave behind all that was familiar. When she enlisted, she had nothing left to lose. Nate had been in an entirely different situation.

"And then, of course, he met Michelle and everything changed. I suppose he's told you about her."

Jess wasn't sure how comfortable she was discussing Nate's late wife with his mother. "A little. Sophie has told me about her, too."

"Michelle was beautiful, brave, driven. I liked her very much but could see from the beginning that she wasn't at all the right woman for my son. I can say that now, though I didn't dare tell him how I felt back then."

Jess didn't know what to say, other than to tell Eleanor not to get the wrong idea about her and Nate.

Jess *really* wasn't the right woman for Nate. Not with all her baggage.

"After Nate came home with Sophie when Michelle was deployed, he and his father made their peace. Jack just adored that girl. It was the sweetest thing. He loved to carry her around and sing to her when she was a baby. When she got old enough to walk, she followed him everywhere."

Eleanor took on a distant look and absently rubbed again at her chest.

"Are you okay?"

"Fine," the older woman said, though her features suddenly looked strained. Was she more pale than she had been even five minutes earlier?

"Are you sure?"

Eleanor swallowed, mustering a slight smile. "Actually, I'm not feeling well. Perhaps I should go lie down."

"That might be a good idea."

She had to tell Nate about these episodes before she left. He needed to know Eleanor was acting unwell. She should have told him earlier.

"Why don't you rest in the guest room next door so that I don't disturb you while I'm working in here?"

"That might be...good."

Jess rose from the floor. "Let me help you."

Eleanor waved a hand. "You're in the middle of things. Don't stop on my account. I'm fine."

Before Jess could reach her, she stood. She took two or three steps toward the door then suddenly collapsed as if someone had kicked her legs out from under her, falling forward and narrowly escaping hitting her head on the doorjamb.

Jess gasped and rushed to her. "Eleanor! Are you all right?"

She didn't answer. *Had* she hit her head? Jess hadn't heard a crack.

Her eyes were closed, Jess saw when she rolled her to her back, and her face was deathly pale.

What was happening?

Fear scorched through her, hot and urgent. She tried to shake Eleanor but the older woman didn't stir.

She was still breathing. Jess could see a faint pulse in her throat and her chest was rising and falling, but she wasn't responding.

"Eleanor!" she called again, even as she reached for the cordless phone next to Eleanor's bed so she could call 911.

As soon as she started to dial, she spotted Nate's number. Still trying to rouse Eleanor, she hit the programmed key first, thinking he could rush over while the ambulance was on the way.

She was immediately sent to voice mail after the second ring. "I think something is wrong with your mother," she said quickly on the message. "She suddenly went pale, said she wasn't feeling well and then passed out. I don't know what's going on. She's unconscious but breathing. I'm calling an ambulance. I'll try to keep you posted where they're taking her."

As she ended the call, she saw Eleanor's eyes begin to flutter. "I don't...need an ambulance," she said, voice breathy.

"I'm afraid you do, honey. You passed out and fell down. You've been out of it for at least three minutes now. You need to be checked out."

"I'm just tired." Eleanor tried to get up, but Jess rested a hand on her shoulder.

"That's what you've been telling me for days now. But it's more than that, isn't it?"

Eleanor was quiet, breathing deeply, then she met Jess's gaze, raw fear in her eyes. "I think I might be dying."

Damn it. She should have called 911 first. She quickly dialed the number and spoke quickly into the phone. "Yes. Hello. I'm with a seventy-year-old woman, Eleanor Whitaker, who just passed out. She's awake and conscious now but still pale. She's having chest pain. You are having chest pain, right?" she asked Eleanor, who nodded. "Yes on the chest pain. Please hurry. We're at Whitaker House, just above Sunshine Cove. Twenty-one thirty-five Seaview Road."

"Confirmed. We have identified your location. Please stay on the line while we dispatch emergency crews to your area. I'll be back with you momentarily."

"Please hurry," Jess said.

Sophie and Nate couldn't lose Eleanor, too. Not when they were still grieving for Jack Whitaker.

Jess vowed to do everything within her power to make sure that didn't happen.

34

Nate

AN AMBULANCE. HIS MOTHER PASSED OUT. SICK.
Nate listened to the message from Jess that he had missed after turning off his ringer during a meeting. When had she sent it? Only ten minutes earlier, he saw quickly.

Still, that was ten minutes when he had been unavailable. Anything could have happened in that time. He rose quickly.

"I have to go," he told his team of project leaders in the room. "Apparently my mother is on her way to the hospital."

"What can we do?" his second-in-command, Kevin Hall, asked instantly.

Just pray, he wanted to say. "I don't know what's going on yet. I'll keep you posted."

He hurried out of the room, trying to call Jess's cell phone. Each time it went to voice mail. He tried a third time as he was sliding behind the wheel of his truck and she finally picked up.

"Hi. Sorry. The ambulance just arrived." She sounded breathless and afraid, which ratcheted up his own anxiety. Jess always seemed so contained, so in control. If she was this upset, he knew the situation had to feel serious to her.

"What's happened?"

"I don't know, to be honest. She passed out and she's got chest pain. They are treating it as a possible cardiac arrest and are taking her directly to the emergency room of the Cape Sanctuary hospital."

Cardiac arrest. Good Lord.

"I'm at a meeting in the next town. It will take me about twenty minutes, but I'll meet you there."

He peeled out, heart racing. This couldn't be happening! He couldn't lose his mother, not just months after his father. He still hadn't figured out how to deal with the huge void in his life left by Jack Whitaker's death.

Sophie.

If something happened to his mother, Sophie would be devastated. She still mourned her grandfather, but he feared that losing Eleanor, who had been more of a mother than a grandmother to her, would crush her.

Nate wasn't sure how he made it safely on the coastal road to the regional medical center on the other side of Cape Sanctuary, especially as he likely broke just about every traffic law in the county. When he rushed into the waiting room, he immediately spotted Jess talking at the nurses' station.

"Nate!" she exclaimed. "I just arrived. They didn't have room for me on the ambulance, so I followed them. They've taken your mother back to a treatment room. I was just explaining to the nurse that you would be here shortly to answer questions about advance directives and the like."

Advance directives. He couldn't think about that now. All he could do for those first frenzied seconds was grab hold of Jess and pull her into his arms. She was his rock, the one secure thing to grab onto amid the seething tumult.

She wrapped her arms around him and held on before stepping away. "You should go back and see what's going on. They
wouldn't let me because I'm not family."

She spoke calmly but he saw how difficult it was for her to
be excluded. "That's bull," he snapped. "You likely saved her
life. You were the one who called for help."

"It's fine. You're here now. What about Sophie? Should I get
her from school?"

"I called her friend McKenna's mom and explained what has
happened. For now, I'm going to leave her at school until I have
more information. It's early dismissal day so McKenna's mom
will pick her up after school and let her hang out at their place
until I can give a proper situation report."

"That's smart. No need to upset her until we know what's
happening."

He made a split-second decision. "You should come back
with me. Eleanor loves you. I know she would want you there."

He approached the reception area with Jess in tow. Though
the woman behind the desk, Cheryl Myers, went to school with
him, she stood firm on the hospital policy.

"Right now, we can only allow one person per patient in a
treatment room for security reasons. I'm so sorry, Nate. Wish I
could make an exception for you."

"It's totally fine," Jess said. "I don't mind waiting out here."

"You don't have to hang around if you don't want to. I can
text you with an update as soon as I have news."

"I'll wait," she said firmly. He wanted to hug her again but
knew seeing his mother had to take priority right now.

The nurse gave him a room number and buzzed him back.
When he arrived at his mother's room, he found several nurses
and doctors darting around and his mother hooked up to a mul-
titude of machines. She looked frail and frightened and every
one of her seventy years and then some.

It shocked him to the core.

When she spotted him, he saw relief and also embarrassment. "Oh, Nathaniel. Hello."

"Mom. What's going on?"

"This is all so ridiculous. I'm perfectly fine. Would you tell these people that I don't need to be here?"

"You're exactly where you should be," a kind-looking woman in scrubs who was monitoring a machine said firmly. "Right now, your heat rate is all over the place and we have to figure out why. Hello. I'm Josie, one of the nurses who will be taking care of your mom."

"What's going on? I heard something about a possible heart attack," Nate said.

"That was what the paramedics thought," the nurse said. "It makes sense because of some of her symptoms but we aren't quite sure what's happening. I can tell you the electrocardiogram is showing some unusual activity. Right now, the plan is to run more tests so her team can get a more accurate picture of what's happening. The attending physician should be here shortly to talk to you."

Nate stood beside his mother's bed, feeling helpless and worried for her. She had closed her eyes, as if trying to block out the whole thing, but would open them to answer questions Josie posed to her.

After what felt like forever, the ER doc, who turned out to be a friend, came in. She was more than a friend, actually. Nate's company had just completed a beautiful house for Luz Herrera and her wife, Jade, in the mountains north of town.

"Nate. Hi. Not the best of circumstances to see you again. Eleanor. How are you feeling?"

"Mostly embarrassed at all the fuss. I would like to go home," she answered.

"I'm afraid we can't send you home until we figure out why your heart rate is going from hare to turtle speed and back again," she said calmly. "And you're having chest pain, I understand. How long has that been going on?"

Eleanor looked at Nate with an apology in her eyes. "About three weeks," she murmured. "It comes and goes."

Three weeks! Three weeks and she hadn't bothered to mention it to him?

"We think the reason you passed out is because you were having what's called bradycardia. Extremely low heart rate. Your heart wasn't pumping enough blood to your brain to do its job."

"What could cause that?" Nate asked her.

"Any number of things. Heart disease, genetic factors, chemical imbalance, thyroid issues. That's why we need to run some tests. The tricky thing in your case, Eleanor, is that you seem to be fluctuating right now between bradycardia and tachycardia, which is an extremely high heart rate. It's as if your heart has forgotten how to work right and doesn't quite know what to do. We'll run some initial tests here in the emergency department and then come up with a plan with the cardiology team, moving forward."

"What if I don't want more tests?" Eleanor said.

"Mom. You don't have a choice."

She glowered at him, then sighed. "Fine. Do what you have to do."

She closed her eyes as if she wanted to block out the whole experience.

"We'll try to make this as easy on you as possible," Luz promised gently. She continued looking at his mother's chart, spoke to the nurse monitoring the EKG, said a few more calming words to his mother then prepared to leave.

Nate followed her out into the hall. "What do you really think is going on?"

Luz frowned and looked through the glass wall of the treatment room at his mother. "We really won't know until we run more tests and get the cardiac team down here to consult. I can tell you something like this rarely comes on all at once, without warning. Has your mother been feeling ill?"

"She's had a few episodes over the past few weeks, apparently. I should have made her see a doctor earlier."

"Parents can be stubborn, can't they?" Luz smiled. "But don't worry, Nate. She's in good hands. Everyone in town loves Eleanor. We don't want anything to happen to her either."

"What happens if you can't regulate her heartbeat?"

Luz looked hesitant to answer but finally shrugged. "I should let the cardiac team give you this info but you'll probably just do an internet search after I walk down the hall anyway. One possible treatment is a pacemaker."

"A pacemaker!"

"Believe it or not, it can sometimes be needed only temporarily, until the heart can once more regulate itself. But, again, it's too early to say until we have more test results. I would tell you to settle in for a bit. We'll probably keep her down here for a few hours during the initial testing and my guess is the cardiac team will want to keep her for a few days to do more comprehensive tests."

That fear clutched at him again. He hated this. It had been hard enough watching his father die by inches. "Thank you."

"She's tough, Nate," Luz said with a reassuring smile. "Tough and otherwise healthy, from what I can see of her medical records. We will work on figuring this out and try to get her out of here as soon as we can."

"Thank you."

"You're welcome. Do you have someone to help you with Sophie?"

He suddenly remembered Jess, still out in the waiting room, anxious for news.

"Yes. She's at school right now then going home with a friend."

"Once we have Eleanor in a regular room, she can have more than one visitor."

"Thanks for everything."

The doctor nodded. "She's in good hands," she said again.

"I know."

He returned to Eleanor's room and found her asleep. As Josie, her nurse, was still at her bedside while watching the EKG, he decided to go out and update Jess.

She was thumbing something into her phone when he walked out. As soon as she spied him, she rose and shoved her phone into her pocket.

"How is she? What's happened? Sophie was just texting me. She's pretty frantic. School just got out. Apparently, a classmate told her an ambulance came to the house. She thought it might be you, especially when she tried to reach you and couldn't."

He pulled out his own phone and realized he had somehow activated the do-not-disturb feature. He quickly turned it off and was bombarded with texts from a dozen different people asking about Eleanor.

"I'll reach out to her."

Gram is fine for now. They're treating her well. I'll tell you more as soon as I know. Love you.

She responded with a weird face he guessed was the worried emoji.

"Do you have any more information?" Jess asked.

"Not really. She's sleeping right now but they need to run some tests. She's got an irregular heartbeat, which could result from any number of reasons. Apparently, it's been going on for some time, though she never bothered to mention it to me."

"I knew something was wrong," Jess said guiltily. "I should have told you. She had a few incidents in the time I've been working at Whitaker House. Random moments when she would suddenly go pale for no obvious reason and then have to rest. She told me she had been ill before I arrived and was still recovering."

He did remember his mother being sick but she had assured him she was feeling better. "I think she purposely didn't want me to know anything was going on with her. She knew Sophie and I would both find it upsetting, especially so soon after my father died."

She rested a hand on his arm and just that simple touch seemed to calm him, steadying something wild and worried deep inside.

"How can I help?"

"You already have," he said gruffly. "You called an ambulance and had her brought here, which is huge. And it helps to know you're here."

Those feelings he had been fighting ever since they first appeared seemed to wash over him, stronger than ever. No question about it. He was falling in love with Jess. She was a calm haven to rest from the storm.

For now, anyway. Until she left town.

This was a really lousy time to realize how far gone he was over her, especially when he knew she was planning to load up her Airstream and drive away from Cape Sanctuary in a few days.

"Are they keeping Eleanor?"

"Yes. At least a day or two for tests. Luz, my friend who is the ER doc, said there is a possibility she might need a temporary pacemaker if her heart rate doesn't self-regulate."

"Temporary is good."

It all seemed overwhelming to him. "I guess. But bottom line, the tests will take time and then they're admitting her. You don't have to hang around that whole time."

"I don't mind. But if you want, I can pick up Sophie from her friend's house after school and she and I can go back to Whitaker House and grab some of Eleanor's things that might make her more comfortable during her stay. Her favorite robe, slippers, that kind of thing."

"Great idea."

"What about you?" she asked. "Can I bring you something to eat from the cafeteria before I leave? You might not have a chance to take a break again until they get her settled into a room."

"I don't think I could eat right now. But thanks."

She nodded. "All right. You had better go be with your mom. I'll be back with Sophie in an hour or so."

"Thank you."

Words were inadequate to express his gratitude. Though he knew it wasn't the smartest idea, he grabbed her in another embrace, needing the strength he found there.

"I don't know what I would have done without you. I hate to think about Mom being alone for hours on the floor. Or, worse, Sophie finding her there after school."

"I'm so glad I was there."

Her arms tightened around him. He didn't want to let her go but knew he needed to return to his mother's treatment room.

He lowered his mouth to steal a quick, intense kiss.

She pulled away, looking flustered, her eyes bright and her color high. "I'll see you later tonight," she said.

He nodded and turned away to go back to his mother, wishing with all his heart he could have her by his side…and that he could ask her to stay.

35

Jess

JESS PULLED AWAY FROM THE HOSPITAL, STILL REEL-ing from all the unspoken emotions of that last kiss.

That look in Nate's eyes. She had never seen that before, from him or anyone else. As if she was his everything. His sea and his stars and his sky.

She had wanted to stand right there in the emergency department waiting room and savor the feelings.

No. It was impossible.

First, she must have imagined that look. Second, even if it was real—even if it was somehow possible Nate might be developing feelings for her—so what?

She was leaving in only a few days, three at the most. She had another job scheduled soon and more lined up all summer long.

Anyway, she didn't do relationships. She was happy with her wandering life, never staying in one place long enough to put down roots or build lasting connections. She had left no space in the world she had created for a long-term relationship.

But, oh, if only she had. An ache of longing hit her as she drove, so fierce and hot that she had to grip the steering wheel. Nate was everything she could ever want in a man. Kind, caring, passionate. Each time he kissed her, she only wanted more.

She remembered his sweetness the night before, how he had sat beside her, silently offering steady comfort and strength while she relived that horrible night when her parents had died.

He was the kind of man a woman could count on. Not her, though. She wasn't cut out for happy-ever-after.

By the time she drove to the address Nate had given her for Sophie's friend McKenna, she had almost convinced herself that that moment in the waiting room when he had looked at her with heartbreaking tenderness had never even happened.

Almost.

As soon as she pulled up to the house on a quiet street a few blocks from the ocean, Sophie raced out the door, hair flying out behind her, and jumped into the passenger seat.

"How's Gram?" she demanded. "Dad won't tell me anything, other than they're running tests. I want to see her."

"That's all we know right now. Those tests all take time to get results. I'm afraid you can't see her until they move her out of the emergency department and to a regular room. They only allow one visitor at a time and no minors."

She had learned that much during her time in the waiting room when she'd heard the receptionist turn others away.

"Maybe they've moved her by now. I want to go to the hospital."

"I'll take you," Jess promised. "First you have to give me a minute to say thanks to McKenna's mom for picking you up, okay?"

Sophie huffed out an impatient breath but nodded. The two

of them hurried to the front porch, overflowing with containers of flowers.

Even before she could ring the bell, a woman with short red hair opened the door.

"Hi there. You must be Jess. Rachel's sister, right?"

That wasn't the response she expected. "Yes."

"Sophie told me you were coming. I'm Tess Peterson, McKenna's mother. I'm on a few charitable boards with Rachel. The library board, Arts and Hearts on the Cape. That kind of thing. I just love that woman. She'll do anything for anyone. You only have to say the word."

Maybe that was part of Rachel's problem. She was so busy trying to take care of the world, she didn't spend nearly enough time taking care of herself.

"She's pretty terrific," Jess said. "Thank you for picking up Sophie."

"Oh, that was no problem at all. She's only been here a few moments. It's good you got here so soon, though. I was having a tough time keeping her from walking to the hospital herself."

"I want to see my grandma," Sophie said, unrepentant.

"How is Eleanor? I've been so very worried. She's such a dear."

"Yes. She is. Doctors are running tests now. I don't have much more information than that."

"Well, give her our love. Everyone in town will be pulling for her."

"I'll tell her. Thank you again."

Tess waved her hand. "It's what we do here in Cape Sanctuary. Tell Nate I'll bring dinner over one night next week, okay? I'll be in touch with him to find out what night works best."

"I'll do that," she said, warmed by the woman's concern.

Cape Sanctuary was a nice place. It was no wonder Rachel loved it here so much. Beautiful scenery and kind people. It made a lovely combination.

"We're not going to the hospital," Sophie said as soon as Jess turned toward Whitaker House.

"Not yet. I need your help."

"Now? We can't! We have to go see Gram! What if she dies and I'm not there, like I wasn't there when Grandpa Jack died?"

Her mouth wobbled like she was going to cry and her eyes looked scared. Poor girl! No wonder she was in such a rush.

Jess reached out and grabbed her hand. Sophie's fingers were trembling.

"Eleanor isn't going to die," Jess insisted, praying that was true. "She's in a good place with caring medical professionals who are doing all they can to figure out what's happening with her. Your grandmother is a tough cookie."

"I can't lose her."

"I know, honey."

She turned onto the driveway at Whitaker House and pulled up in front of the house. "Eleanor might have to stay in the hospital for a few days, so I need your help."

"Doing what?"

"You know her better than just about anyone. What are some of the things she might find comforting while she's in the hospital? What do you think she would like most with her?"

"Besides Charlie? I don't know."

"Charlie! I forgot all about him. I left him in his crate when the paramedics came. Poor thing. We had better let him outside."

"We can take him over to be with Cinder. She always likes his company."

"Good idea. Since we can't take Charlie to the hospital, what else do you think your grandmother might like?"

Sophie's brow furrowed as she considered. "Maybe a picture of Grandpa Jack. She has one by her bed and she's always looking at that."

"Great idea. You could also help me find a few of Eleanor's favorite nightgowns and maybe her robe and slippers."

She had always found that people functioned better during a crisis if they had a task to distract them. The theory worked in Sophie's case, too.

At the house, they first took an anxious Charlie down the road and back to exercise him then left him in the fenced backyard at Nate's house with Cinder for company. The dogs had a dog door leading to the kitchen and plenty of food and water.

"Gram will be okay," Sophie said, hugging the little dog close. "She has to be."

Back at the house, Jess and Sophie gathered a pretty flowered robe, two soft nightgowns from her dresser and a pair of pale green slippers as well as Eleanor's reading glasses, a few toiletries, the mystery novel by the side of her bed and her knitting, just in case. By the time they stowed it in a leather overnight bag they found in the closet, Sophie seemed more calm. As they drove the short distance to the medical center, her anxiety returned.

"I don't know what I'll do if I lose Gram. She's…well, she's like my mom. I don't even remember my real mom."

Jess tried to give her a reassuring smile. "She's been terrific, hasn't she?"

Sophie nodded, clutching the overnight bag to her chest. "Do you have a grandmother?" she asked Jess.

She shook her head. "My father's mother died before I was born. My mother's mother died when I was about Ava's age. Five. Maybe six. I only met her once or twice. I just remember that she smelled like roses, gave the best hugs and that my mom cried a lot after she died."

She had forgotten all about that, coming home from school and finding her mother in tears again. If Roni's parents hadn't died, maybe Jess's mother wouldn't have been so emotionally needy. Maybe she would have been able to find the strength to leave her abusive husband.

"I don't remember much about my grandmother. You're really lucky you've had Eleanor all this time."

"I know."

Though she knew this was a sore spot, she was also compelled to add, "You're lucky to have your dad, too. He's been really worried about you. Maybe it's time you gave him a break."

Sophie looked out the window. "It's not that easy. He lied to me and I don't think I can ever forgive him."

Jess jerked her gaze from the road. Sophie had told her Nate lied to her but she had an even harder time believing this now than she had then. He struck her as scrupulously honest.

"Your dad is a good man. I'm sure you simply misunderstood something he said."

"I didn't misunderstand," Sophie said bitterly. "I heard him clear as day."

She shouldn't get involved. This was between Nate and Sophie. But if the girl wouldn't talk to her father about it, maybe Jess could at least get to the core of the issue and point Nate in that direction.

"What did he lie about?" she finally asked.

"My whole life has been a lie," Sophie said, with the kind of drama only a thirteen-year-old girl could manage.

"Could you be more specific?"

Sophie looked out the window. "My mom. Nothing he told me about her was true."

Jess tensed, not at all certain she wanted to dive into these particular murky waters with Sophie.

She had opened the door, though, and now Sophie didn't give her any choice.

"All my life, he's been telling me how great my mom was and how much she loved me and what a hero she was. None of it was true."

"You don't think your mother loved you?" she asked carefully.

"No. How could she have? If she loved me, she would have stayed with me instead of choosing to go with the army to such a dangerous place where she would end up killed."

"Your mother had an obligation to her unit. She signed up to serve. She couldn't just walk away."

"She could have, though. She could have deferred her deployment until I was older if she wanted to. She didn't want to. She *chose* to go after she had me. She could have stayed with my dad and me, but she didn't want to."

"How do you know that?"

"I heard my dad and grandma talking about it a month ago. They were outside on our patio talking, but my window was open and I heard the whole thing."

That must have been the trigger for the new tension between Sophie and her father, one overheard conversation.

Jess couldn't completely blame Sophie. She knew what it felt like to be abandoned. Left behind. First by her mother, then by Rachel. It formed a deep wound that didn't readily heal.

"He should have told me what really happened instead of letting me believe all these years that she cared about me," Sophie said, sounding distressed. "Why did he have to lie? I don't know if I can ever forgive him."

She shouldn't get involved in this discussion, she should leave it to Nate and Eleanor. It wasn't Jess's business what Sophie thought about her father.

But she couldn't stay quiet, not when she found it grossly unfair that Sophie was blaming her father for her mother's choices.

"Let me get this straight. You overheard a conversation about how your mother made the difficult choice to go back to her unit after you were born."

"She should have stayed. What kind of woman leaves a baby who is only three months old if she doesn't have to?"

"It's not that simple, Sophie. Your mother faced an impossible choice. I'm sure she did what she thought best at the time."

"It wasn't best," Sophie muttered. "Not for me."

"She couldn't know she would die over there."

"She knew it was dangerous."

"I'm sure she missed you every single day she was there. And she would have tried her best to come home to you safe and sound if she could."

Sophie looked doubtful.

"That's not really the point, is it? Let's talk about your father. The one you're so mad at right now. It seems like you've forgotten that he is the one who stepped up to take care of you?"

Sophie frowned. "Only because he had no choice."

"He had plenty of choices. He could have left you with his mother. He could have put you in the care of someone else. Instead, he was here, day in and day out. He gave up his own military career to come back to Cape Sanctuary and take care of you."

"And lied to me about my mom the whole time! He always told me she had to go, not that she chose to go."

Oh, to have the clear-cut, no-exceptions logic of youth, who saw no room for gray.

"Your dad let you believe a story that might not have been completely true about your mother, probably to protect you from feeling exactly like you're feeling right now. And you're somehow mad about that?"

Sophie frowned. "He should have told me the truth. They were even talking about getting a divorce! He never told me that. But then my mom died. That's what he and Gram were talking about."

"Why did you need to know that? Think about it, Sophie. Why does any of that matter? How does it change the wonderful family you and your dad and your grandma Eleanor and grandpa Jack created?"

Sophie looked uncertain, then jutted out her chin as Jess pulled into the hospital parking lot. "I had the right to know the truth instead of believing a big lie all this time."

She did remember what it was to be thirteen and so certain the world was as unambiguous as Sophie thought, without the

nuances one discovered later in life. That gave her a little sym-
pathy for the girl but she still wasn't letting her off the hook.

"So your father didn't tell you everything about your mom.
Okay. Be mad about it. Stomp your feet and slam doors if you
want. But don't you forget for a moment that your father is a
good man who loves you dearly and wants everything wonderful
for you. He left his own military career to bring you back here
to Cape Sanctuary with his mother so you could have the kind
of nurturing love in your life your own mom wasn't able to pro-
vide at the time. Don't take your hurt and disappointment out
on him. He doesn't deserve it simply for trying to protect you."

Okay, maybe she spoke a little more passionately than she
intended. When she stopped speaking, Sophie stared at her for
several heartbeats, then shook her head.

"Wow. You're really crazy about my dad, aren't you?"

Jess swallowed, feeling her face go hot. She hoped Sophie
couldn't see it.

"Don't be silly," she muttered, pulling the keys out of the
ignition. "This has nothing to do with how I do or don't feel
about your father. It's about you."

She faced the girl, and on impulse decided this was a moment
that demanded raw honesty.

"I would have gladly sacrificed anything to have a dad who
loved me and my sister a tiny percentage as much as your dad
loves you."

"You didn't?"

She shook her head. "Not even close. And from the outside,
I can tell you that I find it very unfair of you to take out the
anger and hurt you might be feeling about not having your mom
around on the one parent who was here the whole time to take
care of you. How would you feel if it were your dad who was
here sick in the hospital, after the way you've treated him lately?"

Sophie seemed struck by that as she gripped the handle of Eleanor's overnight bag. "I still wish he hadn't lied to me all this time," she mumbled.

"You should tell him that. But remember when you do that your father loves you with his whole heart. I saw that the first day I came here. That's what matters most, isn't it?"

Sophie sighed. "I guess."

Jess hoped her words had made some kind of impact on Sophie. It gave her some comfort to hope that after she was gone, the two of them could find some measure of peace together.

They went in the front doors, as Nate had texted earlier that his mother was being moved to a room in the cardiac unit.

"Oh, Sophie. Hi, honey." The woman at the reception desk jumped up and circled the desk to give the girl a hug.

"Hi, Mrs. Aoki."

"I'm so sorry to hear your grandmother was admitted. She's in room 112. Take a left past the atrium and look for signs that say 'Cardiac Unit.'"

"Okay."

The woman gave Jess an appraising look. She braced herself to face off against another gatekeeper spouting off about family and limited visitors. Instead the woman gave her a broad smile.

"And you must be Rachel McBride's sister who has been staying with our Eleanor, right? You look like her."

People rarely said that, mostly because their coloring was so different. "That's right. Do I need to wait out here?"

Mrs. Aoki shook her head. "Oh no. You can go in, too. I'm sure she'll be glad to see you."

The two of them walked down the hall until they found the right unit and then Eleanor's room. Despite what the receptionist had said, Jess wasn't sure whether she belonged there. She hovered outside the room as Sophie hurried in to hug her grandmother.

Through the doorway, she spotted Eleanor on the bed. Her

color looked much better than it had before and she didn't seem as wrung out.

Nate must have been standing in the corner where she couldn't see. He walked out into the hallway, the same warm look in his eyes she had seen earlier.

"You don't have to stay out in the hall. Come in."

In her head, Jess could hear the receptionist in the waiting room of the emergency department telling her visitors were limited to family. As much as she had loved helping Eleanor these past few weeks, Jess *wasn't* family. The sooner she remembered that, the easier it would be to move on Monday without looking back.

How was she ever going to leave the Whitakers? The thought ripped at her heart.

Already she could feel the void they were going to leave in her life. All of them. Eleanor. Sophie.

Especially Nate.

This was the very reason she tried to compartmentalize her emotions when she was working. She didn't *want* to get involved. She didn't *want* to care so deeply about her clients that the thought of leaving them to move on to the next job hit her like a punch to the gut.

On this particular job, she had thrown every one of her personal tenets out the window. What was *wrong* with her? How was she going to drive away when she would be leaving a huge part of her heart behind, here in Cape Sanctuary?

"Everything okay?" Nate asked, and Jess realized she hadn't spoken since they arrived.

She forced a smile. "Super," she lied. "I'm so glad you're feeling better, Eleanor."

"I am. I'm wishing I weren't stuck here in this hospital bed, but other than that I'm fine."

"I'm so glad."

"I was so scared, Gram," Sophie said, resting her head on her grandmother's shoulder.

Eleanor patted her. "I'm sorry I worried you all. Hopefully they will be able to figure out what's going on with my ticker and I'll be out of here soon."

"I hope so, too," Jess said.

She stayed a few more moments while Sophie showed her grandmother what they had brought to help her feel more comfortable. Eleanor exclaimed over everything.

Finally, when the walls of the hospital room began to close in on her, Jess edged toward the door. "I should go."

"You don't have to," Eleanor assured her.

"Yes. Stay. I can go find another visitor chair for you," Nate said.

Jess shook her head. "It's a small room. I don't want to be in the way. And, anyway, we left a mess behind in Eleanor's bedroom. I should go back and finish up, so you have a clean room to come home to when you're done here in a day or two."

"Hopefully sooner rather than later," Eleanor said.

Nate gave her a searching look and she wondered if he could sense her restless feeling of not belonging. It was a feeling she ought to be used to by now, after thirty years.

"Thank you again for everything today," he said. He kissed her cheek and she knew she didn't imagine how his mouth lingered on her skin.

She forced a smile, gave Eleanor and Sophie each quick hugs then hurried out of the room.

She would return to Whitaker House to finish cleaning out Jack's closet and then turn her attention to the remaining work.

With a few more hours of hard effort, she could be done by midafternoon the next day.

The sooner she finished the job she came to do, the quicker she could hitch up her Airstream and drive out of town.

36

Nate

NATE WATCHED JESS RUSH OUT OF THE ROOM AS IF the nurses were chasing after her with giant needles. What was her big hurry? She had looked as if she couldn't wait to get away. Eleanor looked at the doorway through which Jess had disappeared. "She's the sweetest girl, isn't she? I'm so glad I had the good sense to hire her to help me clean out that big house. Isn't she wonderful?"

"Yes," Nate said, then looked away, not wanting his mother to see how much meaning that single world held.

She was wonderful. And beautiful. And stubborn.

His feelings were a wild, confusing jumble in his chest. Now was *not* the time to sort them out, when he needed to focus on his mother's health.

"I like her a lot," Sophie said. She gave Nate a meaningful look. "Just in case, you know, anyone felt like my opinion mattered. You have my permission."

He gawked at her. "Permission for what?"

"To date her. If you wanted to."

Yeah. This wasn't the time or place for this discussion. "We're friends," he said gruffly. "That's all. Anyway, she's leaving town in a few days so there's no point to this discussion."

"I think you should. Ask her out, I mean," Eleanor said. "You have my permission, too. As if you ever needed it."

How had this conversation spiraled out of his control? Nate shifted, more awkward than he had been in a long time. Before he could respond, the door opened and a new nurse came in.

His mother's face lit up. "Hi, Brooke. I was wondering if I would see you while I was here."

The woman was a neighbor who also attended book club with his mother. That was one of the perils and joys of a small town. All of their lives seemed to intersect in multiple ways.

"Lucky me, I get to be your night nurse."

"Oh wonderful. You can catch me up on all the good gossip around the hospital."

"Ha. I'm a battle-ax when it comes to my patients. No gossip here, just making sure you take your meds, try to rest and do what the doctors tell you."

Eleanor made a face. "You're no fun at all."

"Hospitals aren't supposed to be fun. Hasn't anybody told you that yet?"

His mother laughed. It was weak, thready, but Nate still felt as if a huge weight had been lifted from his shoulders.

Only then did he fully acknowledge how worried he had been. For the first time since he listened to that voice mail from Jess, he felt the stirring of optimism.

If his mother could try to manage his love life, she must be feeling better.

They stayed until the nurses brought Eleanor dinner, then he and Sophie ate a quick meal in the cafeteria before heading home to take care of Cinder and Charlie.

They were almost to Whitaker House when the topic of Jess Clayton came up again.

"I'm sorry I teased you before. About Jess, I mean," Sophie said out of the blue. "But I do like her. She's nice and she's smart and she's easy to talk to."

He agreed with all of those things. Added to that, she was compassionate, caring, generous.

He really had it bad.

He glanced over at Sophie before turning back to focus on the road. "While I appreciate the, er, vote of approval, I'm afraid it's not going to happen."

"Why not? Don't you like her?"

"That's not really the point." He was falling in love with her, but he really didn't want to have that conversation with his daughter right now.

Sophie was quiet for a long time. When she spoke again, her voice was hesitant. "Jess basically told me today that I've been acting like a jerk to you. Usually that would make me mad but it didn't. Especially because she's right."

Nate held his breath, wondering if he was finally going to get to the bottom of Sophie's seismic mood change a month earlier.

"She told me I should apologize to you and tell you why I've been so mad."

"I'm listening."

He was exhausted from the tumultuous afternoon and evening spent in the hospital but if he and Sophie had any chance of returning to their previous easy, affectionate relationship, he would sit here all night.

"I overheard something I don't think I was supposed to hear a month ago. Something about my mom."

Nate tensed. "Something I said?"

"Yes. You and Gram. You were talking about me and how much I had grown up and looked like my mom. And then you talked about when we first came back to Cape Sanctuary, how hard it was knowing my mom would never get the chance to know me and how different my life might have been if she had chosen to defer her deployment. And you told Gram that even if my mom hadn't died, you probably would have ended up divorced because you didn't want me to ever know I wasn't my mom's first priority."

She sniffled and Nate closed his eyes, cursing himself for not making sure Sophie hadn't been within earshot when he and his mother had that indiscreet conversation.

He rarely talked about Michelle. That brief part of his past seemed a lifetime ago. She had given him his most precious gift, Sophie. Other than that, he didn't think about her much.

He could remember that particular night clearly. It had been the night of what would have been his wedding anniversary and he had been feeling low, a little lonely as he looked back at the path he had chosen to travel as a single father.

"I'm sorry you heard that," he finally said.

"Yeah. It was a lot easier when I thought she was some kind of war hero like everyone else does."

Damn it. He had never wanted this. The wounded hurt in his daughter's voice broke his heart.

"She was, Sophie. She was. Your mom was an amazing woman. She gave her life to protect other people from a terrorist attack. I still call that heroic."

"All this time, you let me think she was the big love of your life, the reason you hardly ever date anybody else."

He had never said that to her. Had he?

"I did love your mother," he protested.

"How could you? You said you were going to divorce her!"

He sighed, wishing they didn't have to have this conversation right now. He wanted his daughter to always believe in happy endings. It was his fault. If only he had kept his mouth shut, instead of making a few half-forgotten comments to his mother in passing.

"Your mom and I...we weren't a good match. I know this might be hard to understand but you can love somebody with all your heart and still not be a good fit together."

The words resonated in his chest. He was doing it again. Falling for someone who was completely wrong for him. His life was here in Cape Sanctuary. He had a business here, his mother, Sophie, while Jess had created an entire business model based on being willing and able to travel as needed.

"I loved your mom. If she hadn't died serving her country, I hope we could have tried hard to make it work. We might have figured out a way."

"It hurt that you lied to me all this time."

"I'm sorry."

This was the crux of the matter. She felt betrayed that the worldview he had always created for her was only one perspective of the wider picture.

"I was trying to protect you. I can see now where you would feel like I kept important information from you. I'm sorry for that. I don't blame you for being upset with me. I wish you had told me this a month ago, though, so we could have avoided all the slamming doors and cranky comments."

"Jess basically yelled at me and told me to stop being a baby. She didn't use those words but that's what she was really saying."

"Was it?"

"She told me it wasn't fair to take out my anger at the parent who stayed and took care of me all this time."

Warmth and gratitude seeped through him along with more of those tender feelings he didn't know what to do with. Nate had to swallow hard before he trusted himself to answer. "I guess that's one way to look at it."

"Yeah. I hadn't thought of it that way. She's kind of right. I'm...sorry. Next time, I'll talk to you before I go all pissy for weeks at a time."

"I hope there's not a next time. I missed you."

"Same."

She rested her head on his shoulder for a minute, just as she used to do when she was small and sleepy from a long car ride, and Nate felt emotions rise up in his throat again.

He had Jess to thank for this, too, this rare and precious peace with his child. Just another reason he was falling for her. She was amazing. Strong, feisty, loyal.

How was he supposed to simply stand by and let her walk away?

37

Nate

NATE DROVE HOME FROM THE HOSPITAL LATE SATurday completely exhausted.

He found it quite odd that he could work on a construction site in the hot summer sun for twelve hours straight and be perfectly fine, yet a day sitting around in a hospital while his mother underwent testing left him so drained.

If he was tired, his mother had been completely wiped out. She was sleeping soundly when he left. He didn't think she would stir for most of the night, even when the nurses came to check on her.

He pulled up in front of his house feeling guilty about leaving Sophie all day but she would have been bored senseless hanging out in a waiting room.

After Sophie had spent a long visit with her grandmother in the morning and had been all but climbing the walls, Jess had popped in to check on Eleanor and had asked Sophie to help her finish a few cleaning projects at Whitaker House.

He suspected the request had mostly been a ruse to distract his daughter from driving Eleanor too crazy with her restlessness. It had worked wonders, though.

He'd checked on them around dinnertime with a phone call and Sophie told him they were going to walk down to the beach and do some beachcombing and have a picnic.

That had been three hours earlier. He imagined Jess must have gone back to her trailer hours ago, but no lights were on when he drove past and pulled around to his house.

To his surprise, he found her at his kitchen table, working on a laptop. A fierce yearning hit him hard. How wonderful would it be to come home to her in his kitchen, in his house, in his bed on a regular basis?

She smiled a greeting, obviously with no clue what crazy things were running through his head. "Hi. How's your mom?"

"Doing well for now. She's sleeping. The cardiac docs are saying she can probably go home tomorrow."

"Really? That's great news."

"It is," he agreed. "The verdict is in, though. She does need a pacemaker, which she's not too happy about. They're talking about putting it in later in the week."

"So soon?"

"Believe it or not, they're hoping it will be an outpatient procedure and she won't have to stay overnight again."

"Wow. That's amazing!"

"Definitely." He looked around. "Where's Sophie? Has she gone to bed?"

Jess gestured over her shoulder to the small family room he had added on to the house, with floor-to-ceiling windows overlooking the water. "Asleep in there, last I checked. We had been watching *The Princess Bride*, which she said is her favorite movie, but about halfway through, she fell asleep, so I came in here to take care of some paperwork."

"I don't think she slept well last night. She was too worried about Mom."

"I don't blame her. I didn't sleep well either."

Why? Because of his mother? Or because of something else?

"I still can't believe my mom never told me she hadn't been feeling well."

"I don't think she wanted to admit it," Jess said.

"You could be right. She also said she didn't want to worry me, so soon after losing my father."

Jess gave a soft smile that made him wish he could drag her into his bedroom and spend the night with her wrapped in his arms.

"She loves you. You're her miracle baby."

He made a face. "She told you that?"

"Yes. She told me about the miscarriages and the stillbirth of your sister. It breaks my heart to think of all the pain your parents went through."

"Yeah. Makes me wish I hadn't been such a shitty teenager."

"You've more than made up for it in the years since, from what your mother says."

He raked a hand through his hair, concern again edging through him. Despite the doctors' claims that the pacemaker would help, he still worried. He also couldn't believe his mother had had what appeared to be a mild heart attack and even she hadn't known it.

In the past thirty-six hours, he had learned more than he ever expected about how women experience heart attacks differently from men and often discount their symptoms or attribute them to something else, like acid reflux or normal aging.

He had learned that while heart disease was the number one killer of women, it often went undiagnosed.

His mother might have had another more serious, even fatal,

heart attack, if Jess hadn't been there to call 911. He didn't even want to think about it.

Jess must have sensed some of his turmoil. She rose and rested a comforting hand on his arm. "Your mom will be all right. Eleanor is tough."

"Not as tough as we think. Or as tough as *she* thinks."

Jess was much the same. He suspected she wanted to put out an aura of invincibility, of toughness and strength and independence, but he sensed a softness at her core, a sweetness she probably would do everything she could to deny.

"Can I do anything else to help get Whitaker House ready for her to come home? Did the doctors say anything about her needing special accommodations?"

"You've spent two weeks doing that. Having the excess clutter cleared out will make a huge difference during her recovery and rehabilitation."

"I'm glad." She folded up her laptop and slipped it back into a simple khaki messenger bag. "Sophie and I finished up the last few things at the house this afternoon. I also put her to work mopping the kitchen and vacuuming where she could, just so it's sparkly clean when Eleanor comes home."

"Thank you. That will help."

"I won't be around tomorrow, unless you need my help with Eleanor coming home. I promised Rachel I would spend the day with her and the kids. We're driving to Redwood National Park."

That would be good for her, especially after their fight the night of her birthday. They must have made up, but he hadn't had the chance to talk to her about it.

"No. Go with your sister. We'll be fine. Thank you so much for all your help with Sophie. You saved the day. Again."

"I was happy to spend time with her. She's pretty terrific."

"She thinks the same of you."

He almost mentioned that Sophie had given him permission

to date Jess but wasn't entirely certain she would appreciate that information.

"She told me you lectured her about her moodiness the past month and told her she should be grateful instead of resentful. Thank you for that. She was like a different person this morning."

"Don't be too hard on her. Being a thirteen-year-old girl is hard work."

"I will try to keep that in mind. I don't think fourteen through eighteen will be much easier."

"Good luck with that."

She smiled, though he thought it looked a little sad. She picked up her bag and threw it over her shoulder. "I should take off so you can get some rest. I'm glad your mom is doing better."

He wanted so desperately to ask her to stay but knew he couldn't, not with Sophie in the next room.

"I'll walk you to your trailer."

She made a face. "You don't have to do that. I'm a big girl and can probably manage to walk two hundred feet by myself."

"Humor me. Maybe I just don't want anything to happen to you."

She looked startled by his words but finally shrugged and opened the door. Cinder and Charlie immediately came out from the TV room, as if they had been waiting for that signal. They both hurried out into the darkness to take care of business.

The night was clear and lovely, the ocean murmuring just down the path as they walked to her trailer, gleaming in the moonlight.

"I really would have been lost without you these past few days," he said when they reached her door. "Thank you."

"I'm glad I was here to help."

"So am I."

Though he knew it would only leave him aching for more,

he leaned down and kissed her. With a sigh, she closed her eyes and returned the kiss.

He didn't embrace her. Didn't touch her with anything but his mouth, just like the first time they had kissed. It was still one of the most emotional, intense kisses of his life. It was soft, sweet, tender, and he never wanted it to end.

They stood together for a long time, while the sea breeze swirled around them and he fell a little harder.

She was the first to break away. He couldn't clearly see her expression in the moonlight but her eyes looked huge in her face.

She opened her mouth to speak but hesitated, swallowed and turned away.

"Good night," she said.

Somehow he had the impression that wasn't what she had been about to say.

"Jess."

He knew what he wanted to say. *Stay. Please stay.* But the words seemed to jumble up inside him in a tangle and he couldn't figure out how to make them work.

She took a step up into her trailer to stand in the doorway. "I'm glad your mom is doing better. I'll try to check in with her tomorrow and then again Monday before I leave."

She hurried inside and closed the door behind her, leaving him standing alone with only the night and his regrets to keep him company.

38

Jess

SHE HAD TO GET OUT OF HERE. FAST.

Monday couldn't come soon enough. Jess sat on her sofa, wishing with all her heart she had been able to drag him inside with her to spend the night.

That kiss.

She was still reeling, a full half hour after he had walked back to the house. She could still taste him, still feel the tenderness and intensity of it.

She knew she needed to leave Cape Sanctuary but had no idea how she was supposed to walk away from a man who kissed her like that, as if she were everything he had ever wanted or needed.

She was in love with him.

If she had any doubt, that kiss had sealed it. Somehow Nate Whitaker had burst past all her careful defenses like they were nothing.

When she went through basic training, she had faced one obstacle course that had kicked her ass time after time, a ridiculously complicated thing with insane jumps, climbs, nets.

Some of the soldiers she trained with didn't even seem to work up a sweat as they made their way through.

Nate would have been one of those soldiers. Somehow, she knew it.

She thought she had been so careful to protect herself but she had fallen for him anyway.

What was she supposed to do now?

Nothing.

Jess let out a shaky breath. Nothing at all. Okay. So she was in love with Nate. What did that change? Exactly nothing. Monday, she would hitch up her trailer and drive away from Cape Sanctuary. It was her only option.

Yes, leaving him would hurt, but she would get over it, eventually.

Wouldn't she?

"I so wish you didn't have to go."

Jess, sitting beside Eleanor's bed at Whitaker House on Monday morning, picked up her friend's hand and pressed it.

The older woman still seemed frail, with no makeup on and her hair not as carefully fixed as usual. But her color was much better and she was obviously happy to be home in her own bed.

"I know. But my job here is done. I have to move on to the next one."

She was aware that every passing moment was leading her inexorably toward that moment when she would drive out of town.

Not yet.

She had promised she would say goodbye to Eleanor first, so here she was, though she had been half-tempted to slip away in the pearly predawn, when she wouldn't have to face any of them.

Eleanor turned her hand over and squeezed Jess's fingers.

"This old house won't feel the same without you. I will miss our long talks."

Jess mustered a smile. "So will I," she answered. It was true. This had been her most enjoyable job ever. She had loved every moment of helping Eleanor.

"If only I had four or five more rooms for you to clean out. But I suppose you're tired of Whitaker House by now and ready to move on."

"I'm not tired of it at all. I've loved the house, the town, the scenery. I've especially enjoyed getting to know you. Thank you for sharing your life with me. But the job is done now. It's time for me to go."

"You've been so wonderful. Whitaker House has never looked so good. It's almost like a new place, now that you've cleared away all the extraneous things."

"Amazing what a difference decluttering can make, isn't it?"

"Such a difference."

Eleanor shifted to a different position, sitting up more. "I'll tell you the truth, before you came, I had been thinking I should sell this old house and move into something smaller without all that upkeep. Or even trade houses with Nate and let him worry about all the things falling apart here while I live in that cute house he has fixed up so nicely."

"Were you?"

"Yes." Eleanor looked around. "But here's the thing. I don't want to sell Whitaker House, especially now that everything seems so fresh and new. Those two nights I was in the hospital, I could only think about coming home. Sleeping in this bed that Jack and I shared for all those years. I want to die in this house. Even if I'm too old to walk to the mailbox and have to hire people to look after me, I don't want to go anywhere."

How would it be to feel a connection to one place, to have lived within these same walls nearly all one's life, with the same view and the same trees and the same people?

Once, Jess would have thought that was a cloying, mundane existence.

She was beginning to wonder if she had been completely wrong.

"Your focus right now needs to be on resting and healing, especially after you get your new pacemaker. Before you know it, you'll be running down the path to Sunshine Cove with Sophie and the dogs."

Eleanor huffed out a laugh. "Who knows? Now that I'm going to have all this new energy, maybe I'll take up surfing."

Jess had to smile. "You should. I would love to see that."

Except she wouldn't be here to see it. She might be in San Jose or Boise or Omaha. But she wouldn't be here.

They visited for a few more moments, until Jess could tell that Eleanor was tiring. She rose. "Thank you for everything. I promise, I'll stay in touch."

"We both know I'm the one who should be thanking you." Eleanor sniffled. "I will miss you, darling. You've brought so much sunshine and joy back to my house."

"It has been my pleasure."

She hugged her, inhaling the scent of lavender and vanilla that Eleanor favored. She would never be able to smell that particular combination of scents without thinking of this woman who had been so very kind to her.

"Have you said your goodbyes to Sophie and Nate yet?" Eleanor asked when she pulled away.

Jess tried to ignore the hard kick to her chest. "No. I knocked on their door earlier but no one answered."

"They slept here last night to watch over me but Sophie had a special end-of-year awards assembly this morning at school. I told them I would be fine by myself for an hour. They should be back shortly. You could wait."

It would probably be easier not to see them before she left, though she knew that was the coward's way out.

"I don't think I can wait. It's time for me to go."

"Oh. They'll be so sorry to miss you. You've touched all of our lives, darling."

"I won't ever forget my time here with you," she said quietly.

"You know you're welcome back anytime."

"Thank you."

"I have something for you. It's in the bottom drawer of my chest. Would you mind grabbing it?"

Curious, she opened the drawer and pulled out the knitted throw Eleanor had been working on at various times during her stay here. It was made of soft, chunky yarn in colors that perfectly matched the interior of the Airstream.

"Oh. I can't take this."

"Yes, you can. I insist. I wanted to give it to you for your birthday but I didn't quite finish it in time. I came home after your party last week and completed it."

"It's beautiful." She ran a hand over the textured knit, already imagining a storm beating against the aluminum of the trailer while she was safe and warm with a mug of cocoa and this blanket.

"Thank you."

"It's a small thing but I hope when you use it, you can remember there are people here in Cape Sanctuary who love you."

Jess hugged Eleanor one more time, trying hard not to cry. Leaving a client had never been so hard. She had been running Transitions for years and this was the first time she felt so shredded at finishing a job.

This place and these people would live on in her heart.

After she said her final goodbye, assuring Eleanor she would check in with her after the pacemaker surgery later that week, she walked through the house one last time.

She wanted to be like Eleanor someday. Strong, generous, kind. She admired her dignity, her compassion, her sharp, orderly mind.

This job and these people had made lasting imprints on her heart, whether she liked it or not.

She walked outside, to where her pickup was already hitched up to the Airstream. She was almost tempted to walk down to the cove one more time but knew she was only delaying the inevitable. Better to go now, while she could.

She was checking the hitch one last time when she heard a vehicle drive up to the house and saw Nate's truck pull in alongside hers.

Oh. If only she had left five minutes earlier, she could have missed him completely.

As soon as he stopped, Sophie rushed out of the passenger side of the vehicle. She wore a coral-colored dress with a white sweater and an expression of dismay.

"Your trailer is all hooked up." She glared at Jess and then at the hitch.

"Yes. It's time for me to go, especially since you and I finished everything at the house the other day."

"Already? Can't you stay a little longer?"

"I have a long drive and don't want to arrive home too late. I thought you would be in school."

"I came home after the awards ceremony so I could be with Gram this afternoon, since we weren't really doing anything at school. You were going to leave without saying goodbye?"

"I'm sorry. I didn't get back from Redwood National Park with my sister until late last night. I didn't want to wake you up last night. I tried to see you this morning but I waited too long and you were gone."

Sophie looked as if she wanted to cry, ripping off a few more layers around Jess's heart.

"I don't want you to go."

To her shock, Sophie threw her arms around her. As she hugged her back, Jess realized she hadn't only fallen for Nate. She had fallen for Sophie, too. And of course, for Eleanor.

She loved all of them.

"It's not forever," she said gently. "My sister and her family still live in town. I'll be through again. Next time I'm here in Cape Sanctuary to see them, I'll call you and we can meet up. Maybe we can build another sandcastle or go beachcombing."

Sophie sniffled and pulled away. "That would be good. It won't be the same, though."

"You have my phone and my email. You can reach out any-time. In fact, I insist you let me know if you ever get that de-livery of postcards and the gift from Japan."

"I will. I'm going to miss you so much."

"I'll miss you, too, Sophie. Take care of your grandmother for me, okay? And your dad."

She hadn't looked at Nate once. She couldn't.

At that, Nate finally stepped forward. He had on a gray dress shirt and darker gray tie, which he must have worn for Sophie's awards ceremony. It was the first time she had seen him dressed so formally and she had to swallow.

"Why don't you go in and check on your grandmother?" Nate said to his daughter.

Sophie sighed. "Okay. Bye, Jess. Drive safe."

"Goodbye, honey."

The girl hurried into the house, leaving Jess and Nate alone. Jess wanted to call her back, needing the buffer. She hated hav-ing to say goodbye to Nate.

Why, oh why, hadn't she left five minutes earlier? Was it pos-sible she had been subconsciously dragging her feet so she could see them one more time?

"So where are you headed next?" he asked.

"Back to my place in Mission Hills for a few days to take care of administrative stuff before I drive to Las Vegas to help clean out a house for a couple who are going into assisted living."

"Fun."

"Not very. He has Alzheimer's and doesn't want to leave their house but she can't care for him there anymore. I have to help her figure out how to condense a five-bedroom home where they have lived for decades to a two-bedroom assisted-living apartment."

"Good luck."

"Thanks. After that, I'm going to St. George, Utah, where a widow is moving in with her son in Salt Lake City and needs help getting her house cleared out and staged to sell. I've got other jobs lined up all summer."

She loved her job and knew she did important work, helping people. She still didn't want to leave.

"They're all lucky to have you," Nate said gruffly.

"Thanks."

"What you did for my mother. I still have no idea how to thank you."

"It was my pleasure, Nate. Really. I loved working on Whitaker House."

"I meant saving her life. But the work you did on the house was terrific, too."

"I hope Eleanor is able to spend many more years enjoying it."

"She will. I'm sure of it."

He loved his mother, which was one of the things she found most endearing about him.

Okay, she found everything about him endearing.

"I will miss you."

The words seemed to have been dragged out of him. They hovered between them, stark and honest.

Stunned by the intensity of them, she didn't know how to answer.

A muscle flexed in his jaw. "I wasn't going to say anything. I figured I would stand here and keep my mouth shut and watch you walk away. But what the hell. Years from now, I don't want to live with the regret of knowing that I stayed quiet when I should have spoken up."

He stepped forward and gripped her hands tightly in his. "Is there any chance of persuading you to stay longer? Maybe you could do your administrative stuff here."

She could. There was no real reason why she couldn't stay a few more days and then drive straight to Las Vegas from here.

But that would only be delaying the inevitable, wouldn't it?

"You said once that your apartment in the valley is mostly a convenient stopping place between jobs. What if you made Cape Sanctuary your home base?"

"I…what?" The suggestion was so unexpected that she could only stare at him.

"You have people who care about you here. Rachel, Cody, the kids."

"Yes."

"And now you have the Whitakers who all care about you, too. Sophie flat out adores you and of course my mom is crazy about you."

What about you?

She wanted to ask but couldn't seem to grab the scattered words together to form a sentence. "I know we're not as centrally located as LA and you would have to drive a little farther to southern places. Or, you know, moving forward, you could take on more jobs in this area of the state to keep you busy or even up into Oregon and Washington."

"What are you asking, Nate?"

"I'm making a mess of this, aren't I? I'm sorry. I went over and over this in my head last night, trying to figure out the right words." Before she realized what he intended, he pulled one of her hands to his mouth—the hand that was probably oily from hitching up her trailer—and kissed the back of it, just as if she were some kind of grand lady in a French chateau or something.

"I'm asking you to take a chance on this. On us."

She stared, fear and confusion and a deep ache of yearning swirling around inside her. "There is no *us*," she protested.

"All we've done is kiss a few times. I've only been here for two weeks!"

"I know. But two weeks is certainly long enough for me to realize I'm falling in love with you."

She snatched her hands away as if he had pinched them. "You are not."

He gave a rough laugh. "I had the same reaction. Disbelief maybe, mingled with no small amount of dismay. I don't want to fall in love right now. I wasn't looking for it, believe me. But you drove into our lives with your trailer and your courage and your tough attitude and I couldn't seem to help myself."

She swallowed. "Well, you can fall right back out."

"I'm afraid it's not that easy."

Jess could feel panic biting at her. She was wholly unprepared for this. In her wildest dreams, she had never imagined Nate Whitaker professing that he was falling in love with her!

He couldn't be. She was all wrong for him. He needed someone soft and kind like Rachel, not a former staff sergeant who lifted boxes and trailered her pickup across the country for a living.

"I am not the happy-ever-after type of woman, Nate. You knew that about me from the first."

"Only because you've sold yourself that narrative. That doesn't necessarily mean it's true."

"Of course it's true! I'm not my sister."

"Agreed. Rachel is a terrific person. But she's not you. Your lives have been shaped by different experiences."

They had spent thirteen years being shaped by the *same* experiences, though. Experiences that had impacted them in completely different ways.

She was only now seeing that Rachel hadn't been untouched by the pain of those experiences, as Jess had somehow thought.

"You can't love me," she said again. The concept was too huge, too unbelievable for her to comprehend.

He took her hands again and she so desperately wanted to fling herself into his arms and hold on tight.

"How could I *not* love you? I love your strength. Your compassion. Your courage. I love the way you can handle yourself in the toughest of situations. I love your fierce loyalty to those you care about. You are the only woman I want, Jess."

She remembered that kiss in the waiting room of the hospital, as if she was his everything. She couldn't be that. Not for anyone, not even Nate.

She straightened and pulled her hands away.

"Don't do this to me. It's not fair. I told you nothing could happen between us. I made it clear from the beginning. This… this isn't what I want. I have to go."

"Just like that. You're not even going to consider staying?"

"I can't."

She looked at the Airstream that she had worked so hard to restore. It represented so much more than just her home. It was the life she had created for herself, the one where she felt safe and needed.

"I have to go," she said again. "I'm sorry, Nate."

To his credit, he didn't try to stop her. He only stood watching, his expression closed as she climbed into her truck.

Oh, she hated this.

She started the truck and the engine turned right away.

There was nothing else keeping her here.

She put the vehicle in gear and pulled away, feeling the tug of the trailer on the engine, like the weight of all she was leaving behind.

Fighting tears and the heavy ache of impossibilities, she looked in the rearview window only once to find him standing where she had left him, watching after her.

She wanted to leave town immediately, go as fast and as far as she could, but she had promised Rachel she would stop in at her house one more time before she left.

How would she endure another goodbye?

With her throat achy and tight from unshed tears, she drove the short distance to Rachel and Cody's house.

At least she found some comfort in knowing she was leaving Rachel in a much happier state than she had found her when she showed up in town two weeks earlier.

Jess had spent the entire day before with her sister and her family, driving in their minivan through the beautiful national park, and she had been relieved to see Rachel and Cody seemed to have found a new closeness together.

They held hands most of the day as they hiked on a few short trails. Several times throughout the day, Jess had caught them stealing kisses, as if they were newlyweds instead of a busy couple with three children.

At Rachel's house, she knocked and her sister opened the door a moment later, wiping her hands on a ruffled apron.

"Come in. Don't mind the mess."

It *was* a mess, Jess saw, with discarded jackets and toys scattered along the hall. The kitchen was worse. Mixing bowls, measuring cups and flour were spread across the island, the sink full of dirty dishes.

Still, it smelled delicious.

At the table, Silas seemed to be completely focused on more flour and a ball of dough in front of him. The flour was everywhere— the floor, the table, even in his hair.

"Wow. What's going on here?"

Rachel made a face. "For some reason, I woke up in the mood to make homemade bread today. Cody loves it and so do the girls. Silas was helping me make the dough and had so much fun with it that I mixed another batch just for him to play with."

What a good idea. Silas looked in heaven as he pounded the dough on the table and squished it between his fingers.

"He seems to be having a great time."

"Until we have to clean it up, anyway," Rachel said ruefully. "I've got a loaf of bread for you, if you want."

"Thanks. I'll take it with me."

"You're leaving now?" Rachel's face fell. She wiped her hands on her apron. "Oh, I wish you could stay longer. Yesterday was so fun."

All these people who wanted her to stay. Jess was completely unused to it. "I can't. You know I have that job in Vegas waiting for me next week."

"Of course. Well, it's been wonderful having you close these past few weeks."

"I've enjoyed it, too," she said truthfully. Even with the heartache she knew was only beginning for her, she was glad she and Rachel had at least begun to rebuild their relationship.

"How's Eleanor?" her sister asked.

"I've just been to see her. She looks good. Her pacemaker surgery will be at the end of the week." She paused. "Will you keep me posted on how she's doing?"

"Of course. Though you know you could always reach out directly to Nate."

Not now. After she had basically done all she could to push him away. She let out a breath, trying not to press a hand to her heart and the ache there.

"I don't think he'll want to hear from me."

Rachel frowned. "Why not?"

At the innocent question, she pictured him as she was driving away, his features set and his eyes shadowed. Their kiss the other night replayed in her mind, stunning and tender and wonderful.

She was right, wasn't she? Leaving now was for the best. She wasn't the kind of woman who could stick around. As hard as it had been to say goodbye to them all today, how much worse would it be if she let herself become completely entangled in their world?

She would only end up hurting all of them.

While she might know all of that intellectually, her heart was another story entirely.

What if she was wrong? What if she had never been the staying sort because she hadn't yet met the right person she cared enough about?

All the emotions and regrets she had been working to contain suddenly seemed to trickle free. She could feel a tear leak out and tried desperately to wipe it away before Rachel could see.

No such luck. Her sister's gaze intensified.

"Why won't Nate want to hear from you?" she asked again.

Jess wanted to bury her face in her hands and cry. "Because I might have just made the worst mistake of my life," she whispered.

Rachel wiped her hands on her cute frilly apron again and came closer to stare at her. "What's happened?"

Jess didn't want to tell her but somehow the words came gushing out and she spilled everything.

"He said he was falling in love with you? Just like that? How do you feel about it?" Rachel asked.

"Terrified," she whispered.

Only then could she admit to herself that fear was at the core of everything.

She had faced tough soldiers, learning to drive every vehicle under the sun, dangerous conditions with snipers and IEDs and hostiles everywhere she turned.

None of that had scared her as much as the idea of giving her heart completely to Nate Whitaker.

"I…may have feelings for him, too," she finally said.

"That's great. Nate's a wonderful guy! So what's the problem?"

How could she explain to Rachel, who had always been a hopeless romantic, that the idea of love could feel like a trap?

"I'm not cut out for all this." She gestured to the kitchen, to the toddler smashing bread dough on the table, to the Instagram kitchen with its gleaming pots and pans and the Families Are Forever sign on the wall.

"No. You're not. This is my life, the one I love. You've created your own. You're an amazing woman, Jess. Strong, courageous, kind."

Jess swallowed, love for her baby sister seeping through her to heal a few more of the cracks.

"If Nate wanted a domestic goddess like me, don't you think that's the kind of woman he would look for? Instead, he fell for prickly, difficult, wonderful you. You're the one he wants. A smart woman would jump on that like Freckles on a grasshopper."

Jess wanted to believe her. She could picture a life with Nate and Sophie and Eleanor. She wouldn't have to give up her business. She and Yvette had worked too hard to build Transitions. But maybe she could focus more on helping people in this region so she didn't have to travel as much. The idea was tempting... and dangerous.

"What if I turn into Mom?" she whispered.

There it was. The moment the words were out, she realized this was the fear she hadn't even dared voice to herself. If she allowed herself to love someone fully, would she turn into her mother, needy, desperate, pathetic?

"Oh, Jess."

Rachel hugged her close. "We are not our mother. Or our father, thank God. Love—real love—doesn't make you clingy and weak. Just the opposite. It gives you strength to follow your dreams. To stay up all night with a sick baby for days on end. To take on challenges you never imagined with grace and dignity because you know you have someone by your side who will do anything under the sun to help you."

Jess closed her eyes, letting the words and the truth of them wash over her.

She wanted that. So much.

She might never be the sort of woman who would bake bread in the morning on a whim.

That didn't mean she had nothing to give.

Nate told her he was falling in love with her. She felt the same. Didn't she owe it to both of them to take a chance, to see if these fragile new feelings could take root and grow into something more?

If *she* could take root somewhere and grow into something more?

"What do I do?" she asked.

Rachel shrugged. "He wants you to stay awhile longer. Why not? You told me you don't have to be in Las Vegas for a week. Why not stay here during that time? You could be here for him while Eleanor has her pacemaker surgery and spend a little more time with Nate and Sophie. Then you can go on to your next job and see where things take you from there."

She was so very tempted, even as fear still had a tight grip on her.

No. She couldn't let the darkness of her childhood determine the decisions she made as an adult. Rachel had moved on and built a beautiful life here in Cape Sanctuary. She and Cody were happy together, even if their life wasn't always perfect.

Why couldn't Jess have that with Nate?

She wanted it suddenly, with a ferocity that shocked her.

"Besides," Rachel said, "I have an ulterior motive to want you to give Nate a chance, especially if it means I could spend more time with you."

"That would be a bonus," Jess said with a smile.

"Hi, Jess."

She and Rachel both jerked their attention to the table where Silas was still happily squishing bread dough. "Did he just say my name?"

Rachel's eyes sparkled. "It sounded like it. Si, who's that?"

"Jess." He pointed a glob of dough at her and Jess's throat tightened with emotion.

"That's right! Good job, buddy."

"Jess," he said again. "Jess. Jess. Jess."

Each time her nephew said her name, Jess's heart seemed to expand.

She was completely capable of love and here was proof. She loved her sister, Cody, her nieces and Silas.

Why was she so convinced that she couldn't be successful at romantic love?

Nate was a wonderful man. While some part of her might think he deserved someone better, someone more like Rachel, he had chosen her. She would be stupid to walk away from a man like him.

They would face challenges. She traveled most of the time and didn't know how to change that. Still, she could spend her off time in Cape Sanctuary with people she loved and there was always video calling, texts and phone calls.

"I have to go."

Rachel's features fell. "Really? I thought…" She seemed to catch herself. "I understand. Do what you have to do. Safe travels, honey."

She shook her head. "No. I have to go back to Whitaker House and see if Nate has changed his mind or if he's still willing to give me a chance."

Her sister gave a short laugh of relief and hugged her hard. "Good luck," she said. "But I don't think you're going to need it. Nate's no fool."

Jess could only hope her sister was right.

39

Nate

"WHAT'S BOTHERING YOU, DARLING?"

Nate turned away from the view of the endless sea out the window of his mother's room toward the bed where Eleanor and Sophie were playing cards.

"Nothing," he lied. "I just have a lot on my mind right now."

"I understand."

"I can tell you what's bothering *me*, if anybody wants to know," Sophie said. "I miss Jess."

"She's been gone for less than an hour," Eleanor said with a small laugh. "But I know what you mean."

"I wish she could have stayed longer. I want to show her the postcards I get from Japan when they come."

"You can always call her, darling. I know she'll be glad to hear from you."

"I guess. It won't be the same as having her here."

He couldn't do this, stay and listen to his mother and daughter talk about missing Jess. They couldn't have any idea that he was standing here feeling like his heart had been ripped out of his chest.

How would he go on without her?

The world suddenly seemed as bleak and gray as a January afternoon.

"I think I'll go take the dogs on a quick walk down to the cove," he said, seizing on any excuse to escape.

"That's a good idea," Eleanor said. "If you want to go, Sophie, I'll be all right by myself. You two don't need to babysit me all day."

Sophie shrugged. "I'm okay. I want to see if I can finally beat you."

He whistled to the dogs, cuddled together on the floor next to the bed. They both jumped up and eagerly followed him to the door.

"I'll be back shortly," he said.

"Take your time. We're fine," Eleanor said.

He hooked the dogs' leashes on, wishing he could throw on his wet suit and grab his board for a little wave therapy.

He didn't want to take that much time away from Eleanor. Despite her claims that she was fine, she had only been out of the hospital less than twenty-four hours.

He would have to be content with a walk for now.

He headed outside and had only made it a few steps when a vehicle suddenly pulled into the driveway.

A baby blue pickup pulling a vintage Airstream.

He stared, frozen in place as he watched Jess expertly back into the very same spot where she had parked for the past two weeks, overlooking the path to the sea.

She climbed out and reached into the back of her pickup for chocks, which she put behind the wheels.

That was when he finally released the breath he hadn't re-alized he had been holding and took a step toward her, gripping the dogs' leashes hard as wild, fierce hope began coursing through him.

His heart beat hard as he crossed the space between the house and her trailer, where she had started the process of removing the ball hitch and sway bars from her pickup.

She stopped working the electric jack long enough to give him a quick, unreadable look before she continued on with what she was doing.

"Jess. What's going on? Did you leave something?"

She reached down to unpin the emergency brake and the chains from the trailer.

"In a manner of speaking."

"What did you forget?" he asked.

She didn't answer for several seconds as she continued the process of unhitching the trailer.

Finally it was free of the ball hitch and she rose to face him.

"My heart," she finally muttered. "I know, it sounds corny. But it's true."

She looked so uncomfortable that he fell in love with her all over again.

"I'm not ready to leave. I...would like to stay and was wondering if you and Eleanor would mind if I, um, park my trailer here for a few more days."

"You can park your trailer here whenever you want and for however long you can spare," he said. "You'll always have a spot right there."

She met his gaze and only then did she smile. It was bright, radiant, full of promise.

"Thank you."

"Can I pull your truck out of the way?"

"I've got it."

She would always do things her own way, his Jess with the fierce streak of independence. That was fine with him. He wasn't threatened by a woman who could take care of herself. How could he be? He had been raised by Eleanor.

She climbed in and pulled the truck forward. When she turned off the engine and went to climb out again, he stood in the way so she had no choice but to fall into his arms.

"I see what you did there," she said.

He laughed, all the sad restlessness and uncertainty of the past hour floating away on the sea breeze.

She threw her arms around him and kissed him so hard, he fell against the pickup door.

"You know those feelings you were talking about?" she finally said when they both came up for air sometime later.

"You mean when I said I was falling in love with you? *Those* feelings?"

She nodded, looking uncomfortable. "I'm not very good at this but, um, there is a very good chance that I'm falling in love with you, too."

His joy seemed to expand exponentially. "Is that right?"

"I've never been in love before so I can't be a hundred percent sure that's what this is. But it's scary and wonderful at the same time. I think about you all the time and want to do anything possible to make you happy."

He smiled, deeply touched at her words and the quiet sincerity in them. Love wouldn't come easily to Jess, which made it all the more rare and precious.

"That sure sounds like love to me."

How was he lucky enough to deserve a woman like her? He had no idea. He only knew that he intended to do everything he could to show her that giving her heart to him didn't have to scare her. He would cherish the gift, honor it, with everything inside him.

He had never expected to fall in love with Jess when he found her unhitching her trailer that first day but right now, it seemed as inevitable and eternal as the sunrise climbing the mountains, as constant as the sea lapping at the cove.

She was absolutely the right person for him. The only person.

And Nate intended to spend the rest of his life proving it to her.

Epilogue

Rachel

One Year Later

S HE HAD MANAGED TO THROW THE PERFECT WED-
ding, if she did say so herself.

Rachel stood in the sand of Sunshine Cove admiring her
own handiwork.

From the grapevine arbor draped in filmy curtains to the little fairy lights twinkling along the path from Whitaker House
like fireflies, everything was exquisite.

She hadn't done it by herself, she had to admit. Eleanor and
Sophie had helped her string the fairy lights and make the table
decorations, and Cody and Nate and their crews had worked for
two days to build the arbor and the wide wooden dance floor
as well as hauling down all the tables and chairs.

It would have been easier to have the wedding on the terrace at Whitaker House. She had suggested that but Jess and Nate had both insisted on having it here.

This was their wedding. If they had wanted to build a pedestal out in the water to exchange their vows, Rachel would have figured out a way to make it happen.

Fortunately, they didn't. They had only wanted a quiet ceremony near the high tide mark as the sun was beginning to set.

They were right. Having the wedding here in the cove had been perfect. The scenery alone would have been gorgeous enough without any other decorations.

Rachel wasn't sure she had ever been to a more beautiful wedding. Jess simply glowed in the simple yet elegant dress Rachel and Yvette, who shared matron and maid of honor duties, had helped her pick out and Nate looked so hot in his bespoke gray suit, she had seen several other women, both married and single, looking more than a little disgruntled that he was now taken.

The best part for Rachel had been seeing the look in her new brother-in-law's eyes as Jess had come toward him down the path and across the sand. He looked as if Jess was everything he could ever want or need wrapped up in one lovely package, his fierce love obvious for everyone to see.

As for Jess, joy seemed to radiate out of her, spilling out across the cove.

Rachel had a hard time remembering the tough-edged, solitary person Jess had been a year ago when she came to help Eleanor clean out Whitaker House.

The past year had been a time of change and readjustment for all of them.

Jess still traveled with Transitions, though not as often. She was limiting the jobs she did away from Cape Sanctuary to one week a month and had chosen to focus on more regional jobs so she could be home with Nate and Sophie at night.

She and Yvette had hired two other people to help them with the more far-flung projects.

Jess seemed so much happier over the past year. She laughed more, she loved being with the girls and Silas, she had even made other friends in town and had started coming to Rachel's book club.

Rachel loved seeing her more often. They were still busy with their respective lives but made time at least once or twice a month to get together, and talked or texted far more often than that.

She was watching Nate lead Jess out to the dance floor, both surprisingly graceful, when Rachel sensed someone coming up behind her. She instinctively knew it was her husband.

His job throughout the ceremony had been to wrangle Silas and keep him out of trouble while Rachel performed her official wedding party duties.

Out of habit, Rachel scanned the area and spotted their son now with Eleanor, whom he adored, sitting at a table on the edge of the dance floor and eating a piece of cake.

The past year had been challenging with Silas, as well. She had found, though, that as his communication skills improved, his frustration level seemed to decrease.

She knew they still had a long road ahead but being his mother seemed much easier than it had been a year ago, when everything had felt so raw and new and terrifying.

He was a sweet boy who loved their dog, adored his sisters and would follow his father around all day if he could.

"Great job, babe," Cody murmured as he wrapped his arms around her from behind. "Everything is stunning."

"Isn't it?" She sighed with happiness, loving this magical day.

"Especially you," Cody said gruffly.

She turned and found him looking down at her much the same way Nate had looked at Jess.

Rachel's heart seemed to sigh with happiness. She turned and wrapped her arms around him, this man who knew her better than anyone else in the world and somehow loved her anyway.

Life wasn't about reaching a single, perfect destination. Of all the lessons Rachel had learned through her difficult childhood and now raising a child with autism, that might be the most powerful.

Instead, the path was continuous and ever-changing. It might be treacherous at times, arduous, complicated. Amid the hard, though, one could always discover unexpected beauty and grace.

She held her husband, looking over his shoulder at their children, her sister, her foster family—all the people she loved most in the world.

No matter how difficult the road they traveled, the way was made easier and certainly more beautiful because of the loved ones who helped them along the way.

★ ★ ★ ★ ★